D1137002

9030 00007 8485 0

PRAISE FOR *THE SHOT*

'A powerful story of the brutality of front-line journalism. Authentic, provocative and terrifyingly relevant. It will stay with you' Will Carver

'Shocking and visceral, this novel deals with the horrors of war ... a brave, important and utterly compelling book' S.J. Watson

'Gritty, hard-hitting and oftentimes harrowing' Victoria Selman

'A gritty, jarring page-turner' Peter Hain

'As searingly an authentic thriller about what it's like for a journalist to work in war as you are likely to read. Trust me. I've been there. Passionate, disturbing storytelling at its best' James Brabazon

'A powerhouse writer' Jo Spain

'You won't read another book like this in 2022! Raw, authentic, powerful ... you won't see the end coming' E.C. Scullion

'Brilliantly conveys both the exhilaration and the unspeakable horror of life on the international news frontline' Jo Turner

'Sultoon's writing style is mesmerising – jumping right into pulse-racing, horrific action, and it never stops. She has a strange way of highlighting little details ... that pulls the reader completely into a scene with vivid clarity' B.S. Casey

'A haunting and thought-provoking story that ... challenges the reader to think about the ethical issues facing news gatherers. Highly recommended' Michael Stanley

'An extraordinary, stunning story told brilliantly well. It offers a realistic and shocking insight into the incredible impact on journalists of working in war zones ... A must-read' Live & Deadly

'There are tears running down my face ... a powerful, extraordinary, heartbreaking book' Simply Suze Reviews

'A brilliant study of character ... stark and vivid, my reaction to parts of it was almost visceral, but with the whole story backed by a real sense of authenticity, it was almost impossible to put down' Jen Med's Book Reviews

PRAISE FOR SARAH SULTOON

Winner of the Crime Fiction Lover Best Debut Award

'A brave and thought-provoking debut novel ... sensitive handling, tight plotting and authentic storytelling make for a compelling read' Adam Hamdy

'A taut and thought-provoking book that's all the more unnerving for how much it echoes the headlines in real life' *CultureFly*

'A remarkable debut' *NB Magazine*

'A powerful, compelling read that doesn't shy away from some upsetting truths' Fanny Blake

'Tautly written and compelling, not afraid to shine a spotlight on the darker forces at work in society' Rupert Wallis

'A gripping, dark thriller' Geoff Hill, ITV

'A stunning debut ... a powerhouse writer' Jo Spain

'A powerful, intense whammy of a debut that is both uncomfortable and exhilarating to read ... Thought-provoking, tense, and expressive, *The Source* is an utterly compelling debut' LoveReading

'So authentic and exhilarating ... breathtaking pace and relentless ingenuity' Nick Paton Walsh, CNN

'My heart was racing ... fiction to thrill even the most hard-core adrenaline junkies' Diana Magnay, Sky News

'Unflinching and sharply observed. A hard-hitting, deftly woven debut' Ruth Field

'A hard-hitting, myth-busting rollercoaster of a debut' Eve Smith

'I could picture and feel each scene, all the fear, tension and hope' Katie Allen

'With this gripping, fast-paced debut thriller, it's easy to see what made Sultoon such a great journalist. She has a nose for a great story, an eye for the details that make it come to life, and real compassion for her protagonist' Clarissa Ward, CNN

ABOUT THE AUTHOR

Sarah Sultoon is a journalist and writer, whose work as an international news executive at CNN has taken her all over the world, from the seats of power in both Westminster and Washington to the frontlines of Iraq and Afghanistan. She has extensive experience in conflict zones, winning three Peabody awards for her work on the war in Syria, an Emmy for her contribution to the coverage of Europe's migrant crisis in 2015, and a number of Royal Television Society gongs. As passionate about fiction as nonfiction, she recently completed a Masters of Studies in Creative Writing at the University of Cambridge, adding to an undergraduate language degree in French and Spanish, and Masters of Philosophy in History, Film and Television. When not reading or writing she can usually be found somewhere outside, either running, swimming or throwing a ball for her three children and dog while she imagines what might happen if...

Her debut thriller *The Source* is currently in production with Lime Pictures, and was a Capital Crime Book Club pick and a number one bestseller on Kindle. Follow Sarah on Twitter @SultoonSarah.

**Also by Sarah Sultoon
and available from Orenda Books**
The Source

The Shot

Sarah Sultoon

**ORENDA
BOOKS**

16 Carson Road
·West Dulwich
London SE21 8HU
www.orendabooks.co.uk

First published in the United Kingdom by Orenda Books, 2022
Copyright © Sarah Sultoon, 2022

Sarah Sultoon has asserted her moral right to be identified as the author of this
work in accordance with the Copyright, Designs and Patents Act, 1988.

All Rights Reserved. No part of this publication may be reproduced in any form
or by any means without the written permission of the publishers.

*This is a work of fiction. Names, characters, places and incidents are either products of
the author's imagination or are used fictitiously. Any resemblance to actual events,
locales or persons, living or dead, is entirely coincidental.*

A catalogue record for this book is available from the British Library.

ISBN 978-1-914585-08-1
eISBN 978-1-914585-09-8

Typeset in Garamond by typesetter.org.uk

Printed and bound by CPI Group (UK) Ltd, ... YY

For s...e and distribution ... o.uk

**LONDON BOROUGH OF
WANDSWORTH**

9030 00007 8485 0	
Askews & Holts	
AF THR	
	WW21018351

For all the photojournalists.
And for Geoff Hill – a warrior.

Prologue

The man, he's tall, with a ranger's lope and a marked imbalance in the square of his shoulders that characterises years working with a piece of heavy equipment on one side. He's done this many, many times before – there's a heft to his frame, an almost balletic glide to his movements as he sweeps around, camera tucked light in the curl of his arm. But look closer and there's a stoop, a hunch to his back – he's weary of it, even if he's still a master of his own choreography. On the rare occasions his eye leaves the viewfinder it snaps primary-blue in the glare, looking away for just long enough to allow a puff of air onto the sweat beaded inside the tight rubber seal.

The girl, she's slight, but with none of the man's long-rehearsed physical grace. Her dark hair is fighting its cords, wisps escaping from below a cap only to write themselves all over the perspiration on her neck. She's stumbling behind the man, twisting this way and that, peering over her shoulder in random directions but finding no alternative point of focus. She doesn't know where she's going, nothing is as she expected but, thanks to him, she's not lost. While both figures are dressed in the stained fatigues of war, otherwise appropriate to the scene they're in, their manner sticks out from the sepia landscape as much as that of the doctors, white-coated and flitting like sprites around the medical tent, with little they can do for anyone inside.

Here, there are only victims. There are no survivors. Here, enfolded in the vast plains of the Sahara, there is a war raging that no one else wants to see or hear. And here, the unforgiving desert can bury the evidence whole with the merest flick of a sandstorm's tail. It is the cruellest of ironies that the state-sponsored militia pillaging this land have Nature on their side too. By the time anyone is inside this particular medical tent, there is no hope left. The only peace lingers in the air above the corpses – isolated little eddies of it, circling with the flies above shroud after shroud. There are other bodies, but they are the undead, the peaceful fate they crave so close that they can touch it in their wounds, which weep into the air, their eyes having no tears left to shed.

They can no longer feel. No comprehension remains. Here, there is nothing left to live for, only nightmares to dread.

The girl, she is holding a microphone. It's thin, like an extension of her arm, almost too feeble to bear the testimony she is gathering. The man, he still has poise about him, his movements calm and deft, but he gets to watch from behind a lens, from deep inside his own personal bubble. It's not just sweat inside the viewfinder, he's blinking away the tears, but that's his own little secret. No one else need ever know. This is a bubble that always bursts, but for now, it's his only protection against the catatonia of grief, the cacophony of despair, a crossfade of past and present, the here and now blurring with scenes he's long buried in his past. For now, her ears are tin, his eye is blind. Their bodies are operating in a preprogrammed trance.

Look closer, you will see a logo on the girl's cap – letters all twisted together, embroidered neatly in fire-engine red: an international news network, another type of rescue service, another type of microphone, only with a far wider reach. The doctors, the aid workers, they all know that logo, they hope even the slightest amount of overseas attention might bring more relief equipment, more food, more medical supplies to their inadequate arsenal. They even dare to dream it might bring intervention, and so they clear the path towards a long, thin bundle wrapped around another, far smaller bundle – a mother, Yousra, cradling her baby son, Ahmed. You can see the bundles are still breathing, their chests are puffing in and out. But the small one has only minutes left before prolonged malnutrition overcomes his still-nascent heart and lungs.

There are questions, and there are answers. There were men on horseback, there were guns, there was fire, there was death. The language varies, from English to Arabic and back, but never settling on anything that makes sense. Are those really a clump of Sudanese desert flowers, peering beguilingly from just outside the flapping tent doorway? Or is it Nature playing yet another joke at their expense? Still the camera rolls, the shutter clicks, the record is set. And before long, there is film; proof that will end a war, launch a career, and sell millions and millions of magazines. A shot that will tell a version of this story that finally sticks.

But the girl, she's trapped in an endlessly repeating scene inside her own head: a dusty afternoon, a stifling-hot apartment, her father, her paint-box, his camera. She was too young to look at his pictures, so she contented herself with painting her own, filling the weeks he was away working in countries she couldn't pronounce, witnessing events she couldn't understand – dreamlike places that became the centre of her nightmares after one eventually claimed him for good. They'd moved all over the Middle East, from Cairo to Amman to Beirut, in pursuit of his job, but she didn't care, until he never came back.

Here's the shutter, her father had said, brushing a fingertip over her sweaty eyelashes, tapping another against the front of the heavy black case in his lap. That's how the eye traps the light, how it sends a picture of what it sees into the brain. And this, he'd continued, pointing at her eyes, wide in the mirror embedded inside the lid of her paint-box, this delicious chocolate-brown circle is the iris. That automatically regulates the amount of light sent through to the back of the eye by changing the size of the pupil.

So the brain has to tell us what the eye sees? she'd asked, staring into her own eyes, squinting between the traces of powdered paint on the mirror. That's right, her father had answered from between his teeth as he lit a cigarette. The eye just gives us the picture, the brain tells us what it is. But the camera, the camera can give you any picture you want, if you know how to use it. The camera can move the angle, change the perspective, leave clues that the eye might never have registered alone. Sometimes, he'd added, smoke furling ruminatively into the thick air as he tapped his temple, sometimes the camera can do the job of both the eye and the brain.

Her mother had leant over then, pinching out the cigarette between his lips with a look the girl pretended not to see. There'd been lots of those looks, with words she hadn't understood to go with the stories she wasn't allowed to hear. So if you want to make your painting realistic, she'd said, tapping the sheet of paper on the table, you've got to use black in the eye. And if you're framing a shot, her father added as he frowned back at her, that's where the shadows have to be perfect. The darkest part of the human body is the pupil.

But it's only when she saw death up close that she knew they were right.

Because it's only in death that light finds its way into the eyes. They become spectral, with depths suddenly as transient as a last breath. A permanent mark of the moment where possibility becomes impossibility, where hope fades to peace.

The giveaway is always in the pupil.

The girl blinks and blinks until it hits her. The light, blooming from Yousra's telescope-dark eyes – radiant, unmistakable. How frail is the curtain between her world and theirs.

She finds the man, his gaze blue as desert flowers, as sure as blossom that grows from dust.

And then the girl makes sense of it. Her brain catches up. The bubble bursts, the trance lifts. In rushes the storm.

For Yousra was already dead. And the evidence was all on tape.

Chapter 1
Risk

Six months earlier: November, 2003

The red phone rang first. It was the only red one in the tangle of black handsets littered over the news desk. It was nicknamed the 'batphone', but its plastic handset and cradle were the colour of running blood. I don't think anyone had ever noticed that before it rang that day.

I felt it before I heard it, tidying the newspapers strewn all over the place as Diana and I got ready to leave. The vibrations trembled through the pages in my hand a nanosecond before the speaker kicked into gear. Still I didn't dare pick it up, even as everyone else dived for the black phones on their desks. It was like watching a crowd realise they've all boarded the wrong train and have seconds to get off, heads swivelling in sync towards the red phone as the realisation dawned. *The red phone is actually ringing.* Hardly anyone had the number. It could only mean one thing. The mental alarm bells were still deafening long after Penny finally grabbed it.

I saw it before I heard it too: her face leached of all colour before she cried out, dropping the handset like it was as hot as it looked. She recovered almost immediately, wiping a hand on her suit jacket before picking it up again, but I saw it: she was sickened and terrified. I knew what she was going to say before she did.

'Kris has been shot? And Ali too? What happened? Is everyone else accounted for?'

Penny's next sentences came in two halves – one directed at the cluster of us on the news desk, the other to the person on the end of the line. I knew who it was, because I knew what must have happened. Kris was the network's news cameraman covering the war in Iraq. The fighting had been raging for eight months, each one hotter than the last.

'Di, quick, go and get Ross.' Penny sounded like she was being strangled as she issued instructions before turning back to the receiver. 'Where are they now? They were in convoy, surely, so what happened to the other car? Wait – which field hospital?'

Ross managed the photographers. He'd usually be downstairs in the crew room, managing via chatting and sorting through camera gear, his own brand of bringing order to chaos since he'd stopped travelling with his own camera himself. The air was suddenly electric, Diana's curtain of blonde hair lifting strand by strand behind her as she ran off.

Penny covered the receiver with a hand again, shaking her head at the man working on the news desk next to me.

'Mike, I need you to call DC right now – get them to raise their most senior contacts at the Pentagon.' I watched her face colour as she returned to the handset. 'I thought you said it was the Americans running the field hospital?'

Her colour deepened, and Penny didn't colour easily. You stop blushing practically before you've started if you run an international news operation.

'Of course we won't call anyone on the ground without running it through you first,' she replied. Her hand shook as she smoothed hair off her face. 'Who's with them on site? What, you're sending Mohammed out too? Why?'

Acid stole up my throat. I knew exactly where Mohammed would be heading. Ali was an Iraqi staff member, a Baghdad native, paid to translate, fetch, carry, explain, wheedle, arrange, you name it. He and Mohammed were the bedrock of the network's Baghdad operation, taking risks far greater than any journalists did, just by being the ones who helped them. They kept people like Kris safe. Now someone was going to have to tell Ali's family what had happened to him. They would only understand it coming from Mohammed.

Penny's face burned as she scribbled on the pad in her lap. Feeling sorry for Penny should have been way down my list of emotions at that moment, but I couldn't help it. Sure, she enjoyed all the bells and whistles that came with being the managing editor of the industry's pre-eminent international news network. She had the shiny glass corner office, the personal assistant, the responsibility for countless decisions per day that had the potential to change the course of lives around the world – and not just the lives of those who were carrying them out. But I'd heard her pleading with her children after she missed yet another school event, begging someone at the end of the line to take care of family issues for her after yet another late night. I'd seen her eating crisps and chocolate from the vending machine for every meal – even her assistant too busy to buy her a sandwich. Then there was the tell-tale paler circle of skin around the third finger of her left hand where a ring once proudly sat. Penny made sacrifices too. She just didn't make them on tape.

Still I found my sympathy evaporate as I caught her eye, phone jammed to her ear. To me, these sacrifices were ultimately a privilege.

'Can't you leave someone on the line with me before you head out? Andrea's there? Perfect. Andie? Are you alright?' I physically felt the depth of her sigh as she exhaled, noticing that she didn't thank any higher power. Anyone who still did that hadn't seen enough. 'Bear with me, love, OK? I need you to hang on this line for a bit, just until we know what's what. Give me a second to make a few calls and I'll be right back with you, I promise.'

Penny placed the handset down on top of the pile of newspapers I'd tidied, the neat stack holding the phone high above the chaos. No one ever read past the front page but I could never be the one who threw them out. What if we found out we'd missed some critical editorial detail – that our competitors had a nugget of information we'd overlooked? Now all those papers would forever remind us of everything we'd misjudged that day. Was that why Penny sent Di to get Ross, instead of me? Was I already subconsciously connected with failure rather than success?

I looked away, found my comfort blanket – the enormous framed photographs lining the wall leading to the newsroom doors. Mounted like trophies, one iconic shot after another. I squinted as if I could read the credits even though I knew they were on the back. And that Kris was behind every single one of them.

People only ever remember the pictures themselves. They never think about what it must have been like to take them.

'Penny,' Ross huffed as he arrived at the desk, puce in the face from running up the stairs, sweat patches already pooled all over his cargo shirt. 'What the hell happened? How bad is it? Who have you got on the phone?'

'Andie.' Penny tossed her head towards the red handset, another phone already in her hand. 'Hang on before you speak to her though – she isn't with them—'

'I've got an official from the Pentagon on the line,' Mike interrupted, braying from across the desk. 'Jennifer wants to call every US general she can, connect them with the field hospital now, make the doctors aware of who their patients really are. Can I go ahead?'

'Get me on the line with Jennifer,' Penny shot back. 'I need to talk to Katja before she does anything else. But good work, that's great.'

Katja. A shiver went down my back. I was right. It had been Katja on the red phone. The news network's chief field producer. They even called her an executive despite the fact her 'office' was almost always a tent or burned out building. And Jennifer was the channel's US affairs editor at the time. Between them, there was nothing they hadn't seen on the rest of the world's behalf – Bosnia, Somalia, the First Gulf War. Except I knew this was the first time any of this network's staff members had been critically injured.

'How bad is it?' I could barely look at Ross's face as he asked me this time, slicking sweat off his corrugated forehead with a pudgy hand.

'I don't know,' I whispered below Penny issuing sharp instructions to a sea of different people. 'I don't think anyone does. It's only just happened. I heard Penny ask about a second car – I don't even know who was travelling with them, or where they were going, just that Kris and Ali—'

'You!' Penny called. It took me a moment to realise who she meant. 'I'm sorry –what's your name?'

'Samira,' I stuttered, swaying as I stood up, a curious mix of excitement and terror coursing through my body, not sure whether to fight or fly. I wanted to be part of this, no matter how bad it was. 'I work with Diana, we … It doesn't matter. What can I do?'

'Just sit on the end of that phone.' Penny pointed at the red handset. 'Don't leave the line unattended for anything. Andrea is on the other end – do you know Andie? Actually, never mind … just stay on the phone. Whatever Andie tells you, tell me. And be there for her, OK? She's already been through a whole lot.'

Penny whirled away before I'd even started to nod, trying and failing to blot my sweaty hand on my jeans before I picked up the handset. All I could hear was scuffles and muffled shouts on the end of the line.

'Hello? Is that Andie? This is Samira, I'm a graphics producer – I work on the morning shows … Hello?'

'Hang on, Mohammed – yes, sorry, hi there.' Andie's cool South African lilt floated down the line, improbably calm. 'Just give me a minute, OK? Samira, you said? I'll be right back with you, I'm just getting Mohammed out of the door.'

'Of course, of course,' I said, swallowing. What she had to prepare Mohammed for was unimaginable. He was an Iraqi staff member too. It could have been him. Now he had to be the one to tell Ali's family that it wasn't. I strained to hear her comforting him, but all I got was white noise.

'Sorry, Samira, I'm back with you now.'

'I'll be on the end of this line at all times if you need anything. And if you could let me know any new developments as you get them, I'll be sure to pass everything on to Penny.'

I knew I was gabbling at her. But if I stopped talking for too long I might hear my own fear.

'Hang on again, sorry, Samira...'

'Everyone calls me Sami,' I told her, even though I knew she wasn't listening. Why on earth would she? What was happening here in the newsroom was nothing to what she was fielding on the ground.

'What's going on?' Penny mouthed from across the desk, a different phone cradled between her shoulder and ear. 'I've got Katja back on this line but the connection is terrible.'

'Penny, look.' Diana's chair fell backwards with a crash as she stood, grabbing Penny's arm. 'They've got it.' She pointed at her computer screen.

All around me, red straplines were flashing on every monitor. Somehow word had got out on the ground that Western journalists had been injured. The news wires had it, and weren't waiting to tell everyone else.

—BREAK: *UK news crew ambushed in Iraq*

—BREAK: *Critical injuries in UK news crew attack*

—BREAK: *Mortars, gunfire heard in Baghdad ambush*

I clenched the red phone, Penny's eyes darting as she replied.

'OK, Di, I need you to get hold of every major news network's London office as fast as you can. We absolutely must ensure a complete news blackout. The victims' families haven't been informed yet. Take any and all offers of help ... Yes, Katja? Katja? Can you hear me?'

'What's going on?' Ross reached for her arm. 'Where is she now?'

Penny gulped before she could continue, covering a receiver with a hand. 'She's on her way to the field hospital. Everything happened right by an American checkpoint, I think, I can hardly hear her. It seems like Kris and Ali were in the rear car, and that's why they took the brunt of it.'

'Brunt of what? The gunfire?'

'I don't know, Ross. I still don't know what actually happened – I don't even know where they were going. I haven't approved anyone setting foot outside the bureau cordon for days. But I have to believe they were travelling in a convoy, no one moves in a warzone without a safety car on my watch. Christ, if I find out this was Kris haring off on one of his own madcap missions I will shoot him myself.'

A cold wash of adrenaline flooded down my back as Andie came back on the line, muffling everything Penny said next. Not that it mattered. I'd heard it all before: the risks Kris took to keep us ahead of the competition. The images he returned with that finally changed the record. My rush intensified, even though I didn't know whether he'd got away with it this time. People like Kris were extraordinary. Anyone who couldn't see that wasn't looking closely enough.

'Sorry, Samira, I'm back with you now.'

'I'm here,' I replied hastily, dragging my eyes away from their tableau. Penny seemed to be getting smaller and smaller, dark suit jacket blurring with her dark hair as she hunched over the desk. Ross, by contrast, seemed to be getting bigger, shirt straining over his chest and cheeks puffing in and out as he took deeper and deeper breaths. Suddenly all the jokes about every year Ross spent behind a desk adding another notch to his ever-widening belt seemed in terrible taste. The reason he sat there the whole time was to anticipate any hidden tripwire that would result in an eventuality like this.

'How are you doing?' The words were out of my mouth before I could stop them. As if Andie would possibly want to engage in small talk. I had played out her field-producer role a thousand times in my head; it was all I'd ever wanted to do myself. Get right to the heart of the story on the frontline, no matter where it was, no matter what it took. No time for small talk. But now here she was replying without even a hint of panic in her cool accent.

I shouldn't have been surprised. That's the emotional load we're all expected to cope with. That's the job. We're supposed to understand it without ever talking about it.

'Yah, we're hanging in there. It all happened so quickly but I think everyone is in the right places for now. Mohammed is on his way. I think Katja has made it to the field hospital – you probably know more about that than me, hey? We were lucky, at least, that it happened close by, and I've managed to get everyone else under the one roof, if you want to pass that on to Penny. It's Samira, right?'

'Everyone calls me Sami,' I repeated idiotically. 'I'll let Penny know as soon as I catch her eye. I think she's on the phone to Katja.'

A sharp intake of breath. 'Katja? What's the latest on the boys? What has she said?'

'Nothing that I can tell, to be honest. It's all a bit crazy in here.' I gazed dumbly around the news desk, every single phone off the hook, everyone on their feet. Usually this sight did nothing but thrill me. Now the balance was completely skewed.

'I'm sure it is,' Andie said. 'My, it doesn't matter how much you prepare yourself. We cover these sorts of incidents all the time, hey? Kris is always the one doing it, too.' I heard her catch her breath again. 'They were just … oh, I don't know. Kris's paperwork needed renewing. They'd barely had breakfast and loaded up, before—'

'So they weren't even going out to film a story? Or at least do an interview?'

I couldn't help but ask, even though she hardly heard me. Later I would reflect on how seedy it felt, but it turned out not to matter in the end.

'—his accreditation had expired. Ah, Katja was furious! You

can't move without a badge around here. And to think we nearly didn't send him out with a security car. They wouldn't have made it to the field hospital without Adam in convoy. We were so lucky.'

Adam must be one of the security advisors in the Baghdad bureau, I thought, nodding as if she could see me. Another role I'd imagined a thousand times. These men were stuff of fable, all former members of the SAS or similar, having left the military to take up one of the thousands of well-paid private security jobs springing up all over the industry after 9/11. Once one media company used them, everyone basically had to follow suit as their insurance companies started writing it into policy. It all sounded so romantic, I'd naively thought at the time. Now even news crews had bodyguards.

'Do you know ... do you know what actually happened?' Maybe it would help her to talk it through, I reasoned.

'Only that their car took small-arms fire. I don't know how or why. I don't even think Katja does, and Adam hasn't had a second to speak to anyone except the medics at the field hospital.'

'I'm so sorry, Andie. You're doing such a good job holding it together at the office. Just hang in there, OK? As soon as I hear anything that you haven't, I'll pass it on, I promise. And so long as we keep talking to each other, we can't lose our connection.'

'You're very kind, Samira,' she replied, as I wondered where my words were coming from, muscle memory in some long-buried corner of my mind. 'Tell me something, anything. I'm all on my lonesome here suddenly. My, I don't think I've been left alone even once since I got out here. What's everyone doing right now in the newsroom?'

I gazed around from my perch on the stack of newspapers. Ross was downing a bottle of water, running a hand through his hair, eyes skyward and fixed on some faraway point deep inside the lighting rig on the ceiling. I knew he was preparing to call Kris's wife, running through his first sentence, then second and third.

What would he start with? Give her a moment to sit down,

collect herself? Insist that someone was with her before he continued? And what would he say? That Kris'd been shot but he didn't know how bad it was yet? I had to tear my eyes away, only to find Penny bent over the desk directly opposite, hunching lower and lower with a phone to each ear. A stream of grave-faced photographers were slowly clustering around Ross, as news of Kris's injuries percolated through to the crew room downstairs. And around the rest of the newsroom, a curious suspended stillness; producers with their hands frozen above their keyboards, frown lines etched into the foreheads, chatter paused mid-conversation, as they watched and realised this was not a breaking-news incident to which they were all so accustomed.

This time, it was happening to us. We were the story. Exactly what journalists should never be. I took a deep breath.

'Well, I can tell you there isn't a soul in here not focused on the boys' survival. There is nothing more important in this room than what's happening to you all right now. Penny is on the line with Katja, and at least ten other people by the look of it. I know everyone else on the news desk is ringing round all the other networks to make sure nothing leaks before their families have been told. And Ross is up here too, along with all the photographers that were still in the building.'

'Does Lucia know yet?' Andie's voice finally cracked. 'Is someone on their way out to their house at least? To tell her in person?'

'I'm not sure I know who you mean?'

I swallowed into the brief silence on the other end of the line. I didn't want to admit to myself why I was making her spell it out. The rumours about Kris and Andie had been all over the newsroom for months.

'Someone must be going to tell Lucia,' she said again, clipped and sharp. 'She'll have prepared for this, of course she will. This is only the hundredth time Kris has been deployed in a warzone. You don't marry someone like that without—' Her voice cracked again. 'Without knowing what you're signing up for.'

'I think Ross is preparing to call her now,' I said softly, looking at my feet. The red phone suddenly felt like a brick in my hand. If I could have thrown it, I would.

'So tell me, Samira,' Andie said after a moment's coughing into the receiver. 'What is it you do in the newsroom? We've not met, have we?'

'I'm a graphics producer,' I said, watching Ross compose himself before walking slowly towards his office behind the news desk, a few photographers trailing after him. 'I've been here almost a year, I was an intern to start with but I was lucky. They were shorthanded on the morning shows when the war started so I volunteered for the graveyard shift.'

'My – so you've been working through the night?'

'I guess so, yeah.' I gazed at the bank of digital clocks running along the edge of the newsroom set, all blinking different times, suddenly aware how tired I was. 'Although it depends which clock I look at. If I linger on Asia Pacific, I can pretend it's the end of the day, even though I haven't had breakfast yet.'

Andie let out a short, hollow laugh.

'So what time is it in Baghdad now?' I asked, even though I knew. The Middle East clock was flashing red directly in front of me.

'It's just gone eleven – wow,' Andie sighed heavily into my ear. 'Last time I looked at my watch none of this had even happened and now...'

'Try not to think about it,' I said confidently, even as at that moment Penny suddenly straightened up, eyes wide with horror. 'It doesn't matter. Nothing can change what's already happened. All that matters now is what happens next—'

'Graphics, you said?' she interrupted, all clipped again. 'What kind? You mean maps, fonts, graphs and such?'

I sighed. 'Nothing that's usually that interesting, unfortunately. Usually it's just the words that run along the bottom of the screen. It sounds mindless, I know, but if a death toll changes or a news story starts to move really fast, then mistakes in the graphics are all anyone ever remembers. It's really important to keep them accurate and relevant.'

'Right, right,' she said quietly, suddenly sounding the miles away that she really was. I plucked at the edge of newspaper bristling under the red cradle. I hated being spell checker in chief. It was just a means to an end.

'And where are you from originally, Samira?' She elongated my name – *Sah-Meer-Rah*. Later I would wonder if it was really just down to her accent or it was something else that made her do it.

'I'm from here, except I'm not. Like loads of us in this business, I guess.' I heard Kris's broad Kiwi accent in my head as I said it. 'My dad was Egyptian. I was born in Cairo but went to school here because my mum's English, and he worked away a lot.' Now I was trying to read Penny's haggard expression.

'So you speak Arabic?'

'Some...' I trailed off as Penny visibly trembled, the pit of my stomach following. 'Yes. It's not perfect but I'm hoping it will get me where I need to be.'

'Samira...' Andie's voice sounded even fainter on the end of the line. 'Has ... has something just happened?'

I'll never know what it was, in that moment, that told her something had changed, something irreparable. But I realise now that I already knew, the minute I saw Penny physically pull herself together, saw Mike and Diana freeze in their seats. The red phone suddenly became as fluid as an open wound as I dropped my head, my eyes filling with tears.

'Samira? Can you hear me back there?' Andie's voice floated somewhere as I tried to compose myself. Penny's face was set to a mask opposite, the only visible sign of emotion the tremble in her finger as she beckoned for me.

'Just one second, OK, Andie? I'll be back with you as soon as I can, hang on.'

I laid down the handset next to its red cradle, positioning both as far inside the square stack of newspapers as possible so they wouldn't be disturbed, before picking my way round the desk to Penny, willing that no tears would escape down my cheeks. Nothing could be worse.

This isn't my story to cry over, I repeated like a mantra in my head.

'It is imperative that Andie does not find out from you, OK?' Penny kept her voice low as I approached. 'You cannot be the one to tell her. Katja will be back soon, or at least Adam will, and they will be the ones to tell everyone locally.'

I nodded even though I didn't know for sure what had happened and Penny had already started to walk away in the direction of Ross's office, running a hand over the brown hair plastered like a cap to her head with sweat.

Diana looked like a ghost as I turned to her, tone blaring from the upturned phone lying in her lap.

'Ali had to be resuscitated,' she breathed, as if whispering somehow might make it a rumour rather than a fact. 'They've got him back, apparently, but only just. He's still critical with almost certain brain damage.'

My hand flew to my mouth.

'But they think Kris is going to be OK. He lost a whole lot of blood but ultimately the bullet just took a chunk off the top of his head.'

I grabbed her chair with my other arm to keep myself upright.

'He's luckier than a cat, that guy,' she continued, turning the handset over and over in her lap. 'But ... oh God. Ali has a family – why else would he do it if not to support them all?'

Blood ran as I blinked furiously at the red phone, motionless and expectant on its bed of old newspaper. At that moment, the only answer I had to this particular question was definitely not the right one.

Chapter 2
Reward

There was always sand in the air in Baghdad. It made it easy to pretend nothing ever bothered you except the weather. There had been a gusty great haboob the day before. So he hadn't even needed to pretend as Katja raged – there was nothing she hadn't seen, there was nowhere she hadn't been, and never had she had it as hard as this.

There was no real journalism to be done in this Second Gulf War. Actually, wait, there was plenty to be done, but none that they were going to get away with, thanks to the military and its preposterous miles of red tape, locking every square inch of the battlefield into a single viewpoint – theirs. He'd been able to rub his eyes all he liked, watching smoke wreathing around her head, ash dropping all over the place from the cigarette in her hand that she was too busy using to point her nicotine-stained finger of blame rather than actually inhale. Kris should have taken more responsibility for himself. Did he honestly need her to keep telling him the stakes were higher than they'd ever been? This was Baghdad at the peak of the conflict, the crest of the West's magnanimous takeover in the Middle East! They were in constant competition with every other news network on the ground in Iraq for the mealiest amount of access. There was no excuse good enough for not being in the right place at the right time. Was someone with a reputation like hers going to let the network fall behind on the next stage of this war because of a dated piece of paperwork? As if she could ever use something as trivial as an incorrect ID badge in her defence. He should have known the expiry date on his press pass as well as he knew his own fucking birthday.

There she had paused, just for a moment, mosaic of lines round her black eyes softening as she reassured him – she thought she knew he was as frustrated as she was. As if changing tack was going to help him open his mouth with all that sand still in the air, gluing his throat fast shut.

For they both knew this war was stage-managed like none other. They both knew that moving around this tortured city, once the pearl of the Middle East, now patchworked with road-blocks, was down to the military and its piles of admin. Making it the wrong side of dangerous for journalists to operate without military cover was both deliberate and deniable. Hell, they were even calling it embedding, as if appropriating a verb that suggested reporters and soldiers were actually getting into bed with each other would make any result the unvarnished, objective truth. Forget about how they'd got the job done in a gazillion other war-zones. These were the new rules of engagement. 9/11 had changed everything. They'd been around the block together for years, hadn't they? Kris and Katja, the king and the queen, only together will the network reign supreme?

But still the sand had lingered as he gulped and blinked at her, wound so tight in her customary black knits that she may as well have been another incoming tornado herself.

Because it was never Katja staring down a lens at kids dying in the street, zooming in on the miniature sandals torn from their little feet, white-balancing on the pages of their schoolbooks flaming on the pavement. It was never Katja bolting towards the fear while everyone else bolted away. Hanging around for just one more shot – the twisted wheelchair, the splintered walking stick, the destroyed remnants of everyday life that really brought it home. The pictures that were worth the risk, that made people choke on their morning coffee. The images that made those in power sit up, listen, and hopefully change the record. Photographs and video of places normal folks only knew existed because Kris was the one who had taken them. Because Kris was the one who'd looked them in the eye so they didn't have to.

The fields of skulls. The vulture waiting patiently for the baby to die. The man's head sticking out of a flaming tyre – necklaced, they called it, as if doing something so unimaginable to another human being should ever transcend to being an actual verb.

And by the time the fireworks started in Baghdad it was only ever Andie's hand at his back – making sure he didn't fall, shielding him from crowds, projectiles, whatever else she could see that he couldn't because he was too busy looking down the viewfinder. By then, Andie was his eyes. Katja had given up long ago. Katja, everybody's, yet nobody's, mother. Kris fingered the outline of the passport stashed in its usual zipped cargo pocket, staring at the featureless English countryside blurring beyond the taxi window as the traffic inched along the motorway. Maybe that was why she couldn't admit she should have remembered his fucking birthday too.

They'd all known for a few days that the airport road was hot. Why else would they all have been benched, ordered not to leave the office under any circumstances, when every news network in the world was desperate to outdo the other on the biggest story in town? You had to travel that thing to get anywhere relevant in Baghdad. And the lot of them had the tip off – it was the same intelligence report doing the rounds. It wasn't as if each news outfit in place occupied a different corner of the city. They were all living in the same street, locked in together in the same fortified houses, behind the same so-called rings of steel. They all partied with each other, even though at home they were kept in their opposing corners. Out where it mattered, where they were the only ones doing the real work, they were all in it together, enemies closer than friends. The local militia had clocked how Western journalists travelled from the start – their armoured cars may as well have been strippers, wearing smaller bikinis every time. If you were a trigger-happy militiaman, you could always bet on an armoured car on the airport road – the only highway in the place that linked anything of note as far as the invasion was concerned. They may as well have named it the Red Zone alongside their so-called Green. That highway just spelled out 'More Idiots Coming into Baghdad'. The definition of an easy target, if you wanted to have a pop. And as soon as Katja sent the intel up to top brass, that was it. House arrest. Locked up by both sides.

It had been a late one, the night before, as usual. Everyone was grouchy, too many people with no place to go, again. Pack a locked room full of folks kept from doing the single thing they know how to, and it will only ever end at the bottom of a bottle of turps. And still there was no such thing as an early night in the sandpit. If Kris wasn't lining up the camera for whichever Tom, Dick or Harry that the news network had parachuted into position to repeat the same thing into the microphone hour after hour after hour, then he'd be editing video he hadn't shot himself because it was getting more and more dangerous for anyone to move around.

He'd known the intel was about a kidnap threat too, of course he had. As if all he ever cared about was his camera, as if his eye alone couldn't possibly compute the bigger picture, the one he wasn't directly looking at. This was hardly his first rodeo. He'd covered the First Gulf War for as long as Katja, never mind that he wasn't the one giving the orders, only carrying them out. It didn't take a genius to figure out what the intelligence report actually said. It wouldn't have made sense otherwise. It had to be about Westerners specifically, pinpointing times and locations for an ambush, and not just another load of tribal pop shots. At some point, this frenzy of power and bloodshed had to count for more than just another few bodies.

So Kris had known perfectly well they shouldn't have gone out that day. The reward was nowhere near worth it. He could take a guess at how much pressure Katja was under, but no one was asking for his opinion. No one ever did. And to think he's a man who calculates risk more than any of them.

All anyone ever wanted to do was look at his pictures. It seemed no one else could see that every single one was a measure of risk, even in the most banal of locations. Not just because he is in the literal line of fire. Because if his timing isn't perfect, if his fly doesn't open and close over his shutter at the exact right nano-second, his whole composition will fall apart, he'll end up with a completely different picture, and the whole operation will have been a waste of fucking time. Photojournalism allows no time for practice. The perfect shot only presents itself the once. He is cal-culating, faster than anyone can imagine, before every single frame. So to chance a journey like that for a press pass? An ID badge worth less than the plastic it's made of if the person in the mugshot is dead? In Baghdad, no less, the heart of the Middle East, where karma was worth a whole lot more than minor detail?

This was a zero-sum game. They knew Westerners were the target. They knew the road was a target. And only paperwork lay at the end. It would never have been his call.

Andie tried reasoning with Katja too, of course she did. He was capable of fighting his own corner but it was her job to do it for him, and she was damn good at it. Besides, the sand was in his eyes, his ears, everywhere by then. He couldn't speak. He'd opened his mouth, all he'd found was a scream, had to swallow it. No one seemed to care what Kris ever said, only what he saw. As for Andie, this war was going to define reputations for years and this was another opportunity to show how good of an operator she could be, even though people did things for her just because of the way she asked. That was her gift. If they weren't going to be able to go out and film stories then surely the paperwork could wait another day or two. She even thought there was a way to wrangle a new badge without actually having to go anywhere, using her contacts in Jordan. They've seen his mugshot a thousand times, haven't they, she'd said, trying to make light of it.

Katja'd laughed too, but not in the way Andie wanted. Katja had lost that gift a long time ago. No one ever seemed to clock what was happening when people like them lost the gifts they'd been hired to use.

And then it got worse, Katja insisted he take Ali too, bring along an Arabic speaker just to renew the damn pass. The Americans were the ones they had to sweet-talk to do it, and none of them spoke Arabic. So why risk him too? What hadn't Kris known about the pressure Katja was really under? For two people who had been so close for so long, how could they have found themselves so far apart they were now opposite? Something else he hadn't been able to ask her, but the sand couldn't help with either.

Ali would have walked through fire if they'd asked, he practically already had, there had been so many explosions to film. Katja'd even said it aloud, the tornado curling and tightening as she leant in closer, that Ali would minimise any threat against him just by looking the part. Never mind that both his cameras, which had to go everywhere he went just in case Saddam Hussein himself walked in, were going to look as inoffensive as a fucking chihuahua in a handbag.

So the sand became grit that he had to keep blinking away. His throat closed over, the argument stayed stuck. Katja was going to make them do it. She was going to send them all out anyway, just to keep his paperwork clean.

For her, the risk of being caught short was far worse than any risk he was about to take. For her, the reward was worth it.

All he remembers after that is being sent home. Packed on a plane like registered post and just ... sent home. As if Lucia and the kids would suddenly make it all go away.

Chapter 3
Hero's Welcome

It was a week later, at least I think it was. Overnight shifts had a habit of making you lose all sense of time and place. It would have been worse if Diana and I weren't always on together. At least for us, there was always someone else in an identical position – even better, someone we'd known for years. Di and I had been closer than sisters at boarding school. There was always an untold class-room story we could dredge up during the dead hours before dawn. And the chances were that one of us would be on form even if the other one wasn't. The truth is it was always her. She could take things in her stride in a way I never could.

That night was a busy one even before it kicked off. I was only in the kitchen because she dragged me there, insisting if she needed a break then I needed one too.

'You should eat something too, you know. A proper meal.' My stomach turned with the smell of warm plastic as she dangled a forkful of steaming ready meal in front of me.

'Spaghetti bolognese? At 4:00am? Oh, wait, no, don't tell me, it's lasagne.'

'It is, in fact. I'm being good to myself – it even says so on the box.'

The jaunty branding on the crumpled wrapping blurred as I looked down at my watch, smearing away a fleck of coagulated cheese sauce. It was 4:01am, Diana's face lit as pallid as her low-fat bechamel under the windowless kitchen's strip light. Still she ate like she was in a restaurant, delicately serving herself with proper cutlery.

'You wouldn't feel so horrific if you treated the night shift like normal workday. Eat some cereal when you wake up, have a sandwich at midnight, then a hot dinner like I do.'

I made a face. 'Like microwave lasagne at 4:00am is a proper meal.'

She put her knife and fork together. 'Well, when you let a typo through on your graphics because you can't see straight, you'll wish you'd at least had your last supper.'

I watched her wash up at the sink before reapplying lipstick using her reflection in the vending machine.

'That's nice,' I mumbled.

'Audacious,' she replied, barely moving her mouth.

I raised my eyebrows as she sighed.

'Not you, silly. This.' She turned to me, clicking and unclicking the shiny tube. 'I guess they think calling it ridiculous things will make us more likely to buy it.

'Well, does it?'

'No.' She turned back to the vending machine, smacking her lips at herself. 'It just helps me feel more awake, is all. Don't tell me, yours is called "pout".'

I had to laugh. Her reflection smiled at me before she headed back into the newsroom.

I paused by the snack machine, trying not to look at my own reflection as I retrieved myself a haul of chocolate. I was most definitely pouting. And it was far more desperate than audacious. It had barely been a week. It felt impossible. Someone had been shot, someone else was still on life support, and yet here we were, back on overnights as if nothing had ever happened, living the same day that becomes night that becomes day again. As usual I was still flailing, while Diana hadn't skipped a beat.

'Wow,' Diana muttered, dipping her head behind her monitor as I swung into my seat next to her. 'What is he doing in here this early? Or late?'

I followed her gaze to the news desk lit up along the length of the far wall, to find none other than Kris himself, head complete with hospital dressing, lounging against its far corner like it was the most normal place in the world he might be found at dawn, blue eyes swivelling and popping even from this far away.

'He's not supposed to be anywhere near the office. He's meant to be resting, recovering, anywhere but the newsroom.' Diana's typing gave her muttering a certain tempo.

'Well you know full well he's been in, don't you?'

I tried to say it lightly but I knew it sounded anything but. As soon as he was well enough to fly, Kris had been evacuated to unheard fanfare. It was as if the more superhuman he seemed, the better everyone would feel about what had happened to Ali.

She cocked her head as she replied, even though she wasn't looking at me. 'I was hardly the only one talking to him.'

I knew I sounded resentful, but I was so tired, my guard was right down. Di was always one step ahead of me. And everyone was adopting Kris's story like it was theirs.

I tried to change the subject. 'Can you take a look at what I've done to page eighteen?'

Diana still managed to hum and type as if nothing unusual was happening, even as probably the widest smile I'd ever seen appeared over the top of her monitor.

'Well, if it isn't Lady Diana...'

I caught my breath as a pair of luminous blue eyes flashed at us both, as unmistakable as his clipped Kiwi vowels.

'It's a bit early for the cameramen, isn't it?' Diana's smile came easily; mine just felt inappropriately plastered across my face.

'Not if it's where the action is.' He beamed as he rubbed his hands together.

At least I'm too dark to blush properly, I thought, tell-tale pink staining Diana's creamy cheeks. It's only ever me who knows how I really feel. And spotting Kris in the newsroom, during the dead hour or not, didn't surprise me at all. That's how passionate he was. That's how committed he was.

'I'm not sure I would call this action, and I'm the one producing these programmes.'

'So what's news? Have you two got anything good for me this evening?'

My ears tingled with recognition.

'Not really.' Di fiddled with her computer mouse. 'It's the same story, just a different day. There was a mortar attack in Baghdad an hour or so ago. Shrapnel wounds outside the US embassy.'

I found myself holding my breath, but Kris didn't even flinch. 'That's the best you can do?'

She cocked her head. 'Well, we don't exactly get out much on the overnight shift.'

'Yeah,' I added reflexively, instantly furious with myself. *Yeah?* The pop and crack of his chewing gum echoed round the room as he leant towards us, somehow still smiling while chewing.

'You'll have to join us tonight then. Let me buy you both a drink. You deserve a whole lot more than just one, stuck in here.'

'Overnights start at ten,' I heard myself say. *Oh God, even worse.*

But his laugh was with me, not at me. 'So just think of it as an early start. We're only ever across the street. You may as well be in the office – that's what everyone else tells themselves, so you two can definitely get away with it. I'll see you in there, alright?'

And with that, he waltzed off, still beaming at nothing in particular. 'Be lucky,' drifted through the glass exit door as it swung dumbly on its hinges behind him.

'Overnights start at ten?'

I couldn't tell whether it was humour or pity creased across Diana's face. I rolled my eyes as I rubbed them, digging in with my knuckles. The hour before dawn was always worst of all. Before you knew it, Monday had become Tuesday, with no closure at all if you'd had a bad day. Or night. They were all one big, blurry mass.

'We should go though, shouldn't we?' My vision rippled and curled as I looked at her, still pink in the face. For a moment I felt sorry for her. She could never hide anything.

'Go where? For drinks?'

'Well, yeah. Like he said. We only need to show up here at ten. We can easily swing by first. They'll be in there all evening, probably all day...' I trailed off as I considered this. The rest of the newsroom seemed to think Kris should still be dumb with shock. To me, he was just on top of his game. I wouldn't have expected anything else. Risk being inherent in everything he did was just a fact of the job. And this was a job founded on facts, not emotion.

Diana shook her liquid hair as she stared at me.

'He asked, didn't he?' I tried not to sound defensive.

'I'd hardly call that asking. And since when did you start tolerating the crowds at the bar? I thought they weren't serious enough about the job.'

'It's not like we have to drink to go, is it? Couldn't we just, you know, turn up?'

My ears tingled so hard I was sure she'd be able to tell I was secretly blushing.

'Come on, Sami. You said it yourself. He's not sitting in there on his own. There's a hero's welcome laid on every night of the week. We'll never get off overnights if we screw up after being spotted in there beforehand.'

I scowled as she folded her arms like it might put an end to the conversation, jerking her head at me for good measure.

'You speak Arabic and you're still stuck in the graveyard. It's bad enough that the rest of this lot are reduced to sniffing themselves through it.' She tossed her head towards the glass doors and the entrance to the ladies toilet.

'I thought—'

'...that it was just talk? Nope.' Diana's head dipped below her monitor again as she leant over to whisper, nodding towards the supervisor's workstation a few feet away.

'I know for a fact that Mary, at least, parties all day after her programmes are over. Then sniffs her way sober so she can come back in on time. It sharpens her up, apparently.'

I couldn't help but stare at Mary. Another immaculate Sloane, all high polish and glamour, brushing non-existent lint off her perfect collar while talking to somebody else.

'And Matt?' Di tossed her head towards the lanky dark suit lounging next to Mary. 'I heard he once got so wired he stayed awake for three days straight.'

'He's never let so much as a typo on screen though,' I mumbled. 'If they can do what they like so long as the product doesn't suffer, then why can't we?'

Diana grabbed her water bottle with another snort as she stood up. I knew I was pushing her, but I didn't care. I wasn't going to pass up the opportunity to get closer to the field crews, no way. My motivation was clear and I thought hers was as obvious.

'Let's just see how much sleep we both get today, OK?'

We both jumped as our computers interrupted us with a curt, sharp buzz. Diana dropped back into her seat with a groan. I scanned the breaking-news headline over her shoulder. Urgent, bright-red news wires were flashing across our screens almost faster than I could read them, buzzing as they landed. Only the red ones were programmed to make a sound. Red, again.

'The Green Zone? And they already think at least ten are dead?' Diana murmured to herself.

'That mortar attack must have been a distraction,' I muttered back.

'But an actual car bomb managed to ram the main gates? How often has that happened?'

My heart started to race. And not just because we'd have to change every graphic in the programme. Suddenly the newsroom was a blur of activity, shouts and instructions bouncing off the padded walls at either end of the set, figures whirling back and forth. I sneezed as Mary screeched over in a shop-girl cloud of perfume.

'We'll go straight to our correspondents in Baghdad right at the start, OK, Di?' I sneezed again as she leant over us, gesturing at the programme lined up on Diana's screen. 'Everyone's rushing to get ready now. So keep the introduction as brief as you can – we begin with breaking news out of Iraq, where the death toll is climbing after a series of brazen attacks on the fortified heart of Baghdad ... you know the drill.'

'How do you want me to handle the graphics?' I wiped my eyes as I looked up at her. Close up, I knew instantly that Diana was right about her partying. Mary's face looked like paper – pale and creased, wide eyes darting maniacally from side to side. My stomach twisted. Why should we take instructions about some-thing as important as this from someone like her?

'Keep the numbers out of it,' she said, chewing her lower lip. 'The death toll will change a million times, and I don't want to be caught with the wrong numbers on screen.'

I nodded as I typed, adrenaline coursing through me like an electrical current. At least now the overnight shift had purpose again; better still, we were at the centre of it all. I pushed away the thought that not everyone cared about what was going on in the Middle East as much as I did, and obviously not some of the people I was doing it with.

'And buckle up, ladies, OK? This is a major escalation – we need to start thinking about what is going to happen as a result.'

I tuned her out as I got to work, methodically updating every graphic in order, mentally checking and rechecking timeframes and numbers: yes, it was definitely still November, the war had started in March, so saying eight months ago was correct, and it was just over two years since 9/11. What other stats and references would Mary want to use? Probably none, as the story was already moving so fast, but all the details had to be exact in case they were, and if I missed so much as a spelling mistake – only being perfect would get me a ticket out of here, and out there.

I shook my head as I started to daydream, snapping myself out of it. At that moment, there was still a whole lot more than just distance between where I was and where I wanted to be.

Chapter 4
Warm Bodies

Of course he went into the newsroom. Where else would he go? It wasn't like he had any friends who weren't colleagues. There were so few of them left that did what he did, he hardly had any colleagues either. No one in their line of work had any friends. They'd all let them down a hundred too many times to even pretend to keep calling them that. Weddings, babies, being there for the blowback after catastrophic personal news – you name it, he'd missed it. And his own kids, Lucia – they were so used to not having him around, his absence was just the status quo. Once they'd all had a hug and established his missing chunk of hair was going to grow back and he wouldn't look like a monk forever, the bandage on his head became a lot less interesting, and he was just the man they were repeatedly told was Daddy, lying around the house with nothing better to do than to get in their way, like this was no different to any other return trip. He just looked stupider, and the bar was already low. His own family was a snare, and like any well-oiled trap, you never knew it was one until you couldn't get out.

Kris allowed himself to dwell on it during his cab ride back to HQ, if nothing else to help block out the twinkling Christmas lights already strung all over central London. When you're away more than you're around, of course you'll start to feel inconvenient pretty quickly. If you're comfortable for too long, of course you'll start to think too much. Home never feels like home – or you've forgotten what home is supposed to feel like. Frankly it's not a bad state of mind when all your options are a pale reflection of what you had to start with. Never mind the fact his first version of the place was on the literal opposite side of the world. He found the ridged scar on his wrist, pinched it hard, locked that mental alleyway down before his mind could even wander to the edge.

Time slowed with the cab, long enough for him to squint at the crowd on the pavement outside the office, all lined up to greet him in the manky, tepid rain he only ever seemed to feel in England, and still, it didn't feel like home. Kris didn't even know why he called it that. But everyone went home, that was the thing. The weeks straight that you worked, you were supposed to think about home, you were expected to talk about all the things you'd do when you got there. If you had kids, you were supposed to imagine the activities you'd do together in mesmerising detail. Better still, if you had a partner to do it all with, another apple-cheeked smiler. Never mind the inevitable agony it would cause you when it all fell apart. He leant closer to the window, breath turning it to fog, trying to feel the warmth radiating from them. Instead all he got was a shiver. The door opened before he could hold it shut and try again.

'Nice haircut, Gonzo,' Ross joked as he got out, hugging him practically before Kris could stand up straight.

'You didn't get a laugh at the airport, DeVito,' he replied, returning the squeeze till Ross coughed. Was his manager going to meet and escort him every place he went now? 'How about a laugh for me this time?'

'I'll let you have that.' Ross coughed again before turning to the crowd of other shooters beaming behind him. 'But if any of you lot try calling me Danny DeVito you'll find yourselves filming overnight in the rain for the next month.'

Kris's laugh came easy then. They called him Gonzo because he partied the hardest – Gonzo Gonzales, always after one more shot. The gonzo journalist who never gives up. He was pretty sure at least Ross knew that the guy who actually coined the fucking term – Hunter S. Thompson – said he believed objectivity to be a myth.

That fiction was often the best fact, better still, retold under the influence of vast quantities of psychotropic drugs. So wasn't it the exact opposite of what they were all supposed to be doing? But by then the name had stuck, and even a mountain of Peru's finest couldn't restore the will to argue it out.

Once inside, it took forever for him to move more than an inch. People were stacked up the stairs – forget about the lifts, no sooner did the doors open than he had to stand there, nodding at everyone who came out, never getting a chance to climb in. So the stairs it was, except he could barely climb a step for having to grip and grin, even though he didn't have a clue who half of them were. After a while Ross just manhandled him over to his office in the back corner of the newsroom, by rights the door should have shattered he slammed it so hard. All the management offices were made of glass, as if that in itself would mean they could never hide anything. And finally Kris found a genuine smile, slumping down in one of Ross's red armchairs while propping his feet on another one. He'd slept in this exact spot so often, it felt like a version of home for a second. It was a poxy excuse for an armchair was the truth – hard angles, scratchy fabric, all style over substance. Just like home, he thought as he closed his eyes for a second.

'How's Lucia doing? How're the boys?' Ross bustled about with some cables so he didn't have to look at him.

'You know how that goes. They're sick of me already.' Kris fidgeted, trying to get comfortable. 'Even the dog's skittish. I think she can smell the strays all over me.'

'Ah, she'll be the first to forgive you. Then the kids will follow, don't you worry.'

'Whatever you reckon.'

He deflated a bit then, stopped trying to find the right spot to sit in. The dog stung far more than the kids. Trixie was usually more dependable than Lucia, loving no matter what. And Lucia hadn't exactly followed their usual script either. He closed his eyes, as if it was possible Ross was going to let him sleep there and then.

'Gonzo?'

Kris kept his eyes shut. 'What?'

'I've been there too, you know.'

'Haven't we all.'

'Come on, Kris. It changes things.'

He cracked an eye to find Ross gazing at the wheelchair folded up behind his desk.

'I can see why it did for you, sure.' Kris couldn't help but look at the wheelchair too then, its tarnished silver frame laid in an ugly twist against the wall. Ross had spent months in that thing while he learned to walk again. Probably felt like home after a while, gave him that much support. And all he'd done was fallen hard while he was running away. Nothing had actually hit him.

'I mean for the families. Not for you. It becomes much more clear and present. The danger, that is.'

Silence then, except for a wheeze of the armchair as Kris fidgeted. He didn't think it had changed much for Lucia. And whether it had changed much for his kids? He didn't want to have that conversation with himself, let alone with Ross.

'I think she's alright,' he replied slowly. 'The boys too. This is what they're used to. They don't expect to have me around all the time. And honestly, I think Lucia's happier when I'm not. She'd never had this much control in her entire life before I gave it to her.'

Kris pictured his four sisters-in-law as Ross snorted. Lucia wasn't even the youngest or oldest. To be honest, he couldn't remember where she fit. Just that she was neither number one or five. Those two had always dead-eyed him with a level of suspicion. The others – not so much. They knew what Lucia was after because they were after it too. Individual recognition. A patch of real estate. Something that was wholly theirs.

'And that bothers you?'

Kris looked up in surprise.

'Hardly. How else would I keep doing it if she was in pieces every time I headed out? She's got everything she needs and knows it can't be taken away from her.'

'So what's changed?'

'Nothing, mate. Nothing.'

Ross tossed his head at the wheelchair again.

Kris sighed. 'She was a bit, you know, more wordy this time, OK? There were a few more hearts and flowers than usual. I guess she saw behind the curtain for a second and discovered she didn't much fancy it. It won't last, though. So long as she's got her car, her house, her little, I don't know, projects – something about the garden next, apparently – she'll be good as gold.'

'And is that enough for you?'

'What, that she's going to lay me a new lawn?'

'Kris.'

He kicked at a well-known tear in the carpet. Ross was always trying to drag it out of him. As if Kris could ever let that happen. His well-worn screensaver swam into view – Ross's wife, their kids, blossoming front garden, shaggy, gambolling sheepdogs: his rock-solid foundation. Kris blinked, a sudden flurry, as he tried to conjure his own. It had the same component parts, but still, Kris was somehow always just out of frame.

'The kids, they need their mum, don't they? The dads, especially ones like us – we're more dispensable.'

'We don't get to choose who we are, I suppose. That much is true.'

More silence, as Kris shredded a bit more carpet. That was the problem with kids. They gave both parents an immovable stake in the future. He sighed again.

'So have you spoke to Katja today? What about Andie?'

'Just now, actually.' Ross picked up a cable from the pile under the desk to twist between his fingers. 'Ali's still critical, but stable, at least. We'll know more when the brain swelling goes down, but it's still early days. The doctors told Katja it might take weeks, months even—'

'Yeah.' Kris cut him off. This wasn't the subject he'd wanted to change to, although he should have known Ross would have assumed the opposite. Ross thought the best of everyone.

'Speaking of doctors,' Ross started up again, tapping the end of the cable on his desk. 'Don't you have something for me?'

Kris dug around for the piece of paper crumpled into his pocket. Dr Collingwood, the network's answer to any potential employee lawsuit. His small but perfectly formed consulting room, all dark, oiled wood and velvet armchairs, secreted between the creamy white pillars of Harley Street's obscenely expensive townhouses, all paid for by the right words on a piece of fucking paper. So long as top brass had that guy's signature, they were in the clear. Kris had been frogmarched there direct from the airport, then again by Lucia two days later. He'd only complied for his own benefit, mind. He needed that piece of paper too. He couldn't live any other way than this.

'A medical miracle, eh?' Ross raised his eyebrows over the rim of the paper.

'Typed up in black and white, too.' Kris lifted his feet back into the opposite armchair, back on steady ground now. 'No one can argue with it. But I've lost one of my nine lives, apparently. Like no one's ever tried that joke before.'

But Ross frowned rather than laughed. 'Is that it?' He turned the piece of paper over in his hand.

'That's the lot, skipper.' Kris crossed his legs, lacing his hands over his tummy. 'A medical miracle. It'll be engraved on my headstone next.'

Finally Ross saw the joke, snorting as he placed the piece of paper carefully on top of the overflowing tray balanced on the corner of his desk.

'So, where's next?' Kris said after a moment, thumping a fist into his chest to clear a cough. 'Afghanistan?'

'Come on, Gonzo.'

'Well you read it, didn't you? Eight lives to go and all that? I'm useful anywhere but here.'

Ross's eyes narrowed again. Kris swung his legs to the floor, panic licking at the edges.

'You come on, DeVito. I've ticked the insurance box.'

'Technically yes, but—'

'Technicalities are all that matter. It was a technicality that put us on the damn airport road in the first place.'

'Is this really the time to go over that? Sitting here with your head like a pumpkin on Hallowe'en?'

Kris cracked his knuckles. 'Who said I want to go over it? You lot have got Katja to rinse for that. I'm just saying that technically, I'm fine to go. And technically, you need me to travel. Because technically, all the network needs are warm bodies.'

Ross was on his feet now, wincing. Kris knew he was snapping too easily, but couldn't help it. He couldn't risk being benched in the name of recovery, no way, and sure as shit Ross was going to try it. That idyllic family snapshot he could barely see? Those pudgy, sloe-eyed little boys who only smiled when he was behind the camera? He didn't dare picture Lucia.

'What, like you haven't said the same, haven't laughed about it a million times yourself? You think we don't hear Katja, night after night, yelling about it? You're asking us to do more with less – she could put me on the phone, I know her speech that well. There are thousands dead in the wars all our warm bodies are covering, and you lot still say it – and now suddenly it's in bad taste because of Ali, because of me? He's only still warm courtesy of a machine, by the way.'

'Don't goad me, Kris.' Ross still managed to sound mild as the weather. 'It won't do you any favours. I'm on your side, remember? I am well aware of the demands of this news network. I am also well aware of the demands of the job. This little outburst is giving me plenty of evidence to suggest you aren't ready to return to it just yet.'

Kris held his breath as Ross paused, feeling the sweat prickling out across his forehead but not daring to wipe it away and draw any more attention to the stupid bandage.

'I'm also not dumb enough to think that keeping you at home is going to protect you in any way other than from live ammunition.'

'Well, then,' Kris mumbled through his sigh of relief. This was an argument he knew he had won long before it started, they both did. They knew what kind of company they worked for, what kind of industry paid their bills. But Ross needed at least to feel like he had some agency over the process. Even though the only agency at play here was the hard-news variety.

'So, I can at least trust you to take it easy until I know what's next?'

Kris forced himself to meet Ross's eyes as he nodded. The guy didn't deserve it from him, no way. He'd been in the thick of it so many times himself he'd lost his full mobility in the process, but he'd have to be six feet under before he abandoned the rest of the tribe. Even if that meant stuffing himself behind a desk all day and all night, walling himself in with equipment. And all the Western news networks were the same, all under the same cosh to hold up the mirror to their respective state's efforts to restore their version of order in the Middle East. There were only so many people who could do that to go around, same as the poor sods in the military.

There were only so many warm and willing bodies who could do what they could.

So he went back to the pub. Where else would he go? And slept downstairs in the crew room until the bar opened again the next day. There was no point going back to the house. He was already in the only place he needed to be.

Chapter 5
Aftershock

Unusually, I woke up when the phone rang. Normally it was a bus horn, or a backfiring motorbike, occasionally a football crowd if I was lucky enough to sleep that late. Nonetheless I loved my tiny flat high above the Holloway Road. It may have been a studio but it had a balcony. If I couldn't sleep I could always watch the day rise and fall on the road's many communities. It felt like there was nothing it hadn't seen.

'Sami? Don't tell me you were still asleep?'

Di sounded like she might just have found out I was in bed with her brother.

'I was, if you can believe that.' I hummed through my yawn just to ram it home. 'See? I told you I don't need any of your revolting microwave lasagne for my body to figure this out.'

The receiver pinched between my head and the mattress as I rolled over towards the window, stretching my legs under the duvet. It was already dark outside but at this time of year it could mean it was still as early as 4:00pm.

I yawned again, brain damp with sleep.

Di sighed down the phone. 'You jammy cow. You must have had eight hours. I don't remember the last time I had more than six.'

I leant down to retrieve my watch from under the edge of the rug by my bed.

'Is it really gone seven? Or did I break my watch?'

'Hurry up, would you? You were the one that wanted to bloody go.'

'Go where?' The room swayed as I sat up, clutching the phone to the still-warm side of my head.

'For drinks, remember? We live like aliens, apparently. We're going to go out like normal people.'

'Ah.' The events of the last twelve hours tumbled back into my brain. 'Well, of course you haven't slept all day.'

'That's got nothing to do with it.' I could practically hear her tossing her head as she said it. 'I just couldn't wind down today. I did everything I usually do, but still. Shall we meet at eight, then? That should give us two hours ... Sam? Hulloooo?'

It took me a moment to process, brain still clotted. Sleeping pills had been part of my life long before the overnight shifts started, but Di didn't need to know that. Plus I liked to pretend that work was the only reason I still used them.

'Sure,' I replied, staring dumbly at the crowds moving back and forth on the street below.

'And don't be late, OK?'

Diana suddenly sounded terrified, but by the time I replied, all I could hear was dial tone.

~~~

Outside, the night was sharp and crisp, ink-fresh sky shining over the crowded Soho streets. It never mattered if it was a weeknight. It seemed people always had a reason to be in this corner of town whatever the time was. And outside the pub opposite the office, the crowd was already rowdy. Puddles of beer pooled on the pavement, crumpled cigarette cartons spilled out of the bins flanking the public toilet block on the other side of the pedestrianised street – notorious for people choosing to relieve themselves against its exterior wall rather than try going inside it. Diana may as well have been a mirage, her entire personage gleaming as she walked towards me, picking her way through the detritus of an evening already in full swing, the end of a long day for everyone except us.

'How is it you are earlier than me?' She shook her head at me with a shy smile. 'Thanks for the hustle. I couldn't do this without you. Like everything.'

'Shucks,' I replied, warm from the inside as I linked arms with her. 'This game isn't meant to be played solo, is it. And you look fabulous. Skin like you've slept for a week. Don't get me started on the hair ... Come on. Best foot forward.'

Liquid sloshed over one of my shoes as we stepped inside. Hardly a good omen, I thought, hoping it was just rainwater, knowing that it wasn't. This pub trip was just as much about me as it was about Di. Not that she needed to know that either.

The air inside the bar was so thick with smoke and noise that it had an almost physical quality, and still I found myself gulping it in with every step. I gave Di a thumbs-up as she raised her eyebrows at the bar. Even though the place was packed she had two glasses of soda and a slice between her neatly manicured fingers in seconds.

'Do you see him?' she shouted, so close to my ear I felt the heat of her breath.

'I can't see anyone,' I shouted back, grimacing as I washed smoke out of my mouth with the acid reek of lime cordial. 'Come on, let's try the back.'

I stayed behind her as she wound her way through the crowds at the bar to the endless nooks in the bowels of the pub, cigarette butts and crisp packets thick below our feet. People parted for Di, not the other way around. I could always tell from the surprise on faces if she was behind me. I busied myself scanning every overcrowded table until an unmistakable pair of blue eyes lasered through the smoke.

'Well, if it isn't the ladies of the night after all,' Kris shouted through another improbably wide grin. 'Shove up, lads, will you?'

A finger of ash fell off the cigarette in his hand as he gestured towards the bench next to him, two other photographers who I vaguely recognised shuffling up to the end.

'You made it.' I nodded as he beamed at us, lighting another cigarette only to just hold it between his fingers like a prop. 'What can I get you? Let me buy you one, at least.'

'We're all set, thanks,' replied Di, tapping her red fingernails against her glass.

'That's hardly going to get you through the night.' Liquid slopped out of the two overflowing shot glasses he nudged towards us. 'Get these down you. It's only aftershock … won't touch the sides. Promise. When do aftershocks ever do any real damage?'

I laughed along with the rest of the table. It seemed like the right move. He nodded approvingly as we toyed with our glasses.

'So, who's your friend?'

I felt Di stiffen beside me, we were packed in so tightly. Suddenly I realised I was sandwiched between them both, like some awkward ingredient.

'We work together on programming,' she answered for me. 'Sami does all the graphics on the morning shows.'

My ears tingled as her fingernails tapped away on her glass.

'Sami,' Kris said exaggeratedly, slugging down the shot in front of him. I tried not to smile as I realised it had been mine. 'Sami, Sami, Sami.' I briefly wondered whether he was drunk until it clicked. 'You were the one on the phone to Andie, right?'

'That's me,' I said brightly, suddenly grateful for the cold glass to grip. 'Penny wanted someone at the end of the phone to her at all times while everything was going off.'

'I bet she did.' He downed another shot, empty glasses clattering as they rolled between the smoking ashtrays on the table. 'And you're all ready for another night in paradise?'

Di giggled in time with her nails tap-tap-tapping the side of her glass.

'Ready as we'll ever be. At least it'll be busy after yesterday's attacks. Busy is good. It makes the hours fly by.'

'Can't you get the sandpit off the front page?' Kris took another deep draft of beer. 'All this talk about Baghdad is messing with my juju.'

The rest of the table laughed uproariously. I felt the ghost of Ali as Kris fingered the bandage on his head with a grin.

'Well, we can't make things up,' I said, pretending not to feel Di tensing again next to me. 'It's the only story in town, and it's our job to cover it.'

'Still a believer, I see.' Kris raised his eyebrows as he nudged at another overflowing shot glass. 'Another one of these should sort that out. Show you what your dreams are really made of.'

Di looked aghast as I tossed it back. Frankly I hadn't been expecting to do it any more than she had, but the emptiness underlying Kris's stare reminded me of something I had long tried to forget.

'Wasn't so bad, was it?' That smile reappeared as I swallowed twice, alcohol and sugar still lodged in my mouth. 'So tell me, Sami. What's your story?'

I stared at him as he paused for a gulp from his pint glass.

'You speak Arabic, right? So what's your game? Folks don't sweat on the overnight shift around here just to collect a wage. You're hardly going to stay part of the newsroom furniture for long, are you?'

'I'm not playing any game,' I said confidently, even as I realised he could only know this about me because Andie had told him. Someone hooted next to me at a joke I couldn't hear.

'Don't you want to hold power to account, give voice to the voiceless, shine a light into the darkness – What did I miss? Any new cliches being taught at journalism school these days?' He stood up, continuing through his teeth. 'Back in a tick.'

I swallowed hard as he pushed his way through the crowd to the bathroom.

'What was that about?' Diana's marble-green eyes were wide in her face. 'What on earth did you say to Andie that day?'

'Barely anything.' I gazed through the smoke at Kris disappearing into the gents. 'Penny told me to keep her talking, and she kept asking me pointless questions. So I answered them.'

'Like what? Surely you didn't try to get on her good side at a time like that?'

'Of course not.' I toyed with one of the glasses still rolling on the table, mind racing. 'She asked me where I was from. I told her. She asked if I spoke Arabic, I told her.'

Diana hung her head with a groan.

'What?'

'Andie thinks she's always being passed over for stories in the Middle East because she doesn't speak the language. You must have heard Penny go on about it.'

Di faded as I swallowed and swallowed, but the lump in my throat just got larger and larger. Worse, it seemed irreparably coated in alcohol, a sensation as foul as it was unfamiliar.

'…And everyone wants to get out to Baghdad. Loads of more experienced producers at all the networks are missing out to people like you.'

'That is so ridiculous.' The empty shot glass bounced rather than smashed as I rolled it deliberately on to the sticky floor.

'It's a thing,' Diana said through the side of her mouth. 'We're all only as good as our last story. Haven't you ever wondered why Andie chats to me but she's never said a word to you? It's obvious *I* don't want to go anywhere near the place.'

I sneezed as perfume, aftershave and cigarette smoke became noxious. Diana wore her disdain for fieldwork as glossily as her wardrobe. There was no mistaking her newsroom ambitions. Management all the way.

'Are you sure that's all you said?'

'What does it matter?' I kicked at the glass on the floor, itching to spit. 'I obviously offended her enough in the moment that it came out in pillow talk—'

'Shhhhhhhhhh.' Diana cocked her head at Kris, who had re-appeared with a grin.

'That's better,' he said, sliding back into his seat and lifting a fresh pint to his lips in one fluid movement. I caught my breath as his sleeve rode up, exposing the livid, ridged scar around his wrist.

'It looks worse than it is,' he said, putting his glass down in front of me. Diana let out a nervous laugh.

'Standard Gonzo,' joked the heavily tattooed Australian opposite. Kris laughed back, tugging at his sleeve a beat too long. 'You girls know how he got that?'

'Can it, would you?' Kris reached for another aftershock.

'Amazing what handcuffs can do when put on by the religious police, huh.' The Australian grabbed an aftershock for himself. 'Saudi Arabia's finest.'

Kris tipped his head back, pouring the shot down his throat.

'What happened?' I couldn't help myself. Even the Australian looked surprised.

'She took off her headscarf,' he replied so Kris didn't have to. 'Andie, that is. It was about 120 degrees, mind. But it didn't go well.'

'She may as well have taken off her pants,' I mumbled. I had heard fragments of this story before. A few months earlier Andie and Kris had been arrested in Saudi Arabia for immodesty. There had been plenty of lewd jokes as to why.

'Huh?' Kris looked up then. Next to me, Diana was stiff as a board.

'Nothing,' I gabbled.

He frowned as the Australian mercifully continued talking. I was hardly going to say how the Saudis saw women displaying the hair on their heads as equally blasphemous as flashing the hair between their legs. All I had wanted to show was that I understood. Instead I already seemed as if I didn't.

'Those guys have cut off hands for less. They were lucky. Hey, Gonzo – didn't you have to sign a confession or something?'

'Yeah,' Kris mumbled.

'In Arabic too.' The Australian started to laugh. 'They still don't know what it actually says.'

'Gosh,' Diana said as the rest of the crew round the table joined in the giggles. All credit to her as at that moment, I was struck completely dumb. The truth is Andie will have only got away with any of it because of Kris. The Saudis didn't allow women to drive a car, show their faces, much less travel anywhere without a man. What that confession actually said will have been irrelevant. But Andie would always know she hadn't understood it.

'Isn't it your round?' Kris turned his empty shot glass on its head with a sharp tap.

'Well you're the Kiwi. So of course it's my round.' The Australian stood up immediately, to a roar of laughter. I stood too, suddenly completely wrongfooted. I should have realised long before it became obvious. Andie was my competition. She was never going to be my friend.

'You can leave the bar to him, don't worry.' Kris smiled up at me. 'You should take it as a compliment that he's finally getting his wallet out.'

The rest of the table roared again as I shifted from foot to foot.

'We'd better go, actually.' I looked past him to Di, willing that she stand up too.

'What's the rush? You only just got here.'

'Yes, well, this is just the start of the day for us.' Diana got to her feet. 'Come on, Sami. We better get you something to eat to soak up all that booze.'

Kris snorted, smile finally dipping a little.

'There's nothing in those. Sugar, water, barely a dash of the good stuff. Hardly going to help you go save the world.'

He nudged at a glass on the floor. It was all I could do to follow as Diana made our excuses and headed for the door, the crowd parting for her as usual. The song playing in the background pierced in for a moment, banging on about the year 2000. Disappointment curdled the alcohol in my stomach. The new millennium had once felt so optimistic.

'Come on, what do you fancy? Thai, Chinese, Indian – what?'

An elbow dug into my ribs as someone stumbled drunkenly past on the pavement outside, but I barely felt it.

'How about pizza?' Di continued, brushing non-existent creases out of her skirt. 'We could try that new type of crust – you know, the one stuffed with cheese.'

'More cheese?' I repeated dumbly. 'How is that even possible?'

'I don't know, do I? Shall we try it?'

I blinked at her still smoothing her shirt over her flat stomach into an even flatter waistband.

'What just happened?'

She took another moment to reply.

'It was a bit awkward, wasn't it? But who knows how they all cope with what they do. And I guess you didn't realise you'd hit a nerve with Andie.'

I blinked back into the smoky interior of the bar.

'He's married, though, isn't he?'

'That's not really the point, is it?'

Di couldn't look at me, still concentrating on her shirt. I shifted my gaze to the cigarette butts floating in pools of beer on the pavement. I couldn't possibly voice what the point really was. That Kris could be anything other than the person I'd imagined.

'I just...' I swallowed down the start of a crack in my voice. 'How can anyone be so blasé about everything we do? Especially someone like him. This war, and all the other wars like it – so many people die.'

'Oh, Sami—' She laid a hand on my arm.

'Don't be too kind to me,' I interrupted before she could say any more, shrugging her away. 'You know how that ends. And I'm fine, really I am. I just can't nod and smile when people brush it off. Especially not people who are supposed to make it impossible for everyone else to turn away.'

'I know, love.' I let her squeeze my arm this time, grateful for the sting. 'Just try not to take yourself so seriously in public, that's all. I know why you're doing it, and of course I understand. But you must be able to see why it is wearing to people like Andie, even Kris – they don't know you. All they see is ambition, drive and inexperience. A dangerous combination when you've been through it all a thousand times.'

I leant into her as she pulled me into the adjacent doorway, out of the path of more stumbling revellers. 'Come on. Pizza? We've even got enough time to sit down – it's only 9:00pm.'

I let her lead me away. Di was usually on the right path, even if I never found it as comfortable as she did.

Chapter 6
One-Eyed inside the Kaleidoscope

He stayed in the pub till they threw him out. He could talk a good game even when he was looped as a hula, and the ever-faithful photographers core didn't disappoint – it was war story after war story, as if those were the only kind he ever wanted to hear. But all of a sudden, the room went from straining at its sweaty seams, crowd whipped into a frenzy of delaying the end, to lights on, barrels run dry, smashed glass everywhere, see ya later, time to go, mate.

Kris found space in his racing thoughts to be furious for a second. The money he spent there, they all spent there, it propped up that bar, it was practically their rent. He could have claimed vacant possession if he'd wanted to. Actually, no he couldn't, because if he was paying rent, it wouldn't be vacant possession, but it was still outrageous – he stumbled out on to the pavement as he tried to figure it out. But by then the last cameraman had already sloped off with some warm and willing body he'd found at the bar, the rest of the chattering classes disappeared in a flurry of high-fives. And just like that, he was suddenly alone, abandoned on the pavement opposite the office with nothing but the full moon, appropriately one-eyed and unblinking overhead.

'Aye up, lad – Kris? Is that you?'

Wait, he was in the dead-end alley behind the office now. He blinked at his feet, desert boots as usual, how had they managed that?

'Steady now...'

Rory stuck up an arm from his pit on the floor, but it was too late, Kris was already collapsing, right into the pile of possessions stacked up next to Rory's filthy blankets, which were spread inside the long-vacant doorway next to the office's back entrance.

'What took you so long?' Rory sat up and gave him a patch to himself, the patch next to Lass, no less – his beloved German Shepherd, so old and knackered she rarely opened her eyes.

'I don't know what you mean,' Kris slurred as Lass licked his face.

'She likes you. She'd have chewed anyone else's face off by now.'

'And I like her,' he grunted, wiping spittle out of an eye. 'These days I like just about any old dog. Especially lassies that can't talk.'

Rory shoved him then.

'Sorry,' Kris mumbled. 'I know I'm never polite enough – where you're concerned anyway.'

'Don't be so hard on yourself. You think anyone else pulls up a pew and bothers to talk to me while you're off on another one of your escapades? I'm worse than invisible. They see the cracks in the paving stones before they see me.'

'That is, indeed, true,' Kris coughed, as Rory's craggy face came into focus. 'I take it it's been the fancy no-fro cappa-frappa-cino brigade these last few weeks?'

'That and the theatre crowd, yep.' Rory raked a self-conscious hand through his hair. 'You lot still keep clippers inside?' He jerked an elbow at the darkened back doors to the office. 'I need to shave this lot off, and pronto, it's giving me the jerks.'

Kris saluted with a shaky hand. Rory would always be the lieutenant colonel he once was, like so many others who ended up sleeping under railway bridges. It was always the ones who joined up practically before they could tie their own shoelaces – army family, heritage, expectation, the whole bit. When it all goes pear-shaped their families are even worse at handling it than them. No one is ever willing to admit they still care about them without the rank, status and glory.

'You'll bring them out next time you're passing?'

'Hang on.' Kris tried and failed to stand up. 'I'll get them for you now...'

'Don't be ridiculous, lad.'

Kris propped himself against the wall as he fumbled in his pocket.

'It can't be that easy,' Rory murmured as Kris swiped his press pass against the exterior security pad.

'Ta-dah!' Kris lost his balance as he spread his arms wide in time with the doors swinging open. 'Back in a tick.'

He could hear Rory chuckling as he swiped his way through the second internal door, stumbling along the darkened passageway to the crew room. There were clippers in a bag hanging from a hook just inside the doorframe. No one ever had time to go to a proper hairdresser, the smudged mirror and blunt clippers always had to do. Anyone could have lent them to the guy trying not to look like he was living off scraps.

Kris pushed open the door, fumbling around for the mesh bag. Cutting his hair was the difference between living and existing for Rory. Why could no one other than Kris piece together why? And this was after a night on the turps heavy enough to sedate a small animal.

He stumbled back along the passageway to the alley, Lass yelping as he sat down heavily on her tail.

'Here.' He tossed Rory the mesh bag. 'You better hope they're charged, is all.'

Closing his eyes, he sank lower into Rory's blankets, smiling as he heard the clippers buzz. Rory would get his haircut. There was some harmony in the world after all.

'You don't look half bad, you know, with a bit of hair to your name,' he murmured, leaning into Lass as she licked his face again.

'Well, judging by the state of your heid, son, I'm guessing I must look like the last king of bloody Scotland.'

Kris's eyes flew open. Rory was just holding the clippers in his hand, clicking them on and off.

'You got caught in bed with someone else's dog recently?'

Kris looked away. 'Something like that.' He fingered the bandage on his head. 'It wasn't worth the risk this time though.'

The clippers started up again, this time taking hair with them.

'So where was it this time? Iraq?' Rory cocked his head as he asked, shaving behind his ear. Kris hoiked up a glob of something caught in his throat.

'That bad, huh?' Rory switched sides. 'And which noble military outfit were you with? The Americans? Don't tell me you were shacked up with the Brits in the south.'

'We were barely out of Baghdad.' Lass swooned under Kris's hand. 'The place is locked up tighter than a gnat's chuff.'

Rory snorted.

'You can't move around unless you're in the pay of the military. So all we ever end up with is some one-eyed view of what it is they think they are doing out there.'

'The war on terror, eh? Locating those elusive weapons of mass destruction?'

Now it was Kris's turn to snort. Rory straightened up, running the clippers down the middle of his head. 'Have any of the various idiotic presidents or prime ministers you've run tape for ever been able to tell you what it actually meant?'

'The war on terror, you mean?'

'That's the one.' Rory clicked the clippers off, smiling. Kris reached out a hand, affirming his freshly shorn scalp. It felt like suede.

'Of course not.' He tapped Rory's head for good measure. 'There's no real answer, is there? You can't wage a war in the abstract.'

'Exactly, son. Exactly.' Rory reached up to squeeze the hand on his head before putting it back into Kris's lap. 'But you're not here to talk about that, are you?'

'Here? You mean in your pit with you?'

'Yes, son, yes. Here, on the very pavement with me, hiding down some back alley in Theatreland at dark, yet another place for this city's living dead to come pretend they are anything but...'

Kris coughed, his head spinning. 'Well, I could ask you the same thing. You're hardly going to attract the pound coins in this dead-end corner, are you?'

'Don't you ever wonder why your top brass make you lot come in and out round the back? As if dragging all your camera kit, all those ugly, heavy cases, the stuff that actually makes television, will put everyone off watching it if they actually knew what it took? They say that about sausages too, you know. No one would ever eat them if they saw how they were made.'

'They say that about Aussies and Kiwis too, you know.' Kris tried to make light of it. 'The sausage would separate if you tried to grind both of us together.'

But he had to look away as Rory's eyes suddenly turned to flint. For the actual fact was he knew exactly why Rory pitched himself so far off the main drag, covered in cardboard like some parcel that fell off the line but nobody wanted anyway.

'So what is it that you are actually doing here, Kris?' Rory repeated gently as Lass started to snore, head lolling on Kris's thigh. 'Nowhere else to go?'

They sat in silence for a moment, suspended in a little pool of light as the moon shone its silvery eye into the alley. Lass's tail gave a thump as Rory started to speak again.

'The trouble with you, son, is that somewhere, buried deep inside that patchy head of yours, you think it's still all worth it. That all the tales you bring back from wherever you've been actually mean something other than ten seconds of distraction to people watching them on the box. They turn it off afterwards, you do know that, don't you?'

Lass's tail gave another flicker. Kris tried to find an alternative point of focus, but even the dark, damp alley walls seemed to swim. He could have come back with quantum mechanics – Rory'd have loved it too – but trying to find the words was a lost cause. What had that professor said? There was an interview he'd never forgotten, some story on artificial intelligence. That the human brain can't handle the complexity of a quantum wave function so it organises it into something it understands. Put simply, the reporter had asked, do you mean that the human brain can't see what it can't handle? Back then Kris had been able to laugh. Not anymore.

'Sometimes, they even turn it off in the middle, because they can't bear to be torn away from their beans on toast, or from whatever pathetic conversation they're having with themselves. Let's say they're the newspaper kind and have gone to the trouble of buying the thing, they still think nothing of crumpling it up to do the crossword – or how about a game of hangman? Hah!'

Kris shifted his gaze to the office doors, all wavy silvery lines framing the dark inside. Back then he could also have argued that journalism was doing a far better job than a human brain, staring complexities in the face before translating them for the benefit of the rest of humankind. The problem was journalists seemed to have lost every scrap of actual humanity in the process. Rory warmed to his theme, as if he was inside Kris's head too.

'And don't get me started on the people whose stories you're telling. I know you don't think showing the world their pain is going to make it go away – you aren't that stupid. So why are you still playing along? Do something else, lad. Not this. It's collusion, at its worst. At best, it's … it's not even bearing witness. Most of these people – there's nothing left that anyone could give them that would make it alright. Justice isn't going to come in any form they would recognise.'

Lass yelped as Kris suddenly stood up, stomach churning with bile.

'Over there, son, over there…' Rory motioned him to a far corner as he started to retch. 'I still have to sleep here after you disappear, you know.'

Kris leant his forehead on the cool brickwork, grateful for the clouds scudding over the moon as he fought and lost against the wave of nausea.

'No, you don't.' Rory hauled Lass back into a prone position as she made for the puddles around Kris's feet. 'We don't eat waste in this alley. No, sirree, we do not.'

Kris spat as he straightened up, grunting apologies.

'Ah, it's alright, lad. I've seen a lot worse, I know you have too. Come on, take another pew before you go.'

Kris stumbled as he backed away.

'Sit down, son. Come on. You're in no condition...'

Rory faded as Kris rounded the corner back, blinking into the streetlamps. There was no sand in the air in London. Another reason he was never comfortable in the place. There was nothing to fall back on when he couldn't open his mouth, stop wiping his eyes, stop blowing his fucking nose.

Streetlamp after streetlamp scudded past as Kris started to walk. From this part of Soho, it was an even two miles to Victoria station, where he knew the benches as well as he knew Rory's patch of pavement, and the trains to suburbia would start to run soon enough. His hand closed into a fist around the money jangling in his pocket. There was more than enough there for a taxi but at the risk of more questions? More conversation? Kris sped up as he turned a corner.

Rory's speech was one he'd given to himself a thousand times before, not to mention to plenty of others – he'd tried convincing Katja, Andie, Penny, the lot of them. But coming from a guy like Rory – he had nothing left except cardboard, didn't he? Was that why hearing it from him was shaking up his own personal kaleidoscope so badly, dislodging parts he didn't even know were there? The orphaned kids he'd interviewed on some far frontline, the privacy he'd invaded to film in destroyed homes, the generals robotically repeating the same state-spun reasons why dropping their latest payload was justified. It was bullshit, the lot of it, the whole rancid excuse for news journalism.

Even if it was news to other people, it wasn't news to him, the fact that pain sells, the fact that telling people about it doesn't make it go away. Kris found himself shivering, a toddler screaming from somewhere deep inside the kaleidoscope, before he managed to shake it again. And this time, somehow, in amongst it all, one true thread started to emerge, a magical beanstalk of a thing, all curls and tendrils knotting around the fragments echoing and banging against each other inside his head, bringing them together in one strong, unbreakable cord.

Kris pulled up short as Piccadilly Circus opened out in front of him, its bright lights and big screens flashing pointlessly into the dark. Maybe it was the shot to the head. But it was the best idea he'd ever had.

He turned on the spot, again and again. No more walking away from pictures of unimaginable pain. No more colluding in the myth that pointing a lens into the darkest of corners will make any difference to what it sees. He spat even as he thought it, a cliché so empty it didn't even deserve to be known as a cliché.

The screens blinked again. The kaleidoscope had crystallised and its new picture was dazzling. And no one else would ever need see it, would ever have a clue what he was doing, if he showed them a different shot.

Kris dug his hand into his pocket, finally able to hail a cab. He knew exactly where he was going now.

Chapter 7
Fresh from the Tigris

'Are you going to be alright? I know you're still overthinking it.'

Even Di looked exhausted as we said goodbye at the top of the steps down to the Tube. To the untrained eye her makeup was still immaculate, but I knew her well enough to see the flaws: blood shot through her green eyes, pale shine on her blush, slightly smudged eyeliner that most would find artful, but Di would frown at as mess.

'You mean what happened in the pub? I'm so over it, honestly. Nothing a pacey overnight shift doesn't sort out.'

I pulled my scarf into a tighter knot as I said it. If I choked the air out of my throat I wouldn't say anything else.

'If you say so. Call me when you're up, OK? There's a good gym class on tonight, if you fancy it. Body pump with a twist.'

I pushed my face into a smile at her striking a pose at the top of the steps.

'Is there such a thing as a good gym class?'

'You'd feel better. Don't knock it till you've tried it.'

'And you know I'll never try it.' We squeezed each other before I headed down stairs with a wave. 'Don't wake me up, OK? I'll call, I promise.'

I could hear her snort just before I hit the main concourse, willing myself to enjoy sailing past the throngs crowding to get through the opposite side of the turnstiles.

Above ground again the air was thick, that curiously warm, wet autumn air that would feel optimistic if spring were actually around the corner. I was so exhausted that I was almost sleepwalking until I saw him, stopping traffic with a meaty hand to get to me before I could disappear inside my block.

'Miss Samira ... wait. Wait, wait!'

This time the smile was genuine, even though I knew what was coming as he rushed over to me, all flamboyant with traditional Middle Eastern greetings. Wahid was a mainstay of the Holloway Road. We'd met when I moved in a year earlier, hawking his cartons of cigarettes and other trinkets on the street corner outside the Coronet, a pub that on the face of it, should have been condemned long ago. But Wahid, laughing and joking, and serving sweet tea to anyone who nodded as they walked past, somehow made it feel welcoming. I had tried to speak to him in Arabic, spotting an opportunity to improve mine, but he'd insisted on English, his still heavily accented despite being here for years. It was obvious, though, that he knew far more than he let on. I spotted early on that the street selling was to stay on top of information for his growing community more than anything else. Once he found out I was working in a newsroom, I could hardly ever slip past him unnoticed. And that was just fine with me. In those briefest of moments, a fleeting sensation of family would descend.

I could hardly blame myself for seeking it out, I reasoned. My father was dead, my mother had been sectioned, and all our problems had done the opposite of bringing my brother and I closer together. The nearest thing I'd ever had to a permanent base was a boarding-school dorm – every school holiday seemed to bring with it a new apartment in a different Middle Eastern capital. I'd done my best to erase any mental pictures of the one we were in when we found out Dad would never come back to hang a new portrait on its clammy walls. I had to find a semblance of community somewhere.

'Miss Samira.' Tatty fingerless gloves clasped my hand, pumping it up and down while he kissed both my cheeks.

'How are you? You are well? I wait to see you – ooof, I look all day and all night. How is it today? Tell me, tell me ... oooffff.'

He patted the low wall bordering my estate as he sat, bagfuls of cigarettes and other knick-knacks bulging on either side.

'There are more bombs, yes? There must be, I know it.'

'It's been a busy few nights, that's for sure,' I said as I perched next to him. 'And for you? I take it no one has bought any of those so far today?' His cartons crackled as he shuffled himself into a more comfortable position.

'Very slow, very slow today,' he replied.

I smiled in spite of myself at the Arabic cadence of his English. I am here to learn, Miss Samira, he'd said that first smoky-bright morning. Not to just be Arab in London ... and this, here, drink for you, please ... I'd tried to tell him no Englishman would ever hand over black, overly sweet tea, particularly in a delicate cut-glass teacup, but he wouldn't hear it of it.

'But tell me, tell me,' he continued now with another hip wiggle. 'What has happen? Something big, yes? I know it, I know it ... I try to speak with my family but–' he flicked a dismissive hand at the internet café across the road '–we all struggle. Nothing is coming through from Baghdad, nothing. We try all night, and now all morning ... nothing.'

'Well there was a car bomb at the gates to the Green Zone,' I said, looking at the cracked paving underfoot. I hated giving Wahid bad news. But that's all he ever seemed to get.

'It was after a mortar attack on the American Embassy. Loads dead, when I left it still wasn't clear how many. But they reckon it's the worst attack on coalition soldiers since the start of the war. There will be reprisals ... I'm sure that's why all comms have been cut, or interrupted.'

Cigarette cartons crunched into my side as Wahid slumped next to me, muttering prayers under his breath. At one time I would say sorry, but I stopped a long time ago. There was no point. The safety of the family he had left in Baghdad was completely out of either of our control.

His eyes glistened as he raised them to the white sky. 'And what will the soldiers do now? I cannot even think of it. You go back to work this evening? You will come and see me first, yes? With any new information? I will be here all day, all night.'

He waved at his spot across the road again just as the Coronet doors swung open. It wasn't officially open until 11:00am but people trudged in and out at all hours. It was good for Wahid. His cigarettes usually went in a flash. But even that wouldn't help him today.

'Of course,' I said, trying not to notice the tear gleaming in the rising sun as it rolled into his beard. 'As soon as I wake up, I'll read all my emails and come for tea. Extra sweet, OK?'

I tried not to smile as I said it. Hanging out with Wahid always made me feel at home in a place where it never took much to feel alien.

'For you, anything,' he replied, leaping to his feet as I stood. 'But please, you will try to find out what is happening in my district? Anything, anything at all you can tell me is good.'

'I can't imagine they'll be doing house-to-house raids or anything like that,' I said, blinking away the image of Wahid's wife and five children, his elderly parents and in-laws, people I'd never even met yet could picture so clearly, all huddled together in their tiny flat as doors were kicked in around them, homes searched, possessions trashed, lives turned upside down. Another family destroyed, just like Ali's. I hadn't dared tell him anything about that. It would just make him angry.

'It's pretty obvious where this attack originated. Only the well-organised insurgent groups would have been able to pull off something this sophisticated, and the coalition knows full well where they are headquartered—'

I jumped as he gripped hold of my arm. 'Please, Miss Samira, *habibti*. You know this is most certainly what they will do, I know it too. These soldiers, they know there is no one there to find, but they will do it anyway – these, these operations are always just to make clear who is in charge, who is the boss.'

'I'm so sorry,' I think I said, but it could have been anything. Wahid was suddenly sobbing into a pristine white handkerchief.

'My uncle, Miss Samira. His house, it is still in pieces – it was raided many weeks ago but still, my family, they cannot put it back together, it is impossible. And now everything will get even worse, again it will get worse.'

I swallowed hard as he looked up, his eyes liquid with tears.

'There is already almost nothing left in my district, Miss Samira. Nothing. There is no school, there is no bakery, there are no markets ... and it was once the finest district in all of Baghdad. The *masgouf*, fresh from the Tigris, the finest in the whole of Iraq. And now – there are only bodies in the Tigris, Miss Samira. There are only holes in the walls that are left.'

I had to look away as his voice cracked.

'I promise you, Wahid, I will try to find out as much as I can. I'll ask our people for all the details they have,' I said, even though I knew I wouldn't. How could I? Some nobody on the overnight shift calling the field crews directly, much less calling them with unrelated questions? Fumes belched from a bus pulling up oppo-site, disgorging passengers like it had been holding its breath.

'Thank you, *habibti*,' Wahid mumbled after a few moments, blowing his nose noisily into his soaking handkerchief. 'I ... I...' he waved a hand to the foggy sky, muttering in Arabic under his breath. 'I know you understand.'

I nodded back at him, my throat too thick to say anything else. It was cruel, really, that I kept going back to him, when it would have been just as easy to freeze him out of my life. It wasn't as if anyone other than the drunks holding up the Coronet bar stopped to talk for a while, much less buy his cigarettes. He may not have worked in the newsroom, but I needed Wahid. I needed him far more than he needed me. At least I could make myself feel better about it, even if it was for just a second, by bringing him information, however bad it was.

Chapter 8
Strawberry Thieves

The boys were already at school by the time he finally got home, but Lucia was still upstairs. It turned out there were a few glittering detours in the new kaleidoscope, but no matter, Trixie still slobbered all over him. Trixie never seemed to mind if he smelled of Lass, it was the strays that got to her. She was always skittish if she sensed any of them, like the fact they were looking for a home meant she might lose her own.

Kris found half a smile as she barked and swooned under his hand. Dogs were more intelligent than humans could ever pretend to be.

Lucia shouted from upstairs. 'Trix. What is it, baba? Mumma won't be long, OK? Trix?'

He was on his knees covered in dog by the time Lucia came into the hallway, Trixie practically draped around his neck.

'Kris – good God.' Lucia clapped a hand over her nose and mouth. 'Where have you been? Can you at least shower before I faint?'

Trixie slithered onto the floor in a love-sick heap as he stood, unbuckling his belt and pulling his T-shirt over his head.

'Trixie, that is disgusting,' Lucia said reprovingly as the dog burrowed into his clothes faster than he could shed them.

'She's a very smart dog.' He managed a wink as he reached for the towel wrapped tight around Lucia's still-wet body, water droplets glistening all over her exposed skin.

'You must be joking.' Lucia gave his outstretched hand a coy smack. 'Play your cards right, and I'll get in behind you, but not until I've seen you wash, and properly.'

Kris followed her up the stairs as she turned, relief cascading over the dried-on sweat as blood rushed to all the usual parts.

'What's this?' He eyed the new row of soaps and potions, surely an impossible number for just one person, lined up battalion-straight inside the shower enclosure.

'I couldn't decide, so I got them all,' she said as she perched on the edge of the bath, towel dropping strategically. 'Good job too, looking at the state of you.'

She tangled a set of perfectly painted toenails into his discarded underwear on the floor.

'You'll have to join me if we're to get through all of these,' he said as the water ran, closing his eyes as she giggled.

'Hurry up, would you?'

He opened an eye to find her pressed, naked, into the glass. 'I'm not getting in until you've taken at least the top layer of dirt off.'

A thought with the intensity of an ear worm nagged at him as he soaped himself, lingering on his cock, as she would expect him to. Did she know? Was this performance deliberately exaggerated, even though it was a usual part of their ritual? Could she sense that it didn't reach the parts it used to? Worse, was she putting it on just for him?

He soaped harder, eyes glazing as he stared past her to some random tile, willing his body not to fail, not now, not directly in front of her, not in full unvarnished daylight. On cue, she suddenly spread her legs, pressing a hairless groin up against the glass, as if it wasn't in any way obscene or disgusting, as if it wasn't in any way criminal that he might get off on her looking like a pre-pubescent child. He turned away for another bottle of soap, rubbed even harder, covered himself in pineapple and mint like a mojito, or was it a pina colada? His stomach twisted at the thought, and now the door was opening, she was coming in one slinky, red-toe-nailed foot after the other, acres of brown satin skin, not a hair to be seen except on her head, one leg then the other clamped around him like a koala, thank God he was still hard enough. There were grunts and cries, those were easy enough to come by, until he felt the unmistakable twitch and pulse of her as the shower thundered. But it wasn't loud enough to drown out the fact that he'd failed to match her. He lathered up another smelly soap, pretended he needed another wash, but there was no fooling her. Still, she cupped his face with a wet hand before retreating, grabbing the only other dry towel to wind herself into a tight knot. The only person doing any unwinding after this was going to have to be him.

Kris rested his head on the tile for a moment as the water shut off.

'Here.' Lucia handed him the wet towel she had previously been wearing.

Kris grunted a thanks. Leaving him naked and cold as she stormed out would have been preferable. But Lucia was far too smart for that. The dignity of a wet towel was just a fig leaf. She was going to try and make him talk.

He sighed as he followed her out into their bedroom, finding her perched on the end of an unfamiliar coverlet.

'That looks nice,' he said, waving at it. 'The red bits ... are they supposed to be strawberries?'

She froze as he stepped towards her.

'Funny you should say that,' she replied, running a finger over the pattern on the bed, his bed, apparently, even though it looked like just another hotel room. 'It's called 'Strawberry Thief' – the design is, I mean. It's William Morris.'

'Right.' As if he hadn't already known. He turned away, fumbled with the chest of drawers.

'You could pretend, you know, Kris. You could fake it. For my sake, if not for yours.'

He deliberately caught a finger in the top drawer rather than answer her. Fake it? *Pretend*? Pretend what? Surely she wasn't about to bring up...

'William Morris was one of this country's most celebrated designers – still, probably, the UK's most iconic in terms of textiles.'

He laughed, suddenly, high and mad.

'You want to talk about William Morris?'

She sighed. 'I just thought you'd have noticed all the changes I've made.'

He laughed again. He was a photographer. He dealt in light and detail. Like he hadn't noticed the new wallpaper, curtains and gazillion other home furnishings she'd added while he'd been away. They could have talked about how remarkable it was that the man behind these now-ubiquitous designs also turned down the post of Poet Laureate. How the volume of iconic art he'd produced was in many ways dwarfed by what he'd written. Did she know that William Morris's largest collection outside of England was actually displayed in New Zealand? Instead it was just silence that settled between them as he pulled out a fresh deck of clothes – always the same: lightweight cargos, loose T-shirt under a fleece, waterproof jacket covered in zipped pockets.

He sighed, another interview chiming in from the past, more explanation of perception versus reality. It's not about what you look at. It's only ever about what you see.

'Aaaand his uniform's back on again.' She spoke softly from behind him. 'So where is it next? And for how long?'

'Afghanistan,' he replied, even though he didn't know for sure. It was a safe enough bet. And right then Afghanistan had everything he needed. A cripplingly expensive, politically damaging and unwinnable war, covered in unimaginable pain with no hope left anywhere in sight.

'Delightful.' She was pushing at the carpet with another one of her perfect toes as he turned around. 'Will you see the boys before you go? They'll be home at the normal time today and tomorrow – that's four o'clock, by the way.'

'Yeah,' he muttered, rooting in a drawer for his passport. He had three, so he was always able to keep one at home. The others were effectively office property, one usually in some embassy for visa purposes – yet again, in case of emergency. Another special dispensation he enjoyed because he had to travel so much: governments allowed you multiple IDs as long as they could use you to peddle their bullshit.

'Are you ... are you sure you're well enough to go back out again so soon?'

He started then, elbow deep in a drawer full of junk, old press passes, staples, some ancient hole punch. Well enough? *Well enough?* Surely she wasn't trying another way into his ... his ... *performance*? Worse, turn it into some affliction he needed to fix?

'It was less than a shrapnel wound,' he muttered, rattling junk below his fingers, willing that was what she'd meant. 'The boys have had far worse falling off the climbing frame.'

'I'm still asking,' she said coolly.

'I'm fine, Luce, never better,' Kris tried to scoff as he tucked his passport into the back zip pocket of his trousers. 'You know I love Afghanistan. It'll be a treat compared to the sandpit. It's exactly what I need.'

'Yes, I'm sure it is.' She let her towel drop then, spilling breasts everywhere. She may as well have slapped him in the face. Still, he continued:

'You should try seeing it for yourself sometime. The place puts William Morris in the shade, even though everyone's had a piece of it – the Americans, the Russians, the Brits, and don't get me started on the Taliban. You won't see a more beautiful setting for a city than Kabul, it's surrounded by three separate circles of mountains, all sparkling, bright with snow—'

'Tommy's started asking, Kris.'

He froze, brain snagged on Kabul's high peaks. 'What do you mean, he's started asking? About what?'

'He wants to know whether Daddy's going to die at work—'

She gasped as Kris slammed the drawer shut on all the other junk, palms suddenly so sweaty they slipped on the wood.

'Sorry,' he mumbled.

'They've started to watch *Newsround* at school...'

'What the hell is *Newsround*?' He found himself opening the drawer again even though there was nothing useful left inside.

'It's a news bulletin made specifically for children. It's only ten minutes, and it's usually only on at five o'clock, they must be taping it or something. It's a British institution, we all watched it when we were growing up.'

'Sounds like just another cartoon compared to what I watched growing up.'

Lucia tucked a wet strand of hair behind her ear as she blinked up at him, naked chest staring along with her. He tried to focus on the strawberry thieves as he had another go.

'So you're telling me school has decided to show a news programme that is walking children through the delights of the war?'

'Not exactly.' She had the decency to cover herself then. 'But it is covering the protests against it, and Tommy's smart, he idolises you. He knows that's where you are, and now he knows why a million people are marching through London angry about it.'

'So tell him I'm somewhere else.'

'I do, and I will, but – I don't know. I can handle it, I've always known I could if we had the right set-up.'

A look passed between them, just for a nanosecond, but a look that connected nonetheless, the nod that signified their mutual terms of acceptance.

'But I don't think either of us could have predicted how the kids might process it until it started to happen.'

'So what are you saying? They'll process it just fine when they stop getting what they want because Daddy got fired from the only job he knows how to do.'

'Kris.' She stood up, tucking her towel around herself like armour. 'All I'm saying is we should think about how to talk to them. How to explain what you're doing all the time you're away from us. He asks enough that I have to say something, and I thought you might like to at least be involved in what I tell him.'

His vision blurred suddenly, a riot of strawberry thieves chirping and cackling as they flew rings around him.

'Tommy is old enough to understand that it's important. I could say that without people like you, people like us wouldn't even know what was going on.'

He walked away abruptly, into the bathroom, unzipping his trousers as if to use the toilet but actually more afraid only bile would come out if he opened his mouth.

'We can't expect them to just accept that you're never here, and that's just the way it is. We can easily keep the heat out of it. He doesn't need details, just that it is significant for the world he lives in, and he can feel proud of your part in that. You'd be doing it for him.'

'Who else do you think I've been doing it for?'

He didn't need to be in the same room as her to know that this time there was no mistaking their understanding of each other's position.

'What else do I have to do for you three?' he continued, staring down into the open toilet. 'I even took your name, as if the Spanish Armada would ever have got as far as New Zealand.'

'Don't pretend you weren't delighted to get rid of yours.'

Kris flushed the toilet to buy some time. He knew she was right about that. He had been more than happy to become a Gonzales, he just wished he'd thought of ditching the poison of his old man's name before some Spanish tradition suggested he had to. As if he was ever going to live by any traditions he'd known as a kid in New Zealand. Aotearoa, land of the long white cloud, neither long enough nor thick enough to cover up even half of what actually happened to the people living on it when the white man showed up and called it his own.

'You're about as Spanish as I am,' he said as he walked back into the bedroom. 'Your parents legged it over here rather than wait for Franco to die.'

He paused at the edge of the strawberry thieves, hovered a hand just above her shoulder, too scared to land it in case she shuddered. But what actually happened is she reached up and grabbed it for herself.

'We can't keep it from them forever,' she murmured, staring at him with her dark eyes, little difference between iris and pupil. Black holes, dying stars, collapsing in on themselves.

He nodded as he stared back, gravitational pull doing its thing. That is until he kissed her so she'd close them, cut the connection. He even slobbered like a teenager and still nothing landed. She licked her lips as she pulled away.

'You'll be back later then? Or tomorrow? Before you fly?'

'Something like that, yeah.' He wiped a thumb around her mouth, tried nudging one corner into a smile.

Downstairs, at least the dog swooned all over again before he headed out.

Chapter 9
Blind Cameras

'You're going to body pump now? Seriously? What happened to treating the overnight shift like a normal workday and going to bed first thing?'

I squinted as I looked up at her. The kitchen strip-lighting seemed harsher than ever. As our night shift drew to a close, I felt like my brain was operating somewhere outside of my body.

'I could say the same to you.' Di sounded curt, punching buttons on the coffee machine. She'd clearly spotted me hanging around Ross's office after our shift ended, seeing if there was a shoot I could join.

'At least body pump helps me get to sleep,' Di continued. 'And sleep well at that.'

I sighed as the coffee machine started to beep and wail. I could hardly tell her why I still didn't need any help passing out.

'I'll go with you this weekend, if you want?'

But all Di did was frown as she fiddled with the water tank at the back. 'I've got to go home, actually. I meant to tell you. Three-line whip. We're all due back for Mummy's birthday even though she'll never tell us neither how old she is nor when the actual date is.'

I slugged down my own coffee even though it was still far too hot to drink.

'I've been meaning to ask you, actually, if you wanted to come with?' She busied herself refilling the water tank at the sink.

'What, to Oxford?' Diana's parents didn't live in the city itself but I would always shorthand it to there. English countryside villages still all sounded the same to me, even if this one was steeped in unforgettable memories of weeks-long school holidays playing in the nearby meadows, grass stains so pronounced they marked even my cheeks.

'You know that's not where they live, but yes,' she said, briskly clipping the coffee machine back together. 'Bunny's bringing a friend too, at least I think she is. And apparently Toff's bringing his new girlfriend. They'd all love to see you, and it will be a lot more fun with a few more of us around. Besides, I won't be able to get to sleep until at least 4:00am every night. What'll I do without my fellow night owl?'

I couldn't look at her. I knew why she was doing it, and I didn't trust myself to say anything without my voice breaking. She'd remembered, when, other than me, there was practically no one else left who would. It was almost two years to the day since I had found my mother unconscious on the bathroom floor, fading with every passing second. Would we ever understand what really made her try and end it all for good? At the time, I even tried to blame the shock of 9/11. Realising that her children's funny Arabic names were suddenly going to make their lives much more complicated was what finally tipped the balance between living and dying. As if this profound change in the world order could affect someone living thousands of miles away, the only connection her children had to the attacks their skin colour and their heritage. The truth was so much simpler, but so much harder to bear.

'Besides, you don't have to decide now,' Diana said, tossing her hair as she picked up her cup. 'I'm not getting the train until the afternoon, so I can try to sleep a bit in the morning at least.'

I nodded, still looking at the floor, tiles swimming as my eyes watered.

'I'm leaving now though, OK? The class starts at half past. Call me when you wake up later?'

I nodded again. 'Thanks,' I mumbled, sniffing; she'd know what I was grateful for.

The tiles were still swimming as I shambled out of the kitchen, straightening my clothes. No point pretending that waiting in Ross's office wasn't exactly what I was going to do next. And why should I? I reasoned, trying and failing to tuck my hair smooth behind my ears. I'm only doing it to try and help where I can. I batted away the thought I was only doing it to try and prove myself better than the overnight shift. I had to make my own luck. No one else was going to do it for me.

I pushed open the glass door to his office only to find Ross already hunkered down in a pile of cables in the corner. We both spoke at once, as surprised as the other.

'Hey, Sami. Shouldn't you be heading to the land of nod?' He sat back on his heels.

I paused in the doorway. 'Hey, Ross. Shouldn't you still be getting out of it?'

He snorted, squinting at the four clocks on his wall.

'Depends which clock I look at.'

I laughed, dropping into one of his red armchairs. It was a standard newsroom joke. Made everyone feel better about being either early, late or absent. Ross winced as he stood up, arching his back. His cushions wheezed sympathetically as he dropped into the other armchair, masses of cables still knotted around his hand. The place was overflowing with equipment: hard black travel cases stacked alongside old edit decks, all pockmarked with satellite phones and festooned with yet more cables, so elaborate it could have been the Christmas display at an electrical pawn shop.

'I was wondering if you needed me to help out with any local shoots today? I can fit in sleep around them, don't worry.'

He snorted again. The truth of it was I spent so much time in Ross's office, begging for any work going, that I may as well have slept in one of his cases.

'Fancy helping me untangle these?' He waved a fist at me, boxing-glove thick with cables.

'If that's all you've got, then sure.' I leant down into the pile at my feet. 'But maybe there's an interview on the cards this afternoon and no one wants to hold the reflector? Or an antisocial press conference that no one wants to go to—'

'Give yourself a break, Sami.' I flinched as he interrupted. Ross wasn't in the mood, but I couldn't have known why. 'We all know how capable you are, and how much you want to progress to worthier activities than overnight shifts.'

'I never said that.' I dug my hands into the cables so I didn't have to look up.

'You didn't have to. You're in here more often than the photographers themselves, and manage to land on the news desk with the same regularity as the daily editions. Don't get me wrong, it's not a bad thing – enthusiasm and flair are part of the job description – but so is knowing when to give yourself a break. Not to mention everyone else around you.'

'Has Penny said something?' I swallowed hard.

'No, of course not.' His tone softened. 'But when you've been around as long as me, you know that if you drive too fast, you'll crash. You might swerve a bit, get away with it for a while. But you'll crash in the end, and you don't want to do it in public if you can avoid it, or take others down with you.'

'But if I do something wrong, that's on me, isn't it?'

The cables clattered against the desk as he pulled them off his hand.

'We've all been where you are, Sami. Everyone has to start somewhere. You'll get your break sooner than you can imagine, probably sooner than you're really ready for, given the state of play right now. If you make a mistake – and it doesn't take much, believe me – then it will be in full view of the floodlights. We're flat out, you don't need me to tell you that. It's only a matter of time before you end up on a decent gig, and take it from me, there is nothing worse than having to learn on the job when there's more than just reputation at stake.'

'I don't understand—'

'Do you need me to spell it out for you? Look what's just happened to Ali … and to Kris.'

'But Katja's got more experience than anyone else at the network, hasn't she?'

I turned round as his expression changed, to find Penny standing in the doorway, sleeves rolled up like she'd been at work for hours.

'You won't believe this,' she sighed, batting the door against an equipment case in the way. 'But we need to pitch some folks into Kabul, and we need to do it, like, yesterday. DC just called.'

Ross groaned, dropping his head into the cables on the desk. My pulse went from zero to hero in a matter of seconds. Afghanistan was hotting up again just as Iraq was boiling over? I knew the network hardly had enough staff to go around as it was. There were barely enough cameras for camera operators. Much less reporters for microphones.

'Don't tell me. The secretary of defence is dropping in overnight?' Ross sounded as exhausted as he looked.

'Worse.' Penny banged the door again, almost like she wanted it to shatter.

'You've got to be kidding me…'

'Nope. Air Force One is on its way right now. Apparently they are going to switch to military aircraft in Shannon. Like that won't attract any attention – hah!'

Bang went the door again. I looked between them, suddenly electric, the idea of heading home to bed as far away now as my bed itself. The president of the United States travelling anywhere was a headline. But to drop in unannounced on Afghanistan at a time like this was a front page splash, a top story, a must-cover whether the actual media was print or television.

It seemed like Penny had barely noticed I was in the room, but she smiled gratefully as I got up, motioning that she sit down instead.

'I could have got away with covering the whole thing from

Baghdad had it not been for the fact that Jennifer has managed to wangle an exclusive seat for herself on the plane, and therefore needs a hot fucking microphone to tell everyone on arrival.'

She raked a hand through her hair as I considered this. Jennifer Nicholls must be travelling with the president, a massive coup for the network's US affairs editor.

Ross groaned again.

'Penny – God, I can't. I am literally running cameras blind right now. I've got a freelance cameraman whose paperwork I haven't even seen on the next plane out to Jerusalem because apparently even their non-Jewish shooters are taking the Jewish holidays off. I'm filming an interview myself later because otherwise I'd have to pull someone off programming – and I can barely stand up straight. What happened to all the photographers in DC? They've got more bodies there than we've got across the whole of continental Europe...'

'You think I didn't ask that question? There's only one extra seat on the damn plane.'

Silence descended then, albeit just for a moment. I held my breath lest they noticed I was still there, looked at the clocks on the wall. The day was already in full swing in the Middle East.

'OK,' Ross said from between his teeth. 'How long have I got?'

'I'd suggest approaching this as if we're already very, very late.'

'Jesus, Penny...'

'I know, I know,' she said, mollified. 'But I'm under the gun here, Ross. What about...'

'Forget it.' Suddenly Ross was on his feet, no time to wince. 'It's barely been a week.'

Penny chewed on a nail.

'But he's been through Dr Collingwood three times now, hasn't he? The paperwork's squeaky clean, and he's champing at the bit.'

I gasped as I realised who she meant.

'He was shot in the fucking head, Penny.' Ross's voice was dangerously low. 'He was already conkers to start with and now—'

'It's just a live camera in Kabul. No movement; in, out, finished. He can do it with his hands tied behind his back.'

'That's not the point, and you know it.'

'But what else can we do?' Penny twisted round to look into the newsroom as a sudden squall erupted at the news desk. She looked ten years older than usual – heavy lines across a pale, sweaty forehead, darting eyes wild and bloodshot.

'Anyone is better than him,' Ross said quietly, as a small smile spread across her exhausted face. 'He's not a solution, he's part of the problem. It's a terrible, terrible idea.'

I strained to see past Penny, the glass walls of Ross's office almost completely blocked by more black cases. The squall was getting louder, hoots and high fives weaving through the air to the open door. I fidgeted in spite of myself, Penny's brow furrowing further as she finally noticed I was still there.

'And I'm not carrying the can for the consequences. I've been through this before, and—'

'Kris!' Penny sounded as shrill as a schoolgirl as he appeared behind her in the doorway, blue eyes somehow both laser-sharp and twinkling at the same time. His smile was so wide it felt like the room was illuminated.

'Morning, boss.' He dipped his head at her even as she stood. 'And hey to you too, skipper.' Ross was at this point puce with fury. 'Alright?'

'What do I have to do to get you to stay away from here, Kris?'

'You know my poison, skipper. And you haven't sold me anything nearly good enough.' He turned back to Penny, eyes flickering with recognition as he noticed me shrinking against a pile of cases. 'Mind if I sit down?'

She stood aside immediately, smiling. He threw me a thumbs-up and a wink as he sank into her vacated armchair.

'Funny you should say that,' Penny said brightly, shifting from foot to foot. 'If your poison's still what I think it is, you're in for a treat.'

'Now you're talking.' I couldn't help but smile as he clapped, rubbing his palms together. Sweat was spreading across Ross's shirt faster than spilled water.

'How do you fancy Afghanistan for a couple of days? A quick in-and-out to Bagram Air Base, nothing too taxing. You'll mainly be running a live camera for Jennifer Nicholls – she's on her way in now, bagged herself an exclusive seat on a VIP visit, if you know what I mean. In and out, nice and tidy, and the air base is almost as comfortable as the Four Seasons. What do you say?'

'You had me at hello,' Kris replied, eyes flashing so bright I almost had to look away. 'I'm flying commercial, though, right? She's the one bunking in with the squaddies? No slouching on some military transport hairnet all that way for me, thank you very much.'

'Right,' Penny replied, sagging in the doorway as she practically collapsed with relief. 'Your comfort is my top priority. British Airways' finest awaits to Dubai. I'll even cough up for first class, how about that? But then you'll have to put up with Pamir Airways, or whichever tin-pot jet I can get you on to Kabul that'll arrive in time.'

'You're on.' He rubbed his hands together again, winking. My ears tingled like they were on fire. He couldn't possibly be winking at Penny, could he? 'Pamir Airways – blimey, that's a new one. Let's hope the in-flight entertainment is better than Kam Air.'

'Penny, let's at least send someone with him. If he's got to fly commercial anyway...' Ross sounded like a deflating balloon. Either that or it was the chair finally giving up on him.

'What, to Afghanistan? Forget it, skipper. I know that place better than the palm of my hand.' Kris clapped again, a hollow thud against the glass walls.

'Then you'll know it won't hurt to have someone hold it!' I jumped as Ross smacked his own hands on the desk. 'I mean it, Penny. If this is honestly going to be our solution then he's not going alone, we can damn well dredge a body up off the news desk too.'

Kris's eyes suddenly hardened. 'I'm not a cripple, Ross. I do not need someone to hold my hand, much less wipe my arse for me on a schoolboy shoot.'

Penny's eyes narrowed as the barbs flew back and forth. At the time, I thought she was cross that she'd been backed into a corner, but now I think it was genuine surprise. Everyone knew Kris loved being waited on. His demands for a chocolate bag were legendary. And I think Ross would probably have been surprised too, if he wasn't already so upset he could barely speak properly.

'That's a smart suggestion, now you mention it, Ross. A very smart suggestion indeed.' She floored them both as she interrupted. 'Sami? You're off the clock for the weekend now, aren't you? So you can go. It's as good a place to start as any, don't you think, Ross? I trust you can sort Sami out with some basic transmission kit and caboodle? It seems there are still plenty of flak vests gathering dust in here for her to choose from.'

The room fell away as I stared at her noodling at the bags and cases crowding the floor. Looking back on it, I think it had to be me; I'd heard way too much by then not to be made part of the decision, rather than just be a witness to it. But in that moment, all I felt was elated, exhilarated, thrilled – you name it. Never mind the horror spreading across both Ross and Kris's faces.

I was buzzing, high and loud, a rush that suddenly made me feel like I could fly if I jumped. I was getting out, and not only that, I was going to Afghanistan, and I was going with Kris. A proper, bona fide, frontline news assignment. I'd done it. It may not have made sense to anyone else, but it made perfect sense to me.

Chapter 10
Mission Accomplished

Even Kris, with his warrior-king halo, medical-miracle armour, alleged armloads of luck – man alive, he could barely bring himself to reference the myths without dissolving into an acid coughing fit – but even Kris couldn't have anticipated bowling into Ross's office right in the middle of a ruck over the exact place he'd been intent on going next.

As usual, technicalities were all that mattered. It was that easy. This soon after 9/11, there was too much at stake for the West in both Afghanistan and Iraq for the news media not to be there every time someone had indigestion, let alone when the so-called commander-in-chief showed up to reiterate 'mission accomplished' – which was right up there with 'medical miracle' in the annals of nonsensical slogans and titles. And with Christmas coming, with the whole workforce's eye on its stockings, the network was even more desperate for warm bodies than usual.

But Kris seemed to have misplaced one of his legendary armloads of luck when it came to taking Sami along for the ride. Some woefully inexperienced junior producer, no doubt bursting with one over-enthusiastically misguided idea after another? That was definitely not part of the plan. That was most definitely not another dazzling new detail in the kaleidoscope.

He pushed his face into a grin as he watched nothing but neat joy spread over her face, stomach curdling as he considered the possible consequences. Was it possible she might actually prove useful? So brazenly hungry she might try and keep them in place an extra few days? Jennifer Nicholls, with all her slavish devotion to the military, would be up and out on the first plane available once the top brass had done all their shouting from the rooftops. There was no way they'd let him stay behind to shoot anything else by himself so soon after his injury. The speech played out in his head: we're here now, wouldn't it make sense to do as much filming as possible? At least try and get a look at something other than the military effort? Coming from her, with him in support, it just might work. It was worth the risk, of that much he was sure.

But he didn't bargain on her actually being any good.

She was surprisingly well prepared once they got to the airport. Considering it was like the air had been sucked out of the room the minute Penny disappeared, she must have done it all by herself; Ross looked like he'd been roasted too. Exactly the right sized minivan was waiting by the right alley exit at exactly the right time, with exactly the right cases of gear already loaded on to the trolley ready for the boot. Exactly the right seating was arranged for the plane – someone must have told her he will only ever fly if he is sitting by the window, unless she was just lucky, and as far as Kris was concerned he was the only one with an excess of dumb luck. So once they'd landed he cut her a break over how to get from the airport to Bagram Air Base, even though Jennifer had it all taken care of – the American generals may as well have unfurled a red carpet.

It was a particularly striking morning, all the sharper for his lack of sleep, as always. Sami made all the right noises when she got her first look at the mountains, curled around the city in their jagged circles more perfectly than the setting for any gemstone. That morning the mountains were sharper than diamonds, cutting into the sky like ice picks, ring after ring after ring. Kris took a gulp of air so sharp it burned. Salvation was in his grasp. He was sure of it.

There was barely time to blink, let alone talk, between arranging Jennifer's endless live reports after He Who Must Not Be Named had departed safely. They handed out the microphone to military aide after military aide, but as he'd anticipated, Jennifer was up and out of there on her way back to Washington DC as fast as she could once the air had gone out of the presidential balloon.

And that's when she did it. That's when Sami brought up the hospitals. No mindless small talk, or blushing giggles. Not a second of it. The panic that he might have to leave before he'd got started had less than a nanosecond to rise. He hadn't even had to start thinking.

'You want to pitch a story on the hospitals? What, like text and stills for the website that no one is ever going to read?'

She'd wrongfooted him, so he was babbling, although it was true that no one read the network's news website. It was like some digital add-on, full of transcripts and summaries that became facts because they were posted on the internet under a news banner.

'And how are we going to get ourselves there and back? Walk? Much less get permission to film inside?'

'I thought ... I thought we could ask Major Lacombe,' she replied. She'd got an answer for every little detail, amazing. 'Remember the last interview Jennifer did before she left? The guy who you said looked like Pee Wee Herman...'

Kris pretended to rub sand out of his eyes as she continued. He'd forgotten he'd even said that until then. Bagram Air Base was practically its own city-state, with Western outlet shops, a whopping great gym or three, even a fucking Burger King. It was easy to get swept into the military fanfare of the place, in fact it would have been weird not to, at least on your first trip. So to have cottoned on to some throwaway detail buried inside yet another one of Jennifer's over-enthusiastic interviews was some mind at work.

'Jennifer asked him about any efforts the military were making to preserve what was left of Kabul institutions, and he spun her a line about the hospitals being untouched.'

'And?'

There was no pretending he wasn't staring then. Sami had got it almost word perfect. And the only reason he remembered was because he'd edited it and had to iron out a glitch in the audio.

'Well, we know that's not true, don't we? Because one of them still had smoke coming out of its buildings as we drove in from the airport.'

'How can you be sure of that?'

'I overheard them pointing out the various buildings to Jennifer,' she said, scuffing at the sand with her boot. 'They may as well have thought she was blind.'

He had to let that hang, just for a second. It had been months since anyone had asked about hospitals, or any institutions or developments that weren't part of the latest battlefield tactic.

'So how do you propose getting Pee Wee Herman and his mates to escort us around a wrecked hospital they insist is untouched?'

'Obviously that's not what I'm going to say,' she replied, a quick flash of anger in her dark eyes. 'But I thought we could ask for a tour of the city before we leave. Get the military perspective on how the city continues to function amongst the devastation, that kind of thing. Since he was so keen to push how careful the operations were to leave institutions still functioning, we might ... we might even get access to the hospital itself.'

And then everything just clicked, like the ice picks in the sky coming together to form one perfect, brilliant-cut diamond. What Sami didn't know, or at least couldn't have known about this particular hospital, is that patients were segregated. Women were on the same level as dog shit as far as the Taliban had been concerned, and even with the new administration in place, levelling up wasn't exactly happening overnight. Kris knew these buildings, he'd had a crack at them before, but they were for female patients. Their all-male crew hadn't stood a chance when they'd shown up. And like all stories that required more effort and time than was available, it was quickly shanked into the long grass as the war was moving far faster than anything else, even though those women had stories to tell that would make the hairs fall out of your arms.

But this time, there would be a female producer calling the shots.

This time, the risk was most definitely worth it.

Kris blinked at her, wiry and determined, dark eyes shining from the frame of the makeshift brown hijab trying and failing to contain her untameable hair.

'So we only tell the network about it if we get somewhere? That's your plan?'

'Exactly.' She kicked up a puff of sand. 'We're just going to the airport to get ourselves out, aren't we? I've got nightshifts to be back for, Penny's made that pretty clear. But if we get a tour of the city on the way, and it happens to throw up access to the hospital, and we've got military escorts, why wouldn't we take our chances? Then even if we do come out with a story, we got it completely legitimately. It'll be a bonus.'

He laughed then, high and clear as the wind off the Hindu Kush. He had to. Because it was perfect. It was completely, utterly, totally, perfect. Just like the diamonds, sparkling as they waited to be found, sitting tight all the way down underneath the Afghan mountains.

'You look different,' she said as he smiled at her. 'In London you always look ... oh, I don't know.' She hung her head.

'How would you know how I look? We've known each other for the best part of a week.' He was still smiling as he said it, even as he pictured himself. He knew exactly how he looked in London. Tall enough, broad enough – hell, even enough hair, shot in the head or not, for all the component parts to seem approachable. Even if the sum of them was always listless, restless and uncomfortable.

'I guess so.' She scuffed at the sand again, mumbling. 'You just ... I suppose it's just because you remind me a lot of someone.'

He snorted, tried to rearrange his face into something more familiar, but his cheeks wouldn't co-operate, not one bit.

'One unlucky fella, hey?'

She looked up then, stared straight at him. Her eyes said it all. He felt an altogether more familiar stirring as he returned her gaze.

Chapter 11
Found in Translation

I remember every detail of that first trip to Afghanistan like it happened seconds ago. I hadn't slept in days, had been living an upside-down schedule for almost a year, had found myself in the right place at the right time just by blindly doing the same thing again and again until it finally happened. And yet the moment I stepped off the plane in Kabul I felt as powerful as the jet engines still whirring on the tarmac. Even the fact I hadn't been able to bring myself to return Di's calls before I left had nothing on the sight of the snow-dusted peaks of the Hindu Kush dappling the land far below the jet's tiny windows.

That first lungful of Afghan air stripped me clean of the first half of my life, as sharp and fresh as the mountains piercing the sky, sparkling with possibility. That first glimpse of the far horizon was almost blinding, blue and white, and more dazzling than any ski resort. I had been dreaming of the moment when everything suddenly made sense again, and here it was in technicolour. And this was a city so ravaged by decades of various wars that despair should have clung to the air like the still-acrid and burning jet fuel. Maybe that's how everyone else on the plane saw it when they followed me down the rickety old stairs taking us to the tarmac. But for me, there was nothing but optimism and hope. Even now I can't bear to think that it was only mine.

We walked off the plane straight on to the runway and collected our gear from haphazard piles inside a building so exhausted by war that the ceiling creaked with the mountain wind. The few women amongst the rag-tag mix of soldiers, journalists and security contractors milled around like blue ghosts in their fluttering abayas. I remember blinking at them – were they there or were they not? Were they sprites, figments of my past flickering in and out as I finally let go of all that had gone before? I still wonder what they saw through the gossamer mesh over their eyes, when all I could see was opportunity.

The military transport awaiting us was so smooth and efficient I found myself marvelling instead of despairing, even as we rode through streets torn into zigzags and pockmarked with rubble. An old man sold fruit next to a pile of twisted, burned-out vehicles, and all I saw were fat, bright oranges, so bursting with juice and hope that I swallowed reflexively with thirst. Everywhere I saw the so-called reconstruction, I saw my own. I registered those hospital buildings like I was born there myself. Even twenty-four hours straight of the same reporting about the presidential trip couldn't wipe them out. So when I asked Major Lacombe if the military could be so kind as to take us on a tour of their efforts on our way out to the airport, it only seemed natural that we were able to go inside and witness what we did. Everything in my life had been leading up to that moment. For me, it didn't feel brazen at all. It felt like it was the only reason I had ended up there.

'This here is the female burns unit,' he said as we paused on the cracked paving between two low buildings, having walked what felt like an impossibly small perimeter for an allegedly functioning hospital.

'The husbands don't like the wives being treated by male doctors, but the truth is just making it to a medical facility is a victory in and of itself.'

'How do you mean?' I kept my voice neutral even though I knew the answer.

'There are a whole lot of burns victims in this country, and most of them are female. It's an easy enough fatal injury to self-inflict. Women have access to oil lamps in a way they don't have access to much else round here.' He frowned as Kris coughed next to me.

'So they self-immolate. Or they try to. And of course, it doesn't always work ... So what you have, inside this here building, are the ones that didn't get to the end.'

I made to push open the door when a boot suddenly blocked me.

'Not so fast, young lady,' he said, folding his arms as he appraised us. We were suddenly a very different commodity from just being Jennifer Nicholls' support act.

'I'm so sorry, sir, of course,' I replied, immediately dropping my head deferentially. 'Forgive me, I should have asked first, I just got lost for a moment in what you said. The conditions for women here ... they are just unimaginable to us, aren't they?'

He grunted, although it might have been Kris. I was still looking at the floor.

'That they are,' he replied after a moment. 'And even now we've got rid of the Taliban, it's still like this for some women.'

'Sadly, I don't think people in the West are aware of it in the way they should be,' I said, watching as his foot started to tap. 'It would go a long way towards increasing understanding of the continued military effort here. If there was any way you might allow us to go inside, perhaps even talk to some of these women – only if they are happy to share their stories with us, of course. We might get enough for Jennifer herself to put a story together on it—'

'No, I don't think so,' he cut me off, unfolding and folding his arms again as I looked up. 'None of the doctors speak English, much less any of patients.'

'But if we were allowed to go inside, just for a few minutes,' I pressed on, 'perhaps it would work even better for you if we took Ajmal with us? Not only would he be able to translate, but he would also be able to explain any support the military is offering the civilian institutions that must be supporting some of these cases.'

The swarthiest of the four soldiers accompanying us froze with shock. Ajmal had been front and centre on the journey with us in and out of the airport but was nowhere to be seen on Bagram Air

Base itself. He'd disappeared at the final security gate when we arrived, and reappeared just as we readied to leave forty-eight hours later. Even if we had been blind and deaf we'd have figured out he was working as a military translator, so conspicuous was his absence once we were inside the base. As it was I'd heard his name the whole way in and out, listened to the questions he'd answered, watched as he'd listened intently to what he was required to interpret from the landscape around him. I knew Ajmal would come in with us, if they let him. And I knew, from the instant flash in his eyes, that he wanted to.

'Now, listen here, young lady.' Major Lacombe straightened up. 'Let me get this straight. You want our military translator to come inside this unit with y'all so you can hear from these women yourself? Isn't it enough I've told you what they do to themselves when they get the chance? Y'all need every sordid detail to make it even more blindingly obvious that the previous regime here needed to be gotten rid of?'

'It's more than enough,' a voice said next to me. Kris – I'd almost forgotten he was there. 'For us, anyway. The problem is, Major, and you know this, I'm sure you do, but we aren't the ones it's for. It's those folks licking an ice-cream as they read the paper, sticking their heads into bowls of popcorn as they listen to the news, just because it happens to be on before whatever movie it is they are about to watch. They get it when they see a woman who's deliberately melted herself. They don't when they hear it from a guy in fatigues. Even though they should, hey?'

And then they all laughed, as if hearing it from a man made it funny instead of true. The hairs on my arms stood so high I had to scratch at my sleeve.

'Give me just a minute, sir?' Ajmal stepped forward, looking at Major Lacombe instead of us. 'The only men allowed on the wards are the doctors or the husbands. But I know one of the doctors here ... and if Sami asks the questions it will be OK, I will take care of it.'

I was the one freezing in shock then. He knew my name, and I should have known better than to be surprised. Translators listen more intently than anyone else ever could. This was a man who spoke Dari, Pashto, English and probably plenty of other local dialects besides.

'In and out, OK?' Major Daniels smiled back as he surveyed us, suddenly firm members of his team again. I couldn't help but smile too, even as a shard of glass fell out of the broken pane in the door as it swung behind Ajmal.

~~~

Whenever humans experience any kind of pain, no matter how intense, physical or mental, all we tend to describe is how it feels. It hurts, we say. Make it stop, we might cry. In extreme circumstances we might find ourselves numb, as if in a final act of defiance we simply won't allow the pain to penetrate, when in fact that's the moment when the pain becomes part of our very bones. But inside that ward, inside that one overheated, squalid room, pain was a physical entity. It seeped from the walls, it creaked with the life-support machines, it clung to the fetid air like a shroud.

Row upon row of women lay in various states of bandage and undress, frozen as if sleeping, their swaddled babies on rickety old cots lining both sides of the room. I paused in the doorway as Ajmal sidled between them, murmuring softly. The room was otherwise silent save for the occasional beep of a monitor, and yet my ears buzzed with the weight of screams I didn't want to imagine. I gulped air so heavy it felt like smoke in my lungs until Ajmal turned to beckon us over.

And there she was, in the far corner, her softly swollen, exposed stomach blistered as pizza. Her name was Habiba. She was eighteen years old. I could not help but take her hand. It lay limp in mine. I clung to the fact it was still warm. In spite of all she'd had to endure this was a young woman who still had life left in her.

'Ajmal, could you...' I swallowed another lungful of smoke before I could continue. 'Could you ask Habiba if she would mind telling us what happened to her?'

Beside me, Kris's camera clicked and whirred to life as Ajmal nodded, turning and murmuring to the figure on the bed as gently as a lullaby.

'She was married at fourteen,' he said after a moment. 'She did this for her family, her father is an important man here in Kabul, it was ... it was expected. But he was not a kind man, and he forced himself upon her time and again. She was not prepared to bear his children...'

Ajmal trailed off as a low wail chimed somewhere behind us. I shivered as the hairs on Kris's arm brushed mine.

'Her baby has survived,' Ajmal continued in a low voice. 'She is five months pregnant. But she has injuries that will make the delivery difficult. She is ... she is unlikely to survive. And to her family, she is already dead.'

Another lungful of air went down then, heavy and poison as lead.

'She's just waiting for it,' Kris whispered next to me. 'Her baby too. Ask her if that's what she wants.'

Habiba nodded then, raising her eyes to meet ours. I felt Kris scrabble with his camera as the shot presented itself. Even swathed in bandages and smothered with tubes, she was exquisite, her limitless eyes as moist and dark as olives. I stared, in spite of myself. Just like Afghanistan itself, her beauty felt impossible.

'What did she like doing?' I asked softly, staring at the tears nestled in the corners of her eyes. 'Before all of this happened, I mean. What did she like doing? Did she dream of being a writer? Or a politician? Maybe she loved to sing, or to dance...' I trailed off as Ajmal stared at me, transfixed with shock.

'I'd just love to know more about her,' I whispered, stroking the satin back of the limp hand in mine. 'I want her to know she's more than the sum of her injuries. She's worth far, far more than that to me. To all of us. I want her to know that.'

And Ajmal's face suddenly split into a smile, his eyes twinkling like the far tips of the mountains still visible beyond the cracked windows. The hand in mine grabbed on tight as the whispers murmured back and forth, some colour staining the hollow cheeks on the bed. I squeezed back, probably too hard, but I couldn't help it, I was sure I could feel a pulse accelerate in the bony wrist. Finally Ajmal was able to translate again.

'Everyone calls her Bibi,' he said, blinking hard. 'She wanted to be an artist. She would dye pieces of cloth the brightest purples and pinks with pomegranate juice from the fruit in her orchard. And then she would stitch them together, make clothes for her sisters to wear under their abayas. She would use spices to paint with a finger, the most beautiful mosaics of turmeric, saffron and pepper. But then she—'

The breath paused in my throat as he caught his own.

'She found the oil lamp in the kitchen. That was how she did it, in the end.'

I didn't have any more questions. What could they possibly have been? I just held her eyes for as long as I could before Ajmal murmured that it was time to leave.

'Give me another minute in here, OK?' Kris murmured as I gazed, hardly able to blink. 'It's the only way I'll get any wide shots without you two in the way.'

I think I nodded then, although it could have been anything. My heart, my head, my eyes were full of Bibi. The endless eyes, the satin skin, the face of what life had been like for women under the Taliban. And thanks to us, the world was going to feel her pain, just as much as she had.

Chapter 12
Shock and Awe

Ross's office was so overflowing with equipment, they could barely fit inside, all hunched over an ancient edit deck on the desk, but there was no chance Kris was going to play his tapes out anywhere on the newsroom floor. He'd even tried to get Sami to go home first instead of coming to the office straight from the airport, but she wasn't having any of it. It would get out soon enough that it was a graphics producer with no former field experience who had pulled a story like this out of her hard hat, and there would be plenty enough questions to deal with then. No, Kris needed it to land as quietly as possible, at least initially. Still he had to pin his arms by his sides or else he might actually have hugged himself.

For once, Penny couldn't speak properly, stammering and gurgling away. Ross, at least, could fall back on the technicalities of the photography, but Penny was floored.

'This is … this is, really … Sami, this is really quite extraordinary … and Kris, these images…'

They both smiled then, as if they were pleased by the same thing. Kris could see their reflections in the glass. They looked happy. No doubt about it.

'Explain this to me again, if you would?' Penny flopped into one of Ross's armchairs. No one had bothered sitting down beforehand.

Sami answered as if she'd been rehearsing. 'Towards the end of her trip Jennifer did an interview with one of the units assisting in the reconstruction in Kabul. We thought to ask for a tour of the city on our way to the airport, since they'd told her at length what they were doing to support various institutions and the like. They could only say no, after all, and as it happened, they were only too keen. Once we'd got to the hospital, they explained how the wards were segregated, and we happened to be outside the female burns unit—'

'And they let you use their translator?'

'Yes. That's him.' Sami pointed to Ajmal in the foreground of the screen.

'Well done,' Ross said as he folded his arms. 'Really well done. That is incredibly smart thinking. You too, Kris. Your compositions are as compelling as the story.'

'They do bring it home,' Penny said, standing up. 'Let me talk to the programming execs, see if I can drum up enough interest for Jennifer to write a script to go with the pictures.'

'Would it be OK, Penny, for me to have a go at writing it?'

Kris watched Sami's reflection in the glass as she pulled herself straight. This was what she'd been waiting to say.

'I'm the one with all the information and I know the pictures so well that it might be easier if I wrote a draft first, at least. Then you could pass it on to Jennifer to provide the voice-over.'

Watching Sami became less bearable then, but the glass walls made it impossible to turn away. So instead Kris stared at Ross's straining gut. He could turn him into a Buddhist monk if he concentrated hard enough. Except Ross knew what was coming too, suddenly opening and closing drawers, fiddling with papers, untangling cables.

'I'm happy for you to have a go.' Penny brushed down her skirt as she answered; even she couldn't bring herself to look Sami in the eye. 'It's your story, absolutely it is. And to be clear, you've done incredibly well this trip, for someone with your experience – Jennifer spoke very highly of you, and I don't even need to ask Kris what he thinks. I just need to look at the video. But realistically, and I do hate to say this, I think we're going to struggle to get this any airtime—'

'But why?'

Sami sounded as desperate as Bibi had, even though their languages were different. No news network had time for hearts and flowers even if it wanted to. There were well-meaning – well, deluded – managers that did, sure, but the war itself always overtook sentiment. It was as if the military thought if it moved fast enough no one would have the capacity to remember what they thought at the time. Another reason they thought they could get away with calling it 'shock and awe'.

'There's nothing new here,' Penny said as she made for the door. 'Conditions for women have always been appalling under the Taliban. It was never going to turn around in a hurry. The grisly tactics some are using to deal with it are certainly compelling, hideous as it is to say so. But it is yet more grist to the mill of why – at least some will say why – the regime needed toppling. It has no wider geopolitical implications than that, I'm afraid. It's just sorrow … and it's a bit thin at that, even if we dredge up some sound from Jennifer's original interview on the military efforts to support the reconstruction. But don't lose heart. We'll definitely put it on the website, I'll make sure of that – and you can have a crack at writing that piece too. It will be good practice if nothing else, OK?'

Penny didn't really wait for anyone to answer as she closed the door behind her.

Kris had to leave Sami to it then. Counselling was hardly in the job description. Ross was cuddly enough that there was a chance he might step up for at least a few minutes, but if he did, he knew exactly what she would find herself doing. She'd watch the video on a loop, relive every minute in her head, find a friend to go over it with and discover that this friend, despite knowing her for however many years, couldn't possibly understand, because how could they? And then she'd feel disconnected and isolated, and wonder why, when she'd just done something that had made her feel more alive than ever. She wouldn't be able to sleep, close her eyes even, without seeing Bibi's face in the dark. She'd look down at her own stomach in the shower and see where the scars would be, blistering open before her eyes, as if she'd done it to herself. It would fade, of course it would, because life doesn't stop unless someone or something ends it for you. And then, as soon as she realised, she'd feel inescapably guilty, and try and do it all over again. Only getting back out would make her feel like she hadn't abandoned a part of herself somewhere and she'd never get it back.

~ ~ ~

There were a few 'normal' nights with Lucia and the boys after that. Kris lived every minute wondering if the next was when it would all fall apart. But then a minute became an hour, became a day, and was almost a week before he realised he'd stopped count-ing, the phone hadn't rung, and he wasn't coming to, after losing consciousness on some bar stool. Being Dad didn't feel quite as ill-fitting with Trixie around, always on hand for an unconditional scratch and a cuddle. It was like he'd been sedated, like getting back on the horse so soon after the ambush had somehow swerved him on to a parallel path.

The Kabul hospital story did eventually make it onto the news website – calling the network's digital product its bastard child would have been complimentary, such was the level of attention any of the correspondents paid it. It was a bit long on emotion and short on detail, but it was decent copy, particularly when Sami found out Bibi had died a few days later, so could sharpen up the headline. Suddenly the main shot was all the more tragic, all the more captivating. And this time, the difference was that she was no longer in pain. Not just that they'd told everyone about it. More than anything, this girl had just wanted it to end and now it had. That's what it really meant not to turn away.

That is, until Andie got hold of it.

'Have you been deliberately ignoring my calls?' Andie spat

when he finally picked up the phone. It was either that or throw the handset in the fucking Thames.

'Yah, you have, unless you can prove to me your wife has been umbilically attached to your side since you got back from Kabul.'

He could hear her huffing and puffing as she moved the phone closer to her mouth.

'I've been going out of my mind here, Kris. Out of my mind! Ali, he's still critical, all the Iraqi staff are in pieces over it – and Katja, yah, Katja is madder than ever! We're still under the gun for new reporting every second of every day – it's like we're fighting ourselves, like every day we're actually in combat, rigging up to go win another little war of our own. And you're in Afghanistan all of a sudden? With the stitches probably still in your cracked-up skull?'

He tried to calm her down at that point, but she wasn't having any of it. She was so clipped and sharp by then he could only get every other word. The South African accent is a better chameleon than the lizard itself. One minute it sounds like a song, the next a shooting range.

'Don't even think about spinning me on this, Kris. Don't even think for one second there is any excuse you can come up with that will fob me off. You owe me your time, Kris, if nothing else—'

'Andie, I'm not—'

'Ali is catatonic, for fuck's sake. A vegetable is the best we can hope for, and all the while I'm having to hold the place together, because if I left it to Katja someone else would end up in the soup, and I can hardly have that, can I? Adam is drinking whisky for breakfast, refusing to let anyone else replace him because, apparently, former SAS members can handle far worse than some "amateur raghead ambush". Mohammed, who, by the way, is the only one with any nerve left, won't even stand next to him. Let alone go anywhere with him—'

'You need to calm down, Andie-girl—'

'And I find out, not even from you, I should add, that not only have you gone back out, but you've gone to Afghanistan? You haven't even come back here. And worse, you and some pip-squeak managed to do a real story, the stuff of fucking dreams...'

She faded as adrenaline tingled so hard up his back he started to sweat.

'You know how it goes,' he mumbled, catching the sweat before it rolled into his eyes. 'I had to get out, I couldn't sit on my hands here anymore than you could.'

'So why didn't you come back here?' All the fight went out of her voice. 'I don't get it, Kris. I don't get it at all. It makes less sense than the damn war itself. If the brass were blind, deaf and dumb enough to send you out again, you should have come back. And you know it.'

Kris let the phone rest in his lap for a second, swallowing and swallowing.

'I just needed to talk to you, Kris, OK? Just once, I needed to hear your voice, and you couldn't even do that, you couldn't even sit on the other end of a line a thousand miles away and grunt, just once or twice. I have asked precisely nothing of you for months. Nothing. It's been you, climbing into my bed at night, not the other way around.'

She faded again as he tried to think through his ways out. He'd known this moment would come with Andie at some point – it always does if you haven't agreed on terms, openly or not. And they hadn't. She'd just kept letting him try to find out whether a physical relationship might blot out the emotional blowback. Muscle memory is all that's left when total recall is too much to bear. It's where biology and chemistry meet, where one cancels the other one out. They'd both shared so many of the same night-mares – surely she had no other means left to process it all either? It always takes someone who has been through it too.

But he should have known this was when the moment would come. He knew enough about how insecure she'd become profes-sionally to realise the Afghan story would push her over the edge.

They'd discussed it a thousand times. What could they all do to make blowing smoke up the war's arse pay back in some way? Some of the reporters cared too, but most were happy with just bearing witness, as if the fact everyone could physically see them in the thick of it made it OK they'd actually done nothing except tell people about it. And this tiny little window into Afghanistan – an orgy of grief, sure, but an alternative window onto a war that up until then had largely been about terrorists, and the importance of them being roasted into dust – that was going to get under her skin like little else. She might, just might, have been able to handle it if he'd done it alone. But he'd done it with a nobody. All she could see was it should have been her.

And he didn't blame her. Sami had never been part of the original plan. Kris wiped a clammy hand on his equally clammy T-shirt before lifting the phone back to his ear.

'Andie-girl? Are you still there?'

'Yah, as usual. I'm here for you, Kris. I holy wish I wasn't. But you know why I still am.'

Her voice finally cracked then. They sat in silence for a moment, just breathing at each other.

'I'm going to come back, Andie, I promise. You think I'm going to leave Ali, leave all those guys to keep doing it anyway? I just—'

'Yah,' she said before he could finish. 'I know.'

Trixie wandered over then, fitting her silky head into the hand hanging by his side.

'You should have left too,' he murmured as he stroked the dog. 'You could have played the Christmas card if you'd wanted to.'

'Like hell,' she said softly. 'Me? I didn't take a shot to the head, and I'm not even one of the ones who'll carry the can for it. And if I did leave, exactly how would it play for everyone else out here? Where would Mohammed go?'

'We don't have to take it on for everyone.' Trixie's ears slid between his fingers. 'We just need to keep our heads above the line.'

'And that's why I'm still here. You know that. I wouldn't just lose my head, I'd lose the job.'

Trixie grunted, so he didn't have to.

'But you should have asked for me, Kris. You should have taken me to Afghanistan. You should have found some way. But instead you took...' She coughed into the receiver before she could continue. 'You took Samira. *Sah-meer-rah*. You opened up her heart instead of mine.'

'There's plenty more where that came from, Andie-girl. She was just lucky, and unless you are me, that kind of luck never strikes twice.'

He thought he had this particular round won, when Andie snorted.

'Lucky or not, you sure did get a great tale on your way out of there. She died after you left, right? That girl, the one with the burns? Even better. It's worth a follow-up if your little Miss Samira still has the means to contact the hospital.'

The hand clenched around his phone suddenly stopped working, Trixie snuffling at the handset as it clattered onto the floor.

'Kris? Kris?' Her voice echoed up at him from the tiles, time slowing as the phone's screen blinked like a flashlight. What would he say if he was asked, outright? His stomach twisted at the mere thought – as usual he'd gone in too hard and too fast. He watched his hand reach out for the phone as if someone else was operating it.

'Sorry.' He had to clear his throat before he could continue. 'The dog got hold of something she shouldn't have.'

'I was saying,' Andie continued, more than a hint of ice in her voice this time, 'that you should do a follow-up story on that girl with the burns. Get back in touch with the hospital. Maybe even with her family. She'd been recovering for over a month, hadn't she? So how come she died all of a sudden? She'd never have made it that long with any serious internal injuries, and the burns were all exterior, weren't they? I suppose your precious new producer didn't think to ask that.'

Kris fumbled for a cigarette he knew he didn't have.

'Yah, I bet her family got into that ward in the end and pulled the plug,' Andie continued, warming to her theme. 'An honour killing – ach, I so hate that description. It's murder! It's nothing to do with honour—'

Trixie barked suddenly as his free hand shook so hard it hit her.

'S-sorry,' he stuttered again, reaching out to steady himself on the kitchen countertop.

'So, I'll see you soon, then, will I? If you're clear for Afghanistan then it's only a matter of time before the sandpit rolls around again, hey.'

Kris gripped the edge of the sink. Being sent back to Baghdad if Andie was still there suddenly felt like the worst idea in the world, but he had nowhere else to go. And Andie was dead right. As usual. She always was. He'd set himself up. Worse, Sami too. The die was already cast. They may as well have already been on the plane.

'Kris? Kris!'

He hung up with a sweaty finger as he pretended to greet Lucia.

Chapter 13
Crackers at Christmas

When you've seen your life through the same lens as far back as you can remember, the moment it starts to look like the opposite is always the one you keep coming back to. It wasn't even when my father was killed, doing the job that he loved, that put fire in our bellies – and not just from the food it also put on the table. It would have been a betrayal of his legacy not to see the world the same way he had, even without him in it.

But the moment I realised that even the most harrowing of stories, from the most brutalised of places, could still be used as cannon fodder – that was when the lens became a kaleidoscope, shattering everything into the tiniest of pieces, pieces I kept trying to reform into something beautiful, something meaningful. Something that would have made sense to both my parents, not just to my dad. But I could never get the landscape back to how it was. The pieces would never fit together.

'I just think if journalists told more human stories, more stories like Bibi's, instead of—'

Diana groaned before draining the last of her coffee, congealed and rancid in the plastic cup beside her. It had been a very long night for her, too. Almost no one in London made themselves available to work over Christmas unless they were as junior as we were. I still find that unacceptable. As if the news stopping in the West means we stop caring what's happening anywhere else too.

'Can we give this a rest?' She didn't look at me as she stabbed at her keyboard. 'I can't bear to talk about it anymore. It was hideous enough to start with—'

'That's just it,' I interrupted as I thumped my desk. 'I can't bear to hear that either. The fact it is so hideous should force us to talk about it, to consider it, to try and do something about it.'

Diana was already exclaiming as she whipped round from her computer monitor.

'And that's exactly what all the military talking heads, the politicians, the analysts will all tell you is happening right now. How many times do you need to hear it? The Taliban needed taking down long before Bin Laden flew those planes into New York. Saddam Hussein needs the same treatment before he gasses us all. Yes, Bibi's story was horrendous, and the fact women still live like that in Afghanistan is outrageous, but—'

'See? If we just did more stories about it, or news networks prioritised them, then...'

'Then what? What else do you think would happen that isn't already? Who else are you trying to convince?'

'Oh come on, Di ... Di!'

I followed her as she abruptly stood, heading for the kitchen while everyone else on the shop floor pretended to stare at their computers instead of her. Diana rarely lost her cool. In fact, I don't think she ever had, in the newsroom anyway. She didn't just look like an ice queen, she actually was one almost to her core, unless you knew certain things about her past. I caught up to her as she whirled round, cheeks as pink as her lipstick.

'If this is going to be another lecture, Sami...'

'Don't you feel guilty, though? Like even just a tiny bit? Don't you see how unfair it is, how random it is that just by an accident of birth, it's not us lying on hospital cots, so desperate to die that we've poured boiling oil all over ourselves? I'm not lecturing you, I just—'

'Here.' She silenced me with a steaming cup. 'Sorry. I didn't mean to snap. I know this is different for you than it is for me. I just don't want to talk about it anymore, if you don't mind. And I'm sorry, again, if that upsets you. You know I think it must have been unimaginably hard for you to sit in that room, to look that kind of agony full in the face. But you have to try and move on. You're doing yourself no favours obsessing all over it.'

I took the stale mince pie she offered me with a small smile before I noticed her pouring herself another coffee.

'Wait, you're having another one? What's got into you?'

She tossed her head. 'I'm just tired, that's all. I keep thinking we might get a break from these overnights soon, but Mary says the news cycle is just so relentless at the moment that they can't afford to lose producers of our calibre.'

'Your calibre, you mean.' I took a few gulps of coffee, wincing as they burned.

'Really?' She stared at me, green eyes suddenly full of hurt. 'Who actually got off overnights, even if only for a few days? Who found themselves on a trip that even senior producers would give their eye teeth for?'

'At least now we're getting to it,' I muttered, swallowing down a scalding mouthful. I shouldn't have needled her, she didn't deserve it, but I just couldn't let it go, the fact she didn't seem to care as much as I did. Up until then, we'd always been in sync. If I'm honest, she'd always been a step ahead. Brighter, friendlier, prettier, you name it. Di was the one who pulled all eyes and ears. But on the inside, we felt the same. We'd shared too much not to, at least I thought we had.

'I was just in the right place at the right time. It was luck, just as it was luck that I wasn't born in Kabul, that you weren't born in Baghdad, that we weren't born to be brutalised like so many innocent people.'

'You didn't even have the decency to tell me you weren't coming to Oxford. I was so frantic when you weren't returning my calls and your phone went dead, that I even called the news desk to check if they'd heard from you. Bunny thought I'd gone mad, it was so embarrassing.'

'This is what I mean!' I shouted then, I didn't care who heard.

'How can you give a rat's arse what Bunny thinks, when you can't bring yourself to think about what's happening to girls like Bibi?'

'I cannot go over this again, Sami. I mean it. I know Christmas is an especially hard time of year for you, I know you take this job more seriously than a religion, I know people like me have no right to question your motivation...'

'I've never said that.'

'You don't have to.' Di suddenly looked like she was about to vomit, eyes glassy with fury. 'My past has got nothing on yours, has it?'

'I can't believe you would even—'

'Let's be real, for once, shall we? I've still got both my parents; worse, I don't have to convince them of what I'm doing here either. Bunny's still my sister, even if she's very little else. There's still the same thick cream carpet in the hallway, waiting for us to slide around on, even though we're hardly schoolgirls anymore. There's the same sumptuous guest bedroom with your name on the door, the same perfect second sets of clothes hanging in my perfect dressing room. So I can't possibly understand how you feel, can I? And I've got no right to feel anything other than grateful that I was born into privilege, do I? Even if that privilege gave me nothing but insecurities and anxiety the entire time we were growing up.'

'This isn't about any of that. This is about—'

'Bibi.' She finished the sentence for me with a sigh. 'And lo, we begin again.'

I couldn't look at her as I walked out of the kitchen, headed for the door. I didn't want to admit to myself that she was right. I felt entitled to feel the way that I did, and I wasn't going to apologise for it, even to Di. Why should I, and especially now I'd seen it for myself? My father was the most honest, hardworking and objective journalist you could ever meet, and there was still a chance that my mum ... I gulped that thought down with a mouthful of winter night air as I pushed my way through the turnstiles and out on to the street.

The first hints of dawn shimmered behind the tall Soho buildings as I stared into the navy-blue sky. There were times, growing up, when I honestly believed it could only have been divine intervention that ensured Diana was put in the same class as me. She even looked like an angel. To her, I wasn't just the girl with a funny-sounding name and a family that lived at the end of two plane journeys instead of a short hop across a leafy country estate. And to me, she wasn't such an impossibly beautiful creature that she couldn't also be the most approachable, intelligent, funny and caring friend I could ever have imagined. The minute she smiled across to me as I took the seat next to her was the minute it became possible that boarding school might not mean feeling lonely, confused and abandoned the whole time.

I blinked away a tear as the North Star winked, just for a second, before the clouds shuffled in their places. Something just as ephemeral had shifted, and I didn't know how I could shift it back.

'Hey!'

A can rattled away into the gutter as I turned to find Kris lolling in the doorway next to the office, hair still wet from the shower, eyes as bright as the oversized teeth flashing across his face. I suddenly became aware of the heart thumping in my chest. I hadn't seen him since we got back.

'Clocking off early for Christmas, are you?'

'Hey yourself,' I said, kicking the can back at him. 'Aren't you supposed to be doing the same? And no, I'm not. Things just got a bit hot upstairs.'

'Ah yes. Christmas means what it's supposed to mean where you come from, doesn't it.'

'Something like that,' I mumbled as I looked at the pavement. The truth was all Christmas would ever mean to me was losing what was left of an already broken family. 'You must be all set though, right? Stockings, Santa, the whole bit?'

'Fatso's handling it himself this year,' he said with a grin. 'I've lined it all up for him, even the elves don't need to get their groove on.'

'What, you're going back out? You can't be.'

I scolded myself inwardly even as I stared at him. I shouldn't have been surprised. Of course someone like Kris would see Christmas for what it really was too.

'Baghdad calling,' he said, raking a hand through his hair. It was hard to tell where the bullet had landed now, it had grown back so fast. 'Someone's got to beam the soldiers filling their faces back to the turkeys who voted for it.'

'Seriously?'

'What, you don't think the serving military have a right to Christmas too? It would hardly be the West's magnanimous take-over in the Middle East without it, right? Especially so soon after finding big man Saddam's foxhole? It's one big celebration.'

'You mean...'

'I know Christmas isn't your bag,' he said as he stepped towards me. 'But pigs in blankets do it for most people round here. And most of the guys out there are just blind kids under instructions. What's a few devils on horseback if it makes the difference between an average job or a done deal?'

I couldn't drop his stare no matter how hard I tried. His eyes were always so blue they may as well have been battery-powered.

'The military is actually going to sit everyone down for a full Christmas dinner in between rolling tanks in and out? The whole works?'

'Crackers, isn't it.' He didn't even blink. 'There will be plenty of those around too, if you want to check 'em out?'

There was so much I wanted to respond with, but the image of a perfectly bronzed, trussed-up turkey doing the rounds like a trophy made me so queasy it was all I could do to clamp my mouth shut. Still then I didn't understand that those soldiers, kids or not, had exactly the same level of conviction that I did. We just be-lieved in completely different things.

Kris suddenly sounded equally unsure of himself. 'I can find someone else to wear the Santa hat if you really don't want to. I just found myself wondering, now, who do I know that would miss Christmas in a heartbeat, even if there wasn't a field trip in it for her?'

'Wait ... what?'

It was so cold that my breath billowed like clouds as I gaped at him.

'I told Penny you'd be game, and she couldn't say no when Katja begged too. I only had to drop in the fact you also spoke Arabic—'

'Hang on a second. You want ... you want me to go to Baghdad with you?'

Finally his face split into that grin. 'That's right, that's right. Almost everyone else is clearing out for Christmas. But that's only if you want to, mind. There aren't enough turkeys to watch the shop this end either, so I had to pull a little rank.

'Sami, are you alright?'

The swing door clanged behind her as Mary strode outside. 'What on earth are you doing out here?'

I looked between her and Kris, his smile as wide as her frown.

'Ah, Queen Mary,' he said with a little bow. 'I do apologise for distracting one of your loyal subjects, but—'

'Hilarious, as usual, Kris, but I need Sami back upstairs.' She beckoned me. 'Are you OK? You know you've still got work to finish?'

'I ... I'm really sorry,' I stammered, as I tried to process. It was so cold our mouths looked like we were smoking, and yet sweat was slicked across her ghost-pale forehead. 'I just needed ... I just needed to get some air.'

'Well, take another couple of gulps and let's get going, OK?' She plucked at my arm as I swallowed, watching her chew the inside of her cheek. 'Plenty of time for air when your shift is over—'

'The truth is, Your Highness,' Kris interrupted with another flourish. 'You need to clear Sami for immediate assignment to Baghdad. Doctor's orders. The place is sick and needs a staffing injection. If you don't believe me, the prescription is at the top of your inbox.'

'Hilarious again, Gonzo.' I watched in disbelief as Mary's eyes darted between us, makeup black and smudged under her eyes. 'Can we save the wisecracks for after breakfast?'

'I'm serious, Mary.' Kris suddenly sounded anything but funny. 'Check your email. Penny's just sent over our marching orders. Would I be chilling my boots outside the office at the crack of dawn for anything else? I'm here for my kit, and Sami needs to get hers, like, yesterday.'

'What on earth are you talking about?' Mary's grip slackened on my arm as she swayed.

'She's got a flight to catch,' Kris said shortly, jerking his head towards me. 'Only if she wants to, that is. Since this company isn't in the business of forcing anyone to do anything they're uncomfortable with—'

'I am absolutely not,' I gabbled, the words suddenly falling out of my mouth as my body caught up with my mind. 'I mean, I am absolutely not uncomfortable with it. That is to say, I am definitely happy to go. I want to go more than anything.'

Kris snorted as Mary and I both jumped, swing doors creaking behind us. This time it was Matt peering outside, head swivelling on his neck like some sort of frantic automaton.

'Mary? Is everything OK, guys?'

'She can't go,' Mary bleated at Kris as if I wasn't there. 'There is no world in which I can spare anyone from the overnight shift this week. It's Christmas, for goodness sake, I've only agreed to be here myself on a promise. She's already doing the jobs of three people. How am I supposed to pull all that off with no replacement? Penny should have—'

'Asked you first?' Kris folded his arms. 'She's signed it off, Mary.

That's all you need to know. There are bigger things for her to be doing than wiping your nose for you—'

'I've got plenty of time, don't worry, Mary,' I interrupted, panic rising up my throat. Could Mary honestly try to keep me here just to do those three brain-dead jobs? And on what authority? It wasn't the news agenda she was worried about, that was for sure.

'I can easily finish off the morning shows and still meet Kris at the airport in time. I haven't even had time to unpack from Afghanistan, so all my stuff is ready to go.'

Matt stepped out onto the pavement. 'What are you playing at, guys? There are about to be black holes on screen where graphics should be. We can sort all this out later.'

'I'll meet you at the gate, OK?' I shouted to Kris over my shoulder as I hurried back into the office. He and Mary were still rooted to the spot, staring at each other.

'What was all that about?' Matt asked as we raced up the stairs.

'Don't worry about it,' I said hurriedly. 'It's my fault, I know I shouldn't have gone outside for so long.'

'Too right,' he snapped as we barged back into the newsroom. 'One trip out and suddenly you're too big for your boots.'

'I'm sorry,' I muttered, cheeks burning with blush that he couldn't see, at least. 'I just needed some air. I'll get everything done in time, I promise.'

I don't know why I cared about mollifying either Mary or Matt. They weren't doing their jobs with the respect they deserved any more than I was doing mine. But Kris was a different matter. I didn't question him. Why would I? Whether it was Penny, Kris or Katja – whoever had decided my time had come again – I was hardly going to give them the opportunity to rethink.

I ducked my head below my monitor to hide a smile as Mary came back in. I was that sure I knew why Kris had asked for me.

Bibi and Afghanistan had meant exactly the same to him. And we had another shot at making others like them mean the same to everyone else.

Chapter 14
A Taste of Baghdad

Kris watched her from a lazy corner of his eye as the plane began its looping descent into what was left of Baghdad International Airport. Yet again Sami had nailed each and every one of his quirks to get them this far, but he was sure she wouldn't have seen this one coming. Cornered by both friendly and unfriendly fire, the only option for commercial flights to land at this particular airport with a cursory amount of safety was to corkscrew down from directly above the runway. It had most people in nosebags, and he had one ready, folded carefully into a side cargo pocket so he could whip it out for her if necessary. She wouldn't know it had hit her until it was too late. No one ever did, the first time. And they'd get on their way faster if she didn't arrive at the office covered in sick. Everyone would look at her just a little differently, but not really know why.

Except there she was, resting her head against the tattered back of the seat, regular breathing without even the benefit of hard liquor, not a bead of sweat on her forehead. His hand went reflexively to his pocket as the plane twisted, but she didn't flinch. It was suddenly impossible not to feel the rejuvenating spirit of a familiar horizon, even with the spectre of Andie and all her questions hovering on it, circling around them faster than he could blink.

'Do you feel that?' Kris turned to her as they stepped out onto the rickety old steps unloading them direct onto melting tarmac.

'What?' Her smile widened, he could almost see the sparkling halo of idealism twinkling around her head.

'The sand,' he replied, pausing for another deep inhale. 'The wind barrels up here straight off the Sahara. It dumps most of the heavy stuff on the way, so you can still breathe out here – most of the time, anyway. Savour that first lungful. It's a taste of Baghdad.'

And she did, puffing away like a dragon. Even he was able to smile then. That first gulp of sand confirmed his axis had unmistakably shifted. The wind wasn't suffocating anymore.

Katja put on a show, at least, when they arrived. She had the sense to put it all out there from the start, how appallingly sorry she was, how she'd made a near-catastrophic error of judgment, how she would live with the consequences for the rest of her life, how there was now nothing more important to her than Ali's safe rehabilitation, even how much it meant to her that Kris had the strength of character to come back, to sign on, to finish out his time. He wasn't going to go so far as to forgive her – the bit about finishing out his time was almost too much to take – but he got far enough past it to give her a hug. And once he'd inhaled the smoke-riddled black jumper Katja never seemed to take off, rested his face on the spike of her bony shoulder, the muscle memory of how many times they'd huddled together all over the Middle East, with artillery in their ears and explosions flashing in their eyes, just took over. In that moment, Katja made sense to him again.

'What is it?' he asked as she pulled away from him, eyes narrowing to almost invisible in her wrinkles as she squinted at something over his shoulder.

'Well, then, I'm glad we sorted that out,' she replied, suddenly all brisk, brushing his shoulders down before taking a step backward. It only took a glance to see why. Andie was quivering in the far corner behind them.

He steeled himself as he turned around.

'I'll leave you two to it,' Katja snapped, unsmiling as he turned back to her. 'But have the decency to keep it down, OK? We don't all need to go through it too. And if you must play hide the salami afterwards, could you wait until we are all asleep?'

And with that, she beckoned Sami outside, who at some point during their confessional must have set herself up in a dusty corner, already industriously typing away.

'Merry Christmas, Andie-girl,' he said softly, nearby candlelight making shadows dance on her hollow face. Things must have got worse even in the short time he'd been out. Normally they lit the candles after the generator blew, not in anticipation.

'You came back,' she whispered, rooted to the spot, pale and shrunken inside her cargo shirt and pants.

'It would hardly be Christmas if Santa didn't at least try to show up on time, right?'

He swallowed down a mouthful of acid as he said it. But there was more than just a bad taste to what he was about to do.

'You came back,' she whispered again. His stomach twisted as he noticed her hands, clenched into fists by her sides under her sleeves. 'You came back with ... with her?'

Kris moved fast then, grabbing her elbow and spinning her back around through the doorway towards her bedroom. Hers was just off the newsroom, which always made it easy to pretend you'd been in there all along if you wanted to. He pushed that thought away along with all the others, a stinking pile of guilt steaming deep inside his inner ear.

'Don't you dare manhandle me, Kris,' she hissed, planting herself in front of the door. 'What is going on here? You didn't even have the guts to tell me she was coming too? After everything I said, you couldn't call to tell me yourself? You had to let me find out from Katja?'

'Andie-girl, listen—'

'You just have no idea, do you.' She pushed at him. 'Not a fucking clue. You don't even realise that it was me who kept you alive.'

'What are you talking about?'

He held up his hands, let her keep punching him. It was the least he could do.

'Don't fucking patronise me, Kris. I don't have anyone else waiting for me in the dark at home, raising my children, fixing up my garden, plumping the cushions in my spot so it's nice and comfortable for me to slide into whenever I feel like it...'

She faded as Mohammed's shadow started to flicker in the corner.

'And now you've brought along some hyper-ambitious Baghdad badge-girl.'

'What are you talking about?' he asked again, even though he knew exactly what she meant.

'Don't pretend you don't know, Kris. What the fuck is this about? You, of all people, come back out here with yet another pathetic excuse for a journalist, just here to finally notch a war story on to her belt.'

'Sami actually already works on the programming side.'

'And suddenly that counts, does it? To you?'

She started to pace about, flexing and clenching her hands. 'You know damn well how hard it is for me to keep hold of these gigs. If nothing else, that should have been enough for you to at least try...'

He didn't need to turn around to know why she'd trailed off, her face falling into sudden shadow as the door banging snuffed out the nearby candles.

'I'm so sorry, I didn't mean to interrupt,' Sami gabbled from somewhere behind them. 'Katja's just getting our paperwork in order, and I thought to come fill yours out so we can do it in one shot.'

He stifled a snort as he turned to her, dropping his hands to his sides. Technicalities were always what did it in the end. The confrontation was set. With someone else in place who could do her job, there would be no escaping the fact Andie's time had been up long ago, especially if she lost it in public. Katja could get her on the next plane out. Kris felt his heart accelerate just thinking about it.

'Why, you must be Samira.' Andie sounded as clipped as South Africa's most decorated general as she stepped out of her dark corner. 'Everyone calls you Sami though, right?'

'Yes, just like everyone calls you Andie.'

'Gosh.' Andie swallowed down the quiver only he would have heard. 'And what brings you to miss Christmas to join us in Baghdad, Samira?'

'I don't celebrate,' Sami said shortly. 'Truthfully, I'd rather be here than anywhere else. I was just lucky that Kris thought to ask—'

'I beg your pardon?' Andie's head swivelled practically full circle on her neck.

'I...' Sami suddenly started stammering. 'Kris? I ... I just need your passport, if you've got it there. To fill in the paperwork...'

'It was you? You asked to bring her in too?' Shadows danced on Andie's face again as Mohammed relit the candles by the door.

'Here you go.' Kris looked away as he mumbled, pulling his passport out of his back pocket and passing it over to Sami without looking. 'Ta, mind. I hate paperwork.'

And with that Andie let it fly. If he'd gone any limper he'd have fallen over and then it would have been over too quickly. So he let her have it, challenged himself to feel every blow. And still nothing landed.

'I'm really sorry to have interrupted,' Sami whispered, passport slipping from his fingers as she made to scuttle away. Andie flung herself past him like a wildcat out of a trap.

'Do you know that I had to get blood for him? Do you know what I had to do to keep him alive? That it was me who kept him going? That's right, I did, I had to get blood for him, for Kris, for this fucking ungrateful IDIOT.'

'Andie, *habibti*...' He became vaguely aware of Mohammed grappling with Andie as she yelled. What the hell was she talking about?

'He was bleeding out. And they ran out of the stuff, of the

damn blood type they needed to transfuse him from the top down – of course, he'd never be a straightforward A pos, or O neg, oh no, sirree! Kris here, he'd have to be one of a kind, an AB negative, the rarest human blood type there is. And, of course, this country hasn't managed to overturn one of the dumbest laws known to fucking humankind—'

'Saddam was scared of AIDS,' Mohammed whispered to him as she screeched, colour draining from his face with every word. 'He called it the invaders' disease, one of the many curses the West could bring upon his country. Still now, only Iraqis can donate blood here. You have to show your Iraqi papers if you want to...'

'Are you kidding?' Kris stuttered, hands above his head again, even though these verbal blows were far harder than anything else. 'You're telling me no doctor round here will stick a vein without seeing the correct ID papers? You can't buy soap without a bribe but you have to have permission to bleed?'

'None of us could donate, Kris. None of us!' Andie threw herself back at him as Mohammed cowered away. 'And we were all lining up with our arms stuck out – we went through the whole cast at the other networks before we realised it had to be the Iraqi staff. And guess who figured all that out? I managed to find the only two AB negs in the whole Western press corps just to be told that the blood of a white man can only run if it's on the fucking floor.'

'So who...' His voice fell away as he stared at Mohammed quivering against the wall.

'The field hospital ran out of my blood? I would have died without another transfusion?'

'Now he gets it.' Andie actually smiled then, but it was horrible, he'd transfigured her into some maniacal witch. 'Now he gets just the teeniest tiniest bit of what it is we've done for him around here.'

'But why didn't anyone tell me?'

And finally the room fell quiet, quieter than he could ever have imagined Baghdad to be. The war was so hot then that there was always a thud and a crackle in the background, but in that moment Kris could have sworn he could hear someone else's blood pumping through his veins, much as he could feel it powering the heart thudding in his chest.

'I want you to listen to me very carefully, Andrea.'

Kris jumped as Katja's voice cut into the room.

'I need you to calm right down. You are not to say another word. Go wait in your bedroom for me, OK? I'll be in in just a moment.'

He looked between them: Andie wild-eyed and cornered again; Katja wrapped tight in black, another hovering tornado.

'Go on, now, Andrea. Step away. If you do as I say I can take care of this. But one more word—'

Suddenly Andie let out a sob, right from her guts, before turning and staggering into her bedroom like she might never be able to stand up straight again.

'Alrighty, then,' Katja said, unravelling herself as she turned to him. 'Go and take care of that paperwork, Kris, please. Go on, now.'

'Wait a second.' He blinked at her. 'You can't just expect me to—'

'Kris.'

Time slowed, just for a second, as he looked between her, Andie's closed door, and Mohammed's shadow trembling on the wall.

And then he understood.

'It was you?'

Mohammed practically shrivelled before his eyes.

'Kris,' Katja said again, no warning shot this time. 'Drop it.'

And then sand caught, again and again, with every swallow, with every blink, the kaleidoscope shifting into an almost unbearably beautiful new picture, shot through with shards as red as blood and as sharp as needles. Because, of course no one had told him. Mohammed couldn't tell anyone, ever. It was one thing to work for the white man when your other choices were numbering the days till your home was raided or you trod on a tripwire. It was quite another thing to voluntarily save the white man's life. Lots of people might understand, but there would be plenty that didn't. And those types had a certain way of making sure you wouldn't misunderstand ever again. They wouldn't bother killing you. They'd just kill your children, in front of you.

Now Andie had let the secret out in a roomful of people. All he'd wanted was to make her look jealous and overtired; instead he'd cast her as dangerously unhinged. Sometimes all it took to compromise an entire field operation was a whisper to the wrong person at the wrong time. Andie knew that better than anyone and had gone and done it. And it was all because of him. They'd both put Mohammed on the line, and he hadn't even known it.

Kris had never filled in a piece of paperwork voluntarily in his life but busied himself with every last piece of it that day. Andie was on her way home, that was for sure, no one in their right mind could risk her losing control in front of anyone else. The network could hardly afford a mutiny amongst the Iraqi staff, especially not while Ali's machines were still beeping. He'd had to get her out of the picture, but destroying her professional reputation in the process? Kris pressed down hard on his wrists, willing Mohammed's blood to drain away, except that would be nothing short of a fucking disgrace, wouldn't it? Mohammed didn't give it up for him to let it run cold.

He cast a furtive glance at Sami, still typing away while spooling through endless tapes in a corner. There was only one way out of this. And he was going to have to trust her to find it.

Chapter 15
Keep Your Head Down

That first night in Baghdad I slept better than I had in years, waking blissfully numb into a hazy dawn streaming through the heavy shutters on my bedroom windows, protecting the inside of the room from any shattering glass. The network's Baghdad office was a series of houses, former homes of some previously well-heeled families, all joined together by underground garages with interconnecting passageways. The only outside space was a heavily fortified balcony, upstairs in the main house, where the live television cameras operated – and a small internal courtyard usually choked with smokers. Otherwise everything we needed was undercover – bedrooms, bathrooms, a kitchen, even a room rigged with some clunky Jordanian gym equipment. We were all assigned radios on arrival, so if you needed to find someone you just had to radio them and it would reach even the furthest house on the block. It all seemed impossibly efficient for a city disintegrating with every new day. When I rubbed sleep out of my eyes, watching the dust motes dance in stripes of sunlight filtering through the blast windows, the fact it had been one of only a handful of nights in recent memory that I hadn't needed sleeping pills made perfect sense. Why would I need to be sedated to rest in Iraq? The Middle East was always going to be where I felt closest to my parents. In Baghdad, I felt like they were both still with me, somewhere in the atmosphere at least.

I practically skipped underground from my house into the main house, through the underground garage that housed the network's armoured cars and up into the foyer. Katja and at least one reporter and camera operator slept in the bedrooms there, so they'd always be fastest to the camera position. Kris had told me not to make a fuss that I was in the farthest house – it was the best I could expect on the first trip apparently. But I'd have slept on the sofa if necessary. I even poked the lumpy cushions of one of the couches for good measure as the thought popped into my head, just to reaffirm it to myself. Pushing open the door to the kitchen, the smell of thick Arabian coffee overriding the residual explosives on the air wafting in from outside, I felt lighter than breath. And I was wearing head to toe body armour.

'Good God, Sami,' Katja growled from the trestle table against the wall, hunched over a steaming cup with a cigarette smoking between her fingers. 'You don't have to wear that inside. We only put it on if the bangs start to feel too close for comfort. Mo-hammed – go show her where we stash it in the newsroom.'

A finger of ash fell onto the table as she waved a hand at Mo-hammed, who was smiling shyly at me from behind the kitchen counter. It looked like a small canteen, a semi-industrial cooking setup arranged on the other side of a counter that wouldn't have looked out of place in a small service station somewhere off a British motorway.

'After breakfast, *habibti*,' he said, handing me a glass teacup of coffee so thick you could stand a spoon in it.

'Thanks,' I replied, resting the cup on the table as I took off my helmet and flak jacket. 'I ... I don't usually eat first thing.'

'Don't be ridiculous,' Katja scoffed as she stood up, reaching for the plate steaming on top of the servery. 'Round here you need to eat when food is up. You never know when you'll next get the chance. We've got plenty of eggs and cheese at the moment, but it won't take much to get down to dry goods.'

The smell of eggs, bubbling inside a thick tomato sauce rich with herbs, made me sway as I bent to put my helmet next to the jacket on the floor. I'd abandoned breakfast months ago. On the overnight shift, it usually took the form of the best of the vending machine.

'Thanks,' I said again as I sat, Mohammed sliding a fork on to the table next to me. 'Do we all do our own cooking, or...'

'Mohammed and the others take care of it between them,' Katja said, eyes narrowing as she took a drag on her cigarette. 'Don't get too excited, mind. If you don't like kebabs or shakshuka, then you'll be eating bread and cheese until the cheese runs out ... What?'

Mohammed had exclaimed from behind the servery. He'd just opened one of the boxes of cheese we'd brought with us.

'Kris did tell me how much you liked cheese,' I said between mouthfuls of flatbread, so hot and fresh it took the skin of my fingertips. 'I didn't realise it was possible to carry so much of it on a commercial flight.'

'It isn't,' Katja said with a wink as she stood, peering behind the servery. 'Unless you're Kris, that is. See, Mo? I told you. Only Jordan's finest for you, my friend.'

His enthusiasm was so infectious I couldn't help but stand to watch as Mohammed reverently unpacked huge wheels of cheese. Kris had checked the boxes onto our Royal Jordanian flight in from Amman as if they were stationery. There were more types of cheese than you might find in a Parisian market.

'I told *you*, you mean,' Kris boomed from the other end of the kitchen as he walked in. 'It's all yours, Mo – I'd love a little of that cheddar on my eggs, but I know I owe it all to you. None of your green powder, though, thank you very much.' He smiled as he rubbed his belly, nodding at me.

'Alright? I see you've been indoctrinated already.' He jerked his head at my herb-sprinkled plate – za'atar, still as normal to me as salt and pepper.

'For you, *habibi*, anything,' Mohammed answered with a smile.

'That's right, that's right,' Kris replied with a cackle. 'It's a three-egg morning I feel. Isn't that right, Katja?'

Katja tried not to smile, but I could tell even she found Kris infectious.

'Full of the joys of spring, and it's only Christmas Eve. God help us all—'

I jumped to my feet as a sudden crash knocked over my coffee cup, its spilled syrupy grounds the only thing moving slowly.

'Steady on.' Kris grabbed my elbow. 'That will be the first of many.'

Another crash rang through my ears. This time Katja stood with a groan.

'Make those eggs to go, would you, Mo?'

Mohammed nodded wordlessly at her, turning back to the stove as Kris protested.

'Katja! Come on ... A man can't work on an empty stomach. Especially not if the fireworks are going to start this early.'

Another faint boom thudded through the kitchen.

'It's not going to be straightforward, Kris. Adam needs both cars to get Andie to the airport.'

Kris pulled up short by the counter.

'She hasn't left yet? Why not?'

Katja frowned as she extracted her packet of cigarettes from my spilled coffee.

'No, of course she hasn't. How fast do you think I can move people around these days? Just take yourself and your eggs up to the balcony and get the camera ready.'

Kris let out a nervous laugh.

'What's ... what's happening?' I swallowed, fiddling with my plate as I realised how jumpy I must have looked too. Maybe they'd just think I had a mouthful.

'Two bangs – a suicide bomb, most probably.' Katja frowned as she squinted at her watch. 'There are always two blasts. They do a second to get maximum casualties as people flood to the scene of the first.'

'How can I help?' I interrupted before Katja could say anything else. 'I could make some calls, try and get some more information together if you were happy for me to?'

'Just go and get yourself comfortable at a desk.' She scowled at Kris not moving fast enough for her liking. 'And Mohammed can show you where the dishcloths are.'

My ears tingled like they were on fire as Katja swept away past the puddles of coffee I'd spilled all over the table.

~~~

After breakfast, the newsroom was curiously quiet, the bank of television monitors stacked on top of each other on one wall all on silent. There was a central desk stationed opposite that could seat at least ten people, with separate desks pushed into every other corner, and a wall of cubbyholes crammed with labelled sets of body armour.

Mohammed gestured at an empty one. 'You can put your vest and helmet next to mine. You must have it with you at all times, but you don't need to wear it unless Adam tells you to. Or your windows break before he does.' He winked as I slid it into place.

'Thanks.' His eyebrows raised as I replied in Arabic. 'It's a lot to get used to—'

'You speak Arabic?' Mohammed suddenly sounded different.

'Just a little ... I'm a bit out of practice.' I laughed into silence. 'I understand more than I speak. I have forgotten a lot of my words.'

I realise now why he instantly trusted me a little less, but in the moment it was not what I had expected at all. Aspects of the fighting were so factional then that I should have been wiser to it. Why would he trust me just because I spoke some of his language? Why would anyone ever do that?

'Would you mind showing me how to use everything else?' I switched back into English as I gestured at the silent televisions, most showing Arabic news channels.

'Shit!'

We both jumped as Katja came into the newsroom, waving a freshly lit cigarette above her head.

'Quick, get over here. Mo, look.'

I followed as Mohammed hurried over to a small screen perched with a stack of edit decks on a corner desk.

'Where is that, do you think?' Katja frowned at the screen as they both hunched closer. 'The bangs didn't sound too far away so perhaps it's—'

Mohammed let out a cry as they both recoiled. I leant forward only to freeze almost immediately. The video on the screen was as shaky as whoever filmed it, grainy but unmistakable. Frame after frame of what looked to me like the aftermath of a devastating explosion – rubble, smoke and bodies everywhere. My breath caught in my throat as I realised the bloodied leg I was looking at, fabric torn into shreds around it, wasn't attached to anything.

'It must have been a car bomb,' Mohammed muttered behind me. 'That is the street outside the main market square.'

'We can't say that for sure, can we?' Katja reached down for the phone on the main desk behind us almost before it started to ring.

'Yes, I know, I've seen it,' she snapped into the receiver. On cue, two other phones started to ring, loud and insistent. 'And yes, we have a subscription to that news agency so it's OK to use the video, although I suggest waiting until we've established exactly what happened before plastering it all over the screen.'

I stared at her glaring until I realised it was at me.

'I only have the two hands.' She waved as she slammed the receiver down only to pick up another.

'I'm so sorry,' I stammered, trying to tear myself from the video and answer a phone. No part of my body seemed to be working as it should, my legs almost as disconnected as the corpse on the screen. I managed to pick up a phone just as a dial tone blared into my ear, staring as the tape rewound and started up again, this time preceded by a title frame bearing the date and location of its contents.

'At least eight people are dead,' Mohammed gabbed to Katja. 'That's from the Ministry of Information. They have also confirmed the location.'

'Type that up,' Katja called to me. 'Mohammed, can give you the English spelling. But don't send it to anyone until I've checked it over.'

My legs wobbled as I slid into a seat, flicking on a computer. All I wanted to do was watch the video, however gory it was, again and again and again. It was already as if no one seemed to care, not even Mohammed, about the people in it. How their lives had been interrupted, how their spirits had been broken, how their families had been destroyed. All I wanted to find out was more about them.

It still seems unthinkable how quickly the dust settled. And by that I don't mean at the blast site, I mean at the Baghdad news desk. I swiftly realised that Mohammed took care of anything involving spoken Arabic, plus managed operational matters like cooking and laundry with other local staff members. I also figured out what role Andie must have played from what Katja asked of me. It sounds backward, but I was so much happier ploughing my own furrow than if I'd had to let her show me the ropes. Andie and I had been drawn against each other from the word go. And I understood exactly why she had to go home. The laws of the land under Saddam Hussein weren't news to me, even if they had been to Kris or Andie.

'I don't mean to bother you with so many questions,' I said as Katja broke open her second packet of cigarettes. 'But now the death toll has stabilised and we've established the facts of what caused the explosion, would someone usually start working on access to the site itself?'

Katja choked on her cigarette, spluttering and coughing into her other hand.

'You have—' She dissolved into another coughing fit, wiping an eye before she could continue. 'You have noble instincts, young lady. In a less intense environment, on a different day, then yes, absolutely our priority would be to film our own video, to get out and talk to people.'

'So how will we get more information or more video from the blast site today if we're not going down there ourselves?'

Katja inhaled deeply before responding.

'The locals will probably file something else later. Iraqi news agencies. If we're lucky, they will talk to a few survivors, maybe get enough sound on tape so that we can write up a script. Not that any programmes will use it, mind. Unfortunately, these tit-for-tat militia attacks are run-of-the-mill stuff at the moment. Don't get me wrong, I hate it as much as the next person, but unless we are given the space and time to sit down with these people and file something with more analysis then we need to gear up for Christmas.'

She paused, leaning forward to squint at her computer.

'At least Andie had already got all that organised,' she continued through a mouthful of smoke. 'How do you feel about handling that with Kris tomorrow? We've at least three sittings of Christmas dinner in the Green Zone to deal with. That said, it's a very straightforward shoot: you'll be with the military the entire time and there is no editorial to worry about.'

'If that's what's needed, then sure,' I choked out. In that moment I figured I could blame the smoke, wreathed around our heads like fog. Or the sand. It lingered in the air almost all the time.

'If that's what's needed?' She stubbed her cigarette out into the overflowing ashtray on the table. Her chair clattered as she pushed herself away from the desk, glaring at me as she stood.

'Absolutely,' I said with another cough.

She wrapped her black shawl around her shoulders, pulling it tight as the frown on her forehead. 'There's a lot to do around here that you might not like, Sami. Baghdad isn't and never will be the place for a newbie, but Kris insisted. We all pull our weight around here, every one of us.'

'I understand,' I said, balling my hands into each other so I didn't rub my burning ears. 'I'm very grateful for the opportunity.'

Katja nodded rather than smiled before making to leave.

'I've emailed you everything you need to know. Have a read through, and we'll talk with Kris later. And keep an eye on that monitor.' She tapped the nearest screen with a bony finger. 'This one's the Iraqi news agency feed. If anyone sends in any half-decent new video then I'll have a chat with the programming executives. If they still don't have a functioning conscience then I always like to make them say so out loud.'

Finally she smiled, lighting herself another cigarette as she swept out of the room. I turned back to the edit desk, hoping that more pictures would start to roll on the allotted monitor if I stared at it hard enough. Anything, however gory, to detract from having to prepare for a full-throttle Christmas, even it was in Baghdad.

And that was how I found him, buried at the end of the final video reel of the day. The elderly grandfather, only spared from the blast by the warped and twisted frame of his wheelchair. His son and grandson who'd taken him to the market were both killed, and he'd previously lost his wife and three daughters. He was the last living member of his entire family, facing the rest of his days with nothing and no one left.

I knew I could find him for myself, if I could just persuade Katja to let me try. And I knew Kris would back me. I had seen what finding Bibi had meant to him.

Chapter 16
No More Turkeys

Christmas hardly held any comfort for Kris either, but this time he felt curiously elated by the whole lurid spectacle, even with Andie still hovering in the shadows, a loose safety catch on a gun. Breaking a few rules under the radar was only going to work if he played along with most of them. And if they were going to get even half of a chance at covering anything other than turkeys, especially at the peak of the West's effort to restore its own misguided brand of order in the Middle East, they were going to have to pay more than just lip service to the fucking cranberry sauce. It was also probably the only assignment in the whole of Iraq that didn't need to involve a local staff member, so there was zero chance of having to sit next to Mohammed, knowing what danger he'd put him in. So giving Christmas dinner in Baghdad enough lights, camera and action for Saint Nicholas himself was just fine by him.

'Welcome to Camp Victory,' he announced, flexing his best American accent as they drove inside the gates of the sprawling installation encircling what was left of Baghdad International Airport. 'That there over yonder is Freedom Village. You won't find better sleeping quarters in Georgia's finest Best Western. Bunk beds with actual mattresses, no need for roll mats and sleeping bags. And here' – he tapped the window as they rolled past the stalwart Burger King food truck, complete with neon sandwich board – 'this here shopping lane has more purchasing options than a Florida mall.'

'Another actual Burger King?' Sami muttered under her breath; maybe she thought she hadn't said it out loud.

'Mine's a double whopper with fries, if you'll please,' he said, trying a laugh.

'Unbelievable,' she murmured, the van pulling up mercifully past the offending sign. They unloaded their equipment in silence only to be subjected to almost the exact same welcoming speech by their escort, who showed up just as Kris shouldered his camera.

'As well as Victory, we've also got Camp Liberty, and Camps Striker and Slayer.' Their chaperone waved a hand in the air as he continued the lecture. Sami had to play along, but as usual it was easy for Kris to focus on something else, knocking off a few general shots, some pointless loops of fairy lights, a few spotty teenagers in fatigues strolling past in Santa hats.

'Striker and Slayer ... Like a pair of evil twins, hey?' she mused with a wink and a grin, smooth as you like.

'Something like that,' the captain said, beaming approvingly.

Smart, thought Kris, as the tape rolled. He shouldn't have been surprised. Still he felt slightly wrongfooted, trailing behind for a moment as they walked into the main dining hall. But he managed to put it down to the prospect of stomaching far more than just three rounds of vacuum-packed Christmas dinners.

Turkey, stuffing, spuds, cranberries – even that sweet-potato confection covered in marshmallows so beloved in America made an appearance, regardless of the fact it wasn't Thanksgiving. Still thanks were certainly due, Kris mused, but for what? Tray upon tray upon tray of the stuff kept coming out, ladles moving like a factory line. The dining-room doors just kept opening and closing, disgorging more and more soldiers almost faster than they could gorge themselves. By then even Sami couldn't open her mouth, but Kris made sure they all got the works, making everyone and everything look and sound as delicious as anything dished up in Washington. Once they were finally done, there was enough video and sound to ensure everyone got a name-check, even the Santa-cam, of all the more preposterous things to deem necessary at the peak of war. An earnest teenager in fatigues was conveniently on hand to explain to camera without even a hint of irony that the North American Aerospace Command sees fit to track the man himself leaving the North Pole, and has similar Santa-cams up all over America's military installations to ensure the job gets done.

But even Kris couldn't stomach a drink by the time they rolled home. And Sami could barely speak. She just crumpled down in the same chair she'd inhabited since they'd arrived, hunched over an edit deck and yet another of her bottles of water.

'We did well in there, you know.' He swallowed the belch threatening as he looked down at her, pale as her skin tone would let her get. 'What's the matter? Didn't I eat enough of your turkey?'

'I don't see why you had to gorge yourself as stupid as they all were.' Her eyes flashed before she could look away. 'All we had to do, as I understood it, was film little vignettes of soldiers spending Christmas at war.'

'Hey, you don't get a belly like this without putting the hard yards in.'

Kris felt even sicker as he tried to make light of it, patting his bloated stomach. 'Besides, didn't you clock how they all smiled and goofed for the camera when I filled my face too?'

'That's what I mean. Why do we need them to look happy about it? Don't you think it's disgusting? Eating like kings while so many families around here are feeding their kids grass soup? Having the nerve to celebrate Christmas? Western culture has per-verted the thing so much that it's nearly unrecognisable to actual Christians.'

'That's what's eating you so much?'

'It's just ... it's just not a happy time of year for me, I guess.'

Suddenly she was whispering, fiddling with her hands. He tuned out the screams echoing in his ears, yet another alcoholic rage chiming in from the past. Christmas was always the worst of it. The old man was never satisfied.

'Do you want something stronger than that?' He eyed her bottle of water as she shook her head, shredding away at her fingertips, ripping the skin around her nails.

'Those are already bleeding, you know.' He closed a rough hand over hers, he couldn't help himself. Her fingers stilled, clenched in a fist inside his.

'And I've never much enjoyed it either, since you asked. Christmas, that is.' He had to pause for a cough, all that useful Baghdad sand getting stuck again. 'There are a lot of turkeys to swallow in this business, even when it isn't Christmas. It just takes a bit of getting used to—'

'Could I show you something?'

His hand fell away as she interrupted, feeling curiously winded as he watched her spool some tape back and forth on the monitor. That wasn't usually the reaction he got.

'It's this ... it's this video that I found. It came in on the last agency tape on Christmas Eve and I wasn't sure if anyone had seen it yet.'

He locked eyes with her as she gazed up at him, a fox in a hole, wary and desperate. Mohammed's blood started to pump. She had something but it was just out of her reach.

'I just thought, now Christmas was over and done with, there might be interest in returning to that story. The explosion at the marketplace, I mean. Not now, obviously, but maybe tomorrow, or the day after.'

He leant forward, squinting at the tiny screen. Rubble, blood and guts and...

'I found this, you see. There.' She pointed at the mangled frame of a wheelchair, dents covered in ash by the side of a bloodied road.

'A wheelchair, or at least it used to be, right?' He had to straighten up, the rush of fresh blood to his head almost too much.

'Yes, and this.' She spooled forward again, tapping a finger on the screen. 'This is Ahmed, or at least that's what I think his name is. He survived the blast because of it, because of the protection of the frame. But his family were all killed.'

'How do you know that?' Tape wound and rewound as she shuttled the wheel back and forth nervously.

'I slowed it right down so I could make out the audio.' She reached for a set of headphones. 'Whoever was filming managed to talk to him right at the end. He's lost everything, all the surviving members of his family – half of them had died before this. He's the only one left, with nothing, barely even a house to shelter in. I went frame by frame so I could figure out as much as I could.'

He pulled on the headphones as she let the tape roll, the usual devastated soundtrack of shouts and cries framing a face he'd seen a thousand times before. A broken man, bereft in grief, skin white with dust, eyes dark and liquid as melting tar. Except...

'This?' He tapped at the screen, ears so full of rapid-fire Arabic that he couldn't hear himself, let alone hear her. 'This is Ahmed?'

She nodded, a streak of blood on her cheek as she rubbed an eye with her weeping finger. And he let the audio invade, clanging around inside his head as Mohammed's blood sprinted through his veins.

This was it. This was his next story, and he already knew the ending.

Chapter 17
Safe Rooms

'Repeat after me,' Adam said as we huddled in the debris outside the crumbling façade of what was left of Ahmed's house. 'In and out, OK? If we don't find him inside, we hustle back out and shift.'

I flinched along with Adam as Kris slammed the armoured-car door closed. Hamdi, the Iraqi journalist at the local news agency who'd shot the original video, quivered next to us.

'Watch yourself, Kris.' Adam frowned as he brushed himself down, the sudden commotion kicking up clouds of dust into the air. 'Anything else you want to get off your chest?'

'Sorry.' Kris grunted as he shouldered his camera. 'You got it. In and out.'

I swallowed reflexively as I watched him do the same. The air was still thick with dust, hazy with every shaft of sun that peeped out from between the clouds elbowing each other overhead.

'You're good to go, then,' Adam replied with another frown, tapping the radio clipped to his belt. 'And make sure you keep these on. I don't want to be told you turned them off because of some audio problem.'

'Loud and clear, sir. Loud and clear.'

My hands went to my own radio as Kris patted his. Finally we were able to follow Hamdi into what was left of the house.

The air inside had a charged quality, not just because of the dust lingering in it. For a building so close to being completely destroyed there was still so much to take in– the masses of cables hanging from what was left of the ceiling, the broken picture frames with their torn insides, the fluttering, scorched panel of

what once must have been a curtain. I felt like my body was operating from somewhere outside of itself, rotating my head on my
neck as I tried not to stare, but in what other way was it possible
to look at something so alien? It was only when I realised that
Ahmed was already in the room that I was able to snap out of it.
I don't know what I'd expected – that he'd have been in bed,
perhaps? Except of course he wouldn't have been, no Arab would
receive visitors in anything other than the most hospitable way
possible, even if mad with grief.

'Sami,' Hamdi whispered as he beckoned me over piles of
rubble to a semblance of a sofa. I had to stifle a gasp when I saw
the dusty tea tray, four delicate glasses.

'Sami, this is Ahmed.'

And there he was, almost folded onto the floor, a torso propped
on whatever he had left of legs, stuffed underneath him like a
cushion he couldn't feel.

I dropped to my own knees, no care for the debris underneath.

'*Salaam aleikum*,' I whispered, holding a hand over my heart.
'Thank you so much for allowing us into your home.'

He nodded, fresh tears oiling the tracks already dried hard onto
his rumpled face. Behind me, I heard Kris's camera whirr to life.
And so too did Ahmed's story.

War had already taken so much from him, first between Iran
and Iraq, robbing him of his eldest sons. The First Gulf War took
the use of his legs. And now, with the slow, methodical deliber-
ation of the worst kind of torture, this conflict had claimed his
wife, his daughters, and finally his only surviving son and grandson. But still it was pride that burned brighter than the tears in
his eyes as he talked of them all, tracing a torn and faded photo-
graph of his wife Arwa with a gnarled, bruised finger, pointing
out the many shattered remnants of their life together – what was
once a turntable, the space where a bookcase full of vinyl had once
stood, the spot where Arwa had loved to dance. This was a man
who deserved so, so much more than the agony he'd been reduced

to. And he was like so many others. I couldn't help but reach to grasp his hand in mine.

'Is it as bad as you thought?' Kris murmured as I pictured Ahmed, once so urbane, radiating intelligence and charm as he strolled along the banks of the Tigris with Arwa, giggling children dancing at their feet, ice-creams melting in their hands, sun hot on their faces.

'Worse,' I whispered, gulping down a sob, except there was nothing I could do to stop the tears rolling silently from my eyes. 'He's got no one left. Everyone, his entire family, they've all died in the various wars that have screwed over this place in the last seventy years. All he wishes—'

'Do you think your sobbing will make him feel any better?' I flinched as Kris muttered at me.

'No,' I choked out, swallowing dust, dust and more dust. 'I just wish he had something left other than to pray for his own death. Because that's all he wants now. He just wants to be dead too. That's all that can take his pain away.'

Kris suddenly coughed himself, eyes streaming with effort, there must have been far more dust lingering in the air than either of us could have known. It took Hamdi to settle him with a thump to the back before he could finish taking his final shots. But Ahmed saw none of this, his eyes still full of Arwa and his children, the family and home they had built and lost. It was so real I had to tear myself away to let Kris finish the job.

~ ~ ~

Back in the car, I may as well have still been somewhere on the banks of the Tigris, watching a man and his wife enjoy the sunset with their children, with no concept of the horrors that lay ahead. Every time the tyres rolled over another pile of broken bricks, I wondered if my arm somehow reconnected to my hip instead of my elbow, my legs to my wrists. If someone had told me my head was floating somewhere outside of my body, I'd have believed them. All I felt was upside down, inside out, back to front. Everything that had happened up to that point – the sight of Kabul's high mountains, the whip of Baghdad's sand-laden wind – had led me to believe I was finally stepping into what I was sure were my dad's shoes, was finally walking on the right path, one I had chosen for myself, even if Di wasn't on it. But if surrounding myself with reminders of him wasn't going to wipe out the pain of losing him forever, what would? And how could I ever convince my mother that it was all worth it? I was suddenly consumed by grief, all over again, like it was the moment just after the phone call came.

'Incredible,' Kris muttered to himself as the cars jerked their way back to the main road.

I couldn't nod, much less speak. I knew I would cry out loud. It was bad enough that tears were pouring out of my eyes faster than I could wipe them away.

'Even if no one ever watches it, we'll always know we tried,' he mumbled, cracking his knuckles one by one, again and again as he twisted his hands in his lap. 'I've had to walk away enough times before and not been able to say that.'

I blew my nose into my sleeve, I couldn't not.

'It will get easier,' he said roughly, almost to himself. 'You find your own way around it. We all do. Until then, just hold on to the fact that we're the ones with the conscience.'

A sob came out then, and he turned on me, blue eyes suddenly livid.

'Watch yourself.' His voice was low but clear. 'It's not our job to feel it.'

I shrank away from him, leather seats squeaking against my back.

'It's our job to hold power to account, give voice to the voiceless, shine a light into the darkness,' he recited even as a boom echoed in the distance, thudding dully against the armoured outsides of the car. 'Isn't it?'

'Heads up, guys.' Adam's voice crackled out of Kris's radio. 'We're headed straight into the safe room when we get back. No arguments.'

Kris swore, reaching down for the radio clipped to his belt, as I pictured the safe room, a fortified basement behind a steel door off the main garage with enough water and food to outlast a bombardment serious enough that—

~~~

I still wonder what came first, or did everything happen at once? An infinitesimal vacuum of sound and time before a luminous-white flash, a cloud of sound, the wheeze of buckling metal as the fortified skeleton of the car fought total collapse. As I blinked I could only see white, or was it black? Spots warped and changed as they popped in my eyes. A minute passed, or two, or five? And then a volley of coughing and spluttering next to me as Kris came round.

'—I'm OK, I'm OK,' I said as he gestured at me, although I couldn't hear myself. I just know those were the words my brain sent to my throat. A strange plug of fog seemed to be lodged inside my ear canal, the air inside the car equally viscous.

Kris kept gesturing and talking as he leant forward, slapping at the cheeks of the head lolling on the side of the driver's seat. I sent more words to my throat that I couldn't hear, Kris nodding back to me. Our driver was out cold, but breathing. Outside the car, the dust had cleared enough for me to see the crater in the middle of the road, the piles of rubble cutting off Adam's vehicle from ours, the flickers of movement as black-scarfed faces – whose? – readied themselves to approach.

'We need to move, pronto,' Kris muttered urgently, folding my hand into his. 'There's a pattern, a formula. We're sitting ducks here, we've got about thirty seconds...'

My arms and legs followed his without instruction, as if the fact my hearing had suddenly returned was enough to propel the rest of my body into action. One sharp kick at the warped car door and it was open, just wide enough for us to crawl out and run. What had happened? There was no time to think, only time to react. Stones rolled away from our feet as we skittered into the courtyard of a nearby house just downwind from the explosion.

'We can't just leave them both,' I panted, ducking as Kris did, down behind a crumbling interior wall just inside the gate. 'Adam, what about Adam?'

'He'll follow if he's made it,' he rasped back, grabbing at my hand. 'This is what he wants us to do. Come on.'

A few more steps across the open courtyard and we were inside an open doorway ahead. Only then did I become aware of how much my entire body hurt, sensation starting to return with each step. Every joint felt lined with nails that pierced each bone as it moved.

'Get down,' Kris hissed, dropping to his knees just behind the heavy steel door. And then the shouting began, high and frantic, as people approached the scene beyond the gate. A volley of gunfire drowned out anything I'd have been able to hear. My head still felt like it was underwater.

'Kris...' I grabbed at his sleeve. 'We can't—'

'We can.' He cut me off, eyes flashing livid as he turned. 'Marwan will play dead and they'll leave him alone. Adam's either out like we are, or doing the same.'

Marwan? The blood charging through my veins turned to ice as I realised I hadn't even known our driver's name. 'But—'

'Shut up,' he hissed, wrapping an arm around my shoulders as he pulled me closer to him. And there we crouched, as small as possible behind the open door, heads down and hunched together until Kris was finally able to push the door closed with his foot. Rubble bounced off my hard hat from the ceiling as it slammed fast.

'Are you OK?' He swore as he stood, hands on the small of his back.

I stared down at my hands, spreading my fingers wide, flexing my palms into fists.

'What ... what just happened? Where are we?'

'Who knows. A car bomb, most probably. Or an IED.'

'I ... E...'

'An improvised explosive device. Actually I'd say that's definitely what it was, the crater was that close to the car.'

'I ... E ... D,' I repeated dully, rolling the letters around in my mouth.

'Armoured cars can take the brunt of 'em,' he muttered, frantically digging into his pockets. 'Come on, fella, work, please work.'

I blinked numbly at him fiddling with the phone he'd pulled out of his trousers. Where was mine? How could I have forgotten to check? Suddenly my hands caught up where my brain couldn't, retrieving the bulky handset still zipped into my trouser pocket.

'Katja,' Kris barked into his phone. 'We got hit ... Yeah, we're OK. An IED, at a guess. She's with me. Marwan and Adam...' He sighed suddenly, dropping his head into his shirt collar.

'Are they ... are they alright?'

'When? Just now?' he muttered, nodding to me as he looked up. 'That'll teach him to give me any more shit about my luck. Hang on, let me check.'

I blanched as he stared, eyes marble-bright with tears. Of all the things I hadn't expected to happen that morning, Kris looking like he might cry was probably the most shocking of all.

'Sami, your phone – fire it, would you? How's your battery? Signal?'

A cracked screen flashed into life in the palm of my hand.

'She should be on the network now too,' he continued, talking to Katja faster than I could squint at it. 'Can you see us? Hang on.' He pulled the phone away from his ear, muttering as he held down a button on its side. 'There ... Try now?'

I turned the cracked phone over and over in my hand. It seemed impossible that it would work, yet it did. This was a Thuraya, a satellite phone that didn't have to rely on a terrestrial phone network to work. I'd only seen it for the first time that morning, Adam explaining how vital it was that we carried one around at all times. But how would the software back in the office geo-locate us without him to operate it? What if this was more than a lucky ambush? What if there was a firefight, yet to really get going? As I ran through all my questions I realised how stupid they all were. There were no answers to anything out here.

'Katja can see exactly where we are,' Kris whispered to me as his eyes shone. 'Adam and Marwan are out too, close by somewhere. Now we all just have to keep our heads down, sit tight, wait for the cavalry.'

Another volley of thoughts burst into my head, falling dominoes, clattering down one by one. We'd survived whatever it was, and so had Adam and the drivers, but where were they? And how would we get out without them? I looked around the dark, dank hallway in a trance – formerly the entrance to an office building, maybe?

Then it hit me, blinking into the shadows of the dusty corridor. It wasn't a residual buzzing from the explosion that I could still hear. It was a low moan, agonised but clear, coming from another dark corner somewhere behind us. I turned as I stood, my Thuraya clattering away as it slipped from my hand. For there, in the back corner, was the unmistakable glint of two pairs of terrified eyes, crouched just as we had been, further back into the hallway. The rest of the dank room fell away as I stared, the moans and wails of Arabic floating through the air like ghosts.

We'd stumbled into a house, and there were still people in it.

'Kris.' I tugged at his arm. 'Look…'

I could hear Katja repeating his name as he went still.

'It's a child,' I whispered, hand still wrapped round his arm. 'It's a little girl. Her name is Jomana – and that's her mother. She's telling her to stay calm.'

I felt his hand close over mine, still clamped to his arm.

'Katja,' he breathed after a moment. 'There's – there's kids in here too. We're in a house, Katja. We're trapped in a house.'

Chapter 18
Blood and Sand

The satellite phone felt like a fallen brick against his ear, Katja still squawking in between the various bangs, wails and crashes that characterised urban warfare. There were more wretched, victimised people trapped with them – worse, a child with her mother, the definition of two souls with everything left to live for, no matter how much debris rained down around them, no matter how deafening the gunfire outside. Kris clutched at the phone, a sudden anchor for his trembling hands as he blinked away all the stupid fucking sand finally threatening to overcome him.

'We have to help them,' Sami whispered urgently as she shuffled away from him in a crouch. Don't, he silently begged the pairs of eyes, as they shone with hope at her entreaties in Arabic. Don't you expect anything of me, don't you dare, not now, not like this...

'Kris!' Sami hissed, flinching as a shower of dust fell between them. 'She's hurt – the little girl, quick.'

'There's nothing we can do for them...' Kris tried to speak but only a growl choked with grit came out before he dissolved into a coughing fit.

'I need your trauma kit, Kris.' Sami's voice now, sharper than the spraying bullets ricocheting off the broken walls outside. 'I don't have a tourniquet.'

She was flat on her belly now, inching away from him towards the far corner. The shadows on the ground seemed to morph and change until he realised they weren't shadows at all, they were pools of blood, undulating towards him like snakes. He bent down, dipped a fingertip, rubbed blood and sand into glue. How could his particular trauma kit possibly help with a situation like this?

'Kris!' Sami screeched, sand and grit spraying everywhere as she grappled with the figures in the far corner. 'We need you, please.'

The little girl's sudden scream shook enough out of him that he started to move, but no sooner had he reached the other end of the corridor than another crash landed so close that a chunk fell out of the ceiling, blocking their way back to the door.

'It's her arm,' Sami gabbled in between whispering in Arabic. 'It's cut so deep – look, I think we need to tie it off and I can't. I can't hold it down.'

Muscle memory kicked in then, biology and chemistry firing in perfect sequence as he whipped out the tourniquet he always had stashed deep in a cargo pocket, looping and yanking it around the little girl's arm so hard and so fast that she howled as if he'd done something unspeakably different.

'Just pull on it,' he choked out, as he scrabbled around for what was left of the trauma kit stashed in the webbing over his flak vest.

'Can't we give her something? Anything?' Sami alternately begged over the child's screaming, while trying and failing to calm her increasingly hysterical mother. Kris ignored her as he looped another band around the injured arm. He'd seen enough to know this wasn't a critical gash, tying it off would do the job.

'Shouldn't we sterilise it, or something? What about pain-killers? You must have something.'

Another crash then, mercifully loud, a shaft of light appearing overhead as another chunk of roof fell away. Time seemed to still as a sunbeam illuminated their faces for a second: the standard tableau, a child clinging to its mother, one tortured in pain, the other desperate with terror, both sets of eyes as liquid and dark as a desert midnight. But what could he do? There was too much hope in this equation for him to do anything other than hope himself, a sensation as unnerving as it was unfamiliar. The contours of emotion were all wrong.

There was no time to linger on it, not even a second, as pairs of brown hands, five – six? Multiple sets appeared, reaching down into the hole, followed by faces too flooded with relief to be anything other than relatives or friends. Screams became cries amid unmistakable shouted prayers as two men let themselves down into the hole to gently lever the little girl back up to the waiting hands above. Kris knelt dumbly, wiping sand and more sand from his eyes as her mother brushed dust from her abaya and headscarf, tears streaming down her face as she embraced Sami, rapid-fire Arabic clamouring through his ears as the men made to help her up too.

He started as Sami suddenly tugged at him with eyes like flint.

'Surely we can't just let them try and run their way out of this? Isn't there anything else we can do – they've got no protection, they don't even have shoes.'

She stumbled into him as another bang sounded, but not nearly close enough for him to pretend he couldn't hear her.

'What if they get shot or hit on their way out?' She turned back to the melee only to find it almost gone, pleading in Arabic as the men hoisted themselves up and out of their hole. Only then did Kris felt the dull buzz of his Thuraya keening against his leg.

'Yeah, hey, Katja.' He coughed as he answered, spitting a mouthful of grit into the dirt. 'We're OK, we're OK. Yeah, there were people in here, but they've made a break for it. You can call in the cavalry now without a problem—'

'What do you mean?'

'Yeah, I've still got the camera,' he continued, ignoring Sami as she stared at him. 'I didn't shoot anything new, mind – but we've got the original tape.'

Sami suddenly cried out, a sob right from her guts.

'Steady a sec, Katja.'

Kris put the phone down in the dirt, chubby aerial still flashing red with its connection as he leant towards her.

'The tapes, Kris.' Sami slumped as she croaked, covering her face with a pair of dusty hands. 'The Ahmed tapes. I left them on the backseat of the car, I'm sure of it.'

'Not all of them, you didn't,' he whispered as he reached to pat the camera at his feet. 'I've still got the one that matters.'

'But it all matters!' Light caught her face as she stood, streaked red and brown, blood with sand. 'This will all have been for nothing if we can't tell his story.'

He gripped her shoulders, running a thumb down her cheek, red light flashing in the dirt between them.

'You need to keep your head on straight until we're out of here, OK? Panicking now won't help either of us, and Ahmed...'

She fell forward into his chest just as he stalled.

'Look at it this way. Would you rather have grabbed that tape and lost your arm or head doing it? Or cut and run in the only window we had? There's a pattern to this kind of attack – disable the vehicles before diving in for the spoils.'

'I just want to tell his story,' she whispered, face dropping into his hand, warm and soft against his gritty palm. 'I know it probably doesn't make sense to you, but...'

'You haven't abandoned him, even though you think you have,' he replied, thumb finding a bruise on her lip, wiping away a smear of blood. 'And obsessing over one sad, dead old man makes a lot better sense to me than you think.'

'He wasn't dead yet though. You don't even know half of what he said to me – he still has hope, even now, even after the most unspeakably unfair amount of pain, and we can...'

'What?' He felt her flinch as he pulled his hand away. 'We're just hired guns – two pairs of eyes and ears for rent. What could people like us possibly do that will make what's left of his life any more worth living? Do you think we could have made it safer for those two that found themselves canned in here with us?'

A dull boom cut off whatever she was going to try levelling him with next. He leant down for the chubby little aerial still flashing red between them.

'Now we're in business,' he muttered. 'Hey, Katja. Was that it?'

'What do you mean?'

He tried not to watch Sami fingering her bruised lip, covering the receiver with a hand instead as Katja disappeared again to deal with something else.

'She gave our location to our brothers at the top,' he replied. 'Once those other two had made a run for it there was nothing stopping them clearing the place so we can move. Defenceless Westerners caught in the crossfire is definitely not a good look, but neither are avoidable civilian casualties when the news networks know they are there.'

'But what if people get hurt just to get us out of here?'

Now all Kris could see were the eyes of countless orphaned children, no lens to put between them so he didn't have to look. For Kris had only gone and tied himself to someone as pure as he was rotten, as sentient as he was numb. If he'd just stopped to think about it, he'd have realised it couldn't have been any other way.

'Try and see it from the other side,' he finally choked out with a cough, a single tear falling like napalm. 'We're just doing our jobs. We don't deserve it either.'

Chapter 19
Salt and Water

I asked Kris for the tape in the camera as the armoured car completed its heavy swing into the office's underground garage. I'd barely been in Baghdad a week, but at that point it may as well have been a lifetime. The alien rhythms of life behind three rings of steel, communicating by radio across a group of old houses all connected by subterranean tunnels felt comfortingly familiar, heightened, even, by the shock of the ambush. I clung to every crack on the fortified walls, the reek off streaks of oil on the floor, the random bursts of static from nearby radios.

'That's what you want to do first, hey? Most people pick a drink followed by a wash. I don't always bother with the wash, is the truth.'

'I just want to see how much we got away with. And then a drink definitely sounds good.'

My smile back at him came easily. I suppose I shouldn't have been surprised. In that moment life had been stripped back to just that – life. We'd come very close to losing it and hadn't. His own smile widened as he pulled the tape from his camera and handed it to me.

'Thanks,' I replied as I turned it over in my fingers. Even if it was just a few minutes, having a glimmer of Ahmed's story on tape would make some sense of the whole episode. 'Do you think they made it too? That they're alright?'

'Who?'

I shrank back into the ripped leather of the seat as his eyes suddenly blazed at me. The crash of the outer garage doors closing echoed around the basement dungeon.

'The little girl – Jomana. And her mother.'

He grunted as he turned away, pushing open the heavy car door, clapping a hand over the injured portion of his head to duck out safely.

'They didn't even have shoes,' I murmured to myself as I shuffled down the backseat to follow him out.

Outside the car the high-fiving had already started, Adam and Marwan back and waiting for us at the top of the staircase. The air was thick with smoke as lit cigarettes whirled from every hand, all the men embracing one another. I hung back, assuming no one would try to hug me too, but wanting nothing more than to press myself into the warm arms of another live human being.

My hand fluttered to my cheek. I could swear it still felt warm from where Kris had held it.

Up in the newsroom the atmosphere was entirely different, Katja lying in wait, wreathed in smoke and wrapped tightly in her own arms. I huddled behind Kris as he walked inside, trod slower with every step.

'We're not the king and the queen for nothing, are we, Katja?' he said as he pulled his camera strap over his head to deposit all his equipment on the table.

'We most certainly are not.' She coughed into a hand, unwrapping one arm to give him a more awkward squeeze.

'Seriously, Kris.' Her voice cracked then. 'One of these days this is going to end very differently, and I sure as hell hope I'm not around to see it.'

He cut her off by pulling her into a proper hug, her dark eyes fixing on mine from over his shoulder.

'And Sami – let me get a look at you.'

I took a nervous step towards her.

'Are you OK?'

I flinched as her hand landed unexpectedly on my shoulder, but it didn't put her off. I'm pretty sure I nodded, opening my mouth to confirm assent, but to my horror nothing came out except a shuddering sigh, followed by tears spilling out of my eyes like someone – most definitely not me – had just turned on a tap.

'Come and sit down.' I stumbled as she parked me in the nearest chair, shouting over her shoulder for Adam.

'Crying is good,' she continued, taking a deep drag on her cigarette as she dropped into the chair next to me, all the while keeping her hand on my shoulder. 'Don't fight it, it's OK. It means you haven't turned to stone like the rest of us around here.'

I tried to laugh but worse, out came a sob.

'She did great.' I jumped as Kris cut in from somewhere behind me. 'Didn't lose her head, followed instructions. I reckon she clear as saved a little girl's arm in the process, too.'

'What?' I leant into her as Katja's grip on my shoulder tightened.

'There was a kid inside, bleeding pretty heavily. We managed to tie it off though before her family came to get them out.'

'I certainly hope you didn't take any unnecessary risks.'

I tried to twist round to look at Kris. Why was he giving me all the credit? I turned back to Katja as she squeezed my shoulder again.

'Well done,' she said softly, with the beginnings of a smile in the lines around her mouth. 'Not losing your head is all you ever need to remember when the balloon goes up. Panic, and you're finished.'

'It was…' I had to cough before I could continue. 'It was Kris, actually. He was the one who tied the tourniquet.'

'I'm sure he did,' she replied from between the cigarette in her teeth. 'He's always the last to leave if he thinks he can save someone else—'

'Haven't we had enough hearts and flowers for one day?' Kris interrupted. 'And don't come near me with that black bag of yours, Adam.' I turned again to see Adam coming into the newsroom. 'There's only one kind of turps I need right now.'

Adam shoved him with a grin as he came over to me.

'Hey there, Sami. How are you doing?' He peered at my lip as Katja shuffled over. 'Mind if I touch that?'

I shook my head as he snapped on a plastic glove before gently palpating my mouth and lip.

'A couple of butterfly stitches and some alcohol, and she'll be fine,' he said to Katja as if I wasn't there. 'It's best you have a wash first though, OK? You'll need to keep the stitches as dry as possible once I put them on—'

'Alcohol, you say?' Kris interrupted again, pressing a glass into my hand. 'Here. This'll help.'

Katja frowned as whisky spilled into my lap. I lifted the glass with a shaking hand and placed it on the table.

'Thanks,' I managed to choke out, nodding at them all. 'It doesn't hurt all that much.'

'I suppose you're going to tell me you want to look at that first?'

Katja finally smiled as she motioned to the tape clutched in my free hand.

'Is that OK?' Out of the corner of my eye I noticed Kris walk away.

'Of course.' She pulled over a tape deck, still-attached set of headphones clattering across the desk behind it. 'Lose yourself for a while. Just make sure you have a wash and a change so that Adam can patch up that lip though, OK?'

Only then did she loosen her grip on my shoulder, pulling away to stand up.

'The pictures can always make it feel worth it,' she said, as if to herself, before walking away.

~~~

The shower stung as I rubbed my head under the tap, rivers of Baghdad dust trickling brown into the drain, but there was no time to luxuriate. The hot water only ever lasted about five minutes, and that was if no one else was washing in another bathroom at the same time. In any other situation I would have cried out, lip throbbing almost unbearably as I rinsed my hair, but Katja was right. The tape, the merest few minutes that we'd managed to salvage, sustained me. I would have poured the shampoo right on to the wound in return. On cue, the shower suddenly ran cold, but I didn't even flinch, slicking water down my body to get rid of the last of the soap. There was still grit between my toes as I reached for my towel, but it felt like some of it belonged there now.

All of Kris's early shots were gone – the video of what was left of Ahmed's shredded home, the smashed picture frames, the torn fragments of curtains. Most of the interview was gone too, but I hadn't forgotten a word. I could recite Ahmed's story as if it were my own, and that was all I needed to write a piece for the website at least, using the best of the video left to crop out some stills to go with it. The tape left in the camera contained the very end of the interview, when Ahmed was basically immobile, paralysed in grief. And once Hamdi and I had moved out of the way at the end, it turned out Kris had spent a good while shooting his face, zooming in and out far more than necessary, I guessed, but he'd done us a favour there. There were dozens of opportunities to create the pictures I wanted. I felt more than just the ghost of my father as I watched it, returning time and again to the sections where Ahmed seemed to look directly at Kris, nodding into the camera, his sunken eyes wellsprings of pain and despair. It was as if Kris was still asking him questions long after I had gone, even though I knew it could only have been a few minutes. Either way I hadn't needed my father to whisper in my ear where we should make the cuts for the most impactful shots. There was nothing on that tape that wasn't impactful, not a single frame.

I dressed quickly, pressing a smaller towel to my lip. I knew the drill by now. The website would publish whatever I wrote, and I was the only person who could possibly do the material justice. The copper tang of blood ran sharp in my mouth with the regret that I couldn't immortalise Jomana and her mother in some more meaningful way too. The script was the only thought that occupied me as I made my way back through the underground garages to the main house, grinning at Marwan and the other drivers hunched round a couple of upturned crates with a fragrant shisha pipe and a game of backgammon. This was their usual rhythm. How quickly it had become my own.

Up on the main floor, I paused in the doorway to the newsroom. Everyone seemed to be gathering in the courtyard beyond, judging by the faint laughter drifting with the hot wind through the air. But Kris was slumped against the news desk, his back to me, a set of earphones clamped around his head as he hunched over the edit deck I'd vacated barely half an hour earlier. I winced as I smiled to myself under the small towel, injured lip not ready for that yet. This was how he was making sense of it all too.

'It follows you around, hey?'

I jumped as Andie's voice cut into the room. Where was she? My wound splayed painfully under my fingers as I pressed down on the towel, noticing her in the far corner of the newsroom, where all the body armour was kept. Was she readying hers for the journey out to the airport? Surely no one would be heading out again today after everything that had happened to us?

'What does?'

I watched in a trance as Kris's fingers spooled tape back and forth. His headphones were still on, but he can't have been listening to the audio. Just looking at the pictures must have been enough for him.

'Trouble, Kris. Trouble.' I shrank behind the doorframe as Andie stepped further out of the shadows, hard hat in her hand.

Kris snorted.

'That's the best you can do?' She laid the hat on the desk with a soft clunk.

'We only ever see each other in warzones, Andie-girl. We're the ones following it, not the other way around.'

'Once upon a time I might have agreed with you,' she replied with a hollow laugh. 'But now ... now I'm not so sure.'

Kris's fingers spooled back and forth, back and forth.

'Don't you have anything else to say to me?'

'I'm sorry,' he grunted. I noticed his other hand clench around an empty glass.

'That's it?'

I shuffled further away around the doorframe. I desperately didn't want them to see me, but couldn't tear myself away.

'What is going on with you, Kris? Why are you obsessing over these tapes? What happened to "I just shot it, I don't need to see it again"?'

Blood ran into my mouth as I pushed on the towel. Wasn't this what everyone usually did, after a near miss? Hadn't Katja just said so, barely ten minutes ago? Andie knew Kris far, far better than I did, but I still couldn't help thinking that she'd got him all wrong. That I, the newcomer, the pair of fresh eyes, knew better.

'I'm sorry,' he repeated after a moment, voice cracking.

When she next spoke, it was so soft, I could hardly hear her.

'That's what I'm asking. What are you sorry for? I don't get it, Kris. I don't get it at all. I mean, I get why you went to Afghanistan, even though I hate you for it. But I don't get anything else. There I was thinking this was all about a new squeeze – but it's not about that at all, is it?'

I stumbled, steadying myself with a free hand against the clammy tiles on the wall. She couldn't possibly mean me – could she?

'I'm actually wondering enough to be worried, Kris.' She moved over to him, perching on the table next to the edit deck. 'I shouldn't care, I know – I get what 'this' is.' She waved a hand in the air between them, as if to denote the nature of their relationship. 'We all know why we do it. But what I don't get is—'

I jumped as all the phones rang, a sudden rattle of cradles on desks. Andie frowned, leaning past Kris to pick one up.

'Baghdad, this is Andie?'

Silence hung in the fetid air as she listened for a moment.

'They're fine,' she said into the receiver, frowning at Kris. 'Yah, but thanks for asking, they're all fine. Two of the crew were trapped for a short while but otherwise...' I watched her hand tighten around the receiver. 'And how about you? Hamdi, is it? You're OK, I take it?'

I sighed into the towel, which was now almost entirely wadded into my mouth. Hamdi. How could I not have thought to check what had happened to him? He'd been with us every step of the way until we got into our fancy armoured cars, leaving him with not even the protection of a flak jacket to navigate his way back to his local news station. I felt sick as I realised I didn't even know what or where that was. And now he was calling in to check on us? My whole body burned with sudden, acute self-loathing.

'You did what?' Andie straightened then, hand moving to her hip as she stood up, clenching the handset against her ear. 'That's strange, isn't it? Did you notice anything different, at all?'

She turned to Kris, still spooling tape back and forth, back and forth, headphones clamped over his ears even though by then it couldn't have been more obvious he wasn't listening to anything.

'I'll pass the message on, don't worry, Hamdi. I think she's showering at the moment but I'm sure she'll want to give you a call when she's out.'

My ears burned as I realised he must have been asking for me all along. And Andie had been nothing but courteous and professional, caring, almost. What had I been expecting? That she would trash my reputation before I'd even made one for myself? Refuse to pass the message on, place blame for the entire incident squarely at my feet? My clean shirt was now plastered to my body with the heat of shame. I watched dumbly as she finished the conversation, placing the phone back into its cradle with a gentleness I couldn't really comprehend, resting her hand on the top.

'Is this your guy?' She laid her other hand on Kris's shoulder as she asked.

'I don't know what you mean,' he grunted, shrugging her off like a child.

'Ahmed.' I started when she replied, tapping a finger on the screen of the edit deck. 'The guy you went out to interview.'

Kris suddenly pulled off his headphones, pushing his chair away from the desk to stand.

'That was your fixer on the phone,' she continued tonelessly, folding her arms as she stared at his back. 'Hamdi. He wanted to check you were alright. You and Sami. He got caught in the same drama after you left, of course.'

'He's alright, is he?' Kris didn't turn around.

'He is. But he went back to check on Ahmed himself.'

I stumbled across the threshold then, I couldn't help myself, pulling the bloodstained towel out of my mouth as Andie turned in surprise.

'Is he alright?' I stammered thickly, blood pooling in my mouth.

'Hey, Sami,' Andie said, brow creasing again. 'Wow – OK, you need to get that seen to. Adam!' she shouted over her shoulder.

'Is he alright?' I repeated, lisping, wringing the towel in my hand.

'Who?' Andie looked concerned as she turned back to me. 'Here, let me...'

She reached for the towel, pressing it back down into my lip as Adam hurried into the room.

'It's pretty deep,' she said to him as they fussed over me, muted all over again.

'I'll have to stitch it properly now,' he said with a frown. 'What did you do?'

I shook my head, looking between them. What had Hamdi said to Andie?

'I'll be back in a sec, OK? Keep the pressure on it.' Adam gave me a warning look as he sped out of the room.

'You heard the man,' Andie said, frowning as I made to lift away the towel. 'You don't want it to scar, do you?'

'Is Ahmed alright?' I spoke through the towel, biting down, I couldn't help it. 'What did Hamdi say?' I tapped the screen on the edit deck in case she couldn't understand me.

'Ah,' she said softly, looking past me to Kris, still standing and facing away from us, towards the wall. I'd forgotten he was there.

'Your fixer Hamdi called in for you just now.' She spoke more to Kris than me. 'He wanted to speak to you, check you were both alright.'

I nodded vigorously, grunting at her through the towel, willing her to hurry up.

'He went back to check on Ahmed too, he said. The blast was pretty close.'

I know, I screamed into the towel, except I knew she couldn't hear me.

'I'm afraid all he found was a corpse, though. Strange, as his building was pretty much as he'd left it, Hamdi said. And the old man had no obvious new injuries. But there was no pulse. He wasn't breathing.'

'Must have been the shock.' I jumped as Kris cut in. 'Poor sod couldn't have taken any more.'

I bit down on the towel as my eyes filled with tears, reaching out my free hand to trace the face immortalised on the edit deck – the eyes sunk deep into pits like canyons, the saltwater tracks streaked over the worn old face. We had his final testimony. He'd died, then and there. But not before telling everyone how much he'd loved life, and now we could make sure the world knew too. If we could make just this one testimony change just one mind, his death wouldn't have been in vain.

'Strange, though,' Andie repeated as she stood, staring at Kris's back. 'The car took most of the blast, didn't it? Hamdi said nothing had changed, and he had no visible injuries. So you just happened to be there right before his heart finally gave out?'

'It was already broken,' I lisped through a mouthful of blood, salt and water.

I watched her decide not to ask any more questions of Kris before turning back to me. Silence hung in the air between us, weighed down by the sand on the wind whipping through the open door to the courtyard.

'Keep your head down, OK?' She looked right into my eyes as she said it, hand warm on my shoulder. And before I could nod or say anything else, she was gone.

Chapter 20
Occupational Hazards

The accusations fired through his head as he packed up his gear, surveying the room they all optimistically called his bedroom. Obscene pink marble bathroom suite, check – formerly the beauty parlour of some Arabian princess, no doubt. Well, he had his new William Morris bedspread to take its place now, didn't he? Stale whisky burned down his throat as he slugged down the dregs in the glass next to his pillow. The minute the armour on that car had shaken he knew they'd be on their way out – that is, if nothing killed them first. Patch up Sami's face, file the copy, and take no more chances other than the one involved in getting them all to the airport and into the sky. Even the most gold-plated of insurance packages wasn't going to pay out on a guy that still had holes in his skull from the last time he'd got in a bullet's way. And the network would have been toast if anything else happened to Sami, barely out of an internship as she was. Top brass could tell themselves how desperate their staffing levels were until the cows came home. They could see the negligence suit just waiting in the wings and knew their only defence would involve lobotomising various staff members.

And what else could he have expected of Andie? That she wouldn't get them sent home along with her? She was smarter than he'd ever realised – but what exactly did she think she knew, and how did she intend to use it? He cast around the room for another drink, knowing there was nothing left. Katja and Andie, two of the least stupid people on the planet, and he'd tried to play them both for fools.

His eyes travelled the room again – every crack on the tiled walls, each shaft of light that came through the shutters, always angled directly on the pillows to lift him from his nightmares as early as possible. He dug a finger in his ear and rooted around as Andie's laughter tinkled through his head; the only time he ever seemed to hear it was when they were in bed together. It was only ever dirty, exploitative, predatory behaviour, Kris – but wasn't it worth the live charge of fight or flight, turning their whole lives into poetry? Weren't he and Andie just two of life's fugitives, raging and raging against the dying of the light? What, knuckle-heads like him get off on Dylan Thomas too? He knocked the empty glass deliberately on to the floor, but it didn't even do him the courtesy of shattering. This kind of work made prey out of people like them, not the other way around.

Prey. Yes. That's what they were. They were all on the right side, the same side, of this particular line. The business – it was the busi-ness that was their true enemy. The business needed people like them trying to re-amplify themselves. Why else would anyone vol-untarily stare down the barrel at more horror than they'd ever known? Overnight, they'd all managed to laugh, joke and drink their way out of any aftershocks – and Kris put on his best show for months, helped by the fact Andie stayed buried in her room, as if she'd already gone. But if they'd known what was really driving him ... He rubbed at his head as he lied to himself, that damn bullet again, opening up mental cracks that had been almost invisible before.

These days he only needed to blink and out came that useless, worthless cunt of an old man who spent more time doling out beat-ings than anything else. Kris screwed his eyes shut but ended up feeling all over again the bruises he wore more days than he made it to school. *Pop-pop-pop* went some gunfire off in the distance, way too far away to be a threat, and yet ... *Should I shoot her, kid? What d'ya reckon?* Drunk himself blind, deaf and almost dumb, but the old man still had it in him to ask, a tangle of hair knotted round a meaty hand as he pointed his pistol at his mother's head. The old man didn't deserve a peaceful end, but she, she surely did – that was the thought that propelled his eyes open. They landed on the rolled-up carpet sitting in the corner, its rich hues vivid even through the dust in the air. He'd take that back for Rory. It would tickle him pink to spread the finest of Persian rugs, looted – no, removed – from one of Saddam's palaces, in some back alley in Soho. He couldn't think of anyone who deserved it more. And it would be far more comfortable than a cardboard box. Kris suddenly wished he'd thought of it months ago.

'Kris?' Adam frowned as he peered around the door. 'Are you going to be ready? We're leaving in fifteen.'

'Right you are.' Kris stumbled, reaching for the carpet. 'Just paying my last respects to my digs. Something tells me I won't see this particular beauty spot again for a while.'

Adam grunted, leaving the door ajar as he went back down the stairs.

It was hardly a surprise that Sami fell on the right side of that particular line too, Kris mused. Yep, she was right beside him, giving the evil eye back to those predatory business interests on the other side. He staggered just a little as he forced the carpet into his empty flak-jacket bag. He'd have to carry it with him on board once the body armour was stowed, but some unidentifiable rug had nothing on the wheels of cheese Royal Jordanian regularly let him smuggle in for Mohammed. He felt the sting of guilt sloshing with the whisky as he considered how personal her motivation was – she had whimpered out the real story almost as soon as they'd been rescued: how her father had died on the job, how her mum had basically imploded afterwards and tried to kill herself, how all she'd ever wanted to do was continue her dad's life's work to try and change her mother's mind about it. He'd been a photographer too, she'd wept. One of the best around, apparently. Egyptian, even better: easy to fling between every regional shit-show going, absolving the Westerners of any risk. No surprises –

he'd been blown to bits without a final frame to show for it. Kris gave the carpet the benefit of his knee as he forced the zip closed.

He ran a shaky hand through his hair as he surveyed the empty room, devoid now even of memory. What if this really was the last of it for him here? He was leaving behind a small piece of his skull, a decent hank of his hair and all the blood that used to run through his veins. Would the fair pound of his flesh this place had already claimed excuse him everything else?

And that was what stuck with him, all the way along the airport road, then cocooned high in the clouds above the Arabian desert wilderness with Sami by his side, and through the post-Christmas sales traffic on the M4 back up the stairs into Ross's office.

'Hey.' Ross could barely whimper, pale and slumped behind his desk. 'Man, am I glad to see you both back here safe.'

'I can tell.' Kris leant down to give him a squeeze. 'What the hell happened to you? Did you get run down by a sledge or something?'

'Managed to slip my wonky few discs.' Ross grimaced as he tried and failed to stand. 'Not even in pursuit of a decent story this time – I was putting the angel back on the Christmas tree, if you can believe that ... Jesus...'

'And all in the name of celebrating his birth, hey.' Kris's eyes flicked to the locked cupboard where the replacement medical supplies were kept, gleam on its polished door like a twinkle in the eye. 'Don't you have anything strong enough left back there?'

'I just swallowed every painkiller left in Andie's kit. You just missed her, actually.'

Kris stiffened. He had Andie's obsession with gaining her air miles to thank for the fact they'd flown home separately, but he'd counted on dumb luck not to bump into her in the office. She'd be on the road again herself now, wouldn't she? And wasn't she connecting on to Johannesburg? Or was it Cape Town? She should have been well ahead of them on British Airways.

'Hand over yours too, would you, Kris?'

His fingers tangled with his empty cargo pocket.

'I'm all out, sorry, skipper,' Kris replied quickly, shifting from foot to foot as he thought on them. 'I left Adam with everything I had so supplies would last a little longer out there. They weren't sure when we'd next be swapping out the muscle.'

'Please, have mine,' Sami said, handing over her brand-new trauma kit, untouched, may as well still have been wrapped in sterile plastic. Kris felt the beginnings of drool forming at the corner of his mouth as he watched the movement of the leather case across the desk, bulging with all its unused hospital-grade painkillers. Ross grunted a thanks, mercifully still in far too much pain to question why she hadn't left it with Adam too. The guy was paling with every second.

'Andie's already gone?' Kris couldn't help but ask.

'She's somewhere around, I think.' Ross tossed his head towards the deserted newsroom, still in its fugue holiday state. 'Said she wanted to catch up with you, Sami, before you left.'

'I got her message,' Sami replied as Kris flinched again. What could Andie still want with Sami, after all this? 'I'll find her, don't worry, Ross. Shouldn't you be going home yourself?'

'What did she want?' Kris turned to her, failing to disguise his nerves. 'Why is Andie leaving you messages?'

'I don't know.' Sami frowned as she considered Ross. 'She just asked that I call her before I leave the office. Look, Ross – can we get you a car home, or something? Isn't there a doctor we could call that might be able to take a look. What about the network's medical facilities?'

'Thanks, Sami, but I'll be OK.' Ross winced. 'I'll be fine now I've got my hands on the strong stuff. I have to account for everything in there –' He tossed his head towards the locked cupboard behind him. 'And dipping into company morphine on account of drunk and disorderly behaviour is going to get me nowhere fast.'

'Where is Andie, Ross, do you know?' Kris interrupted, gabbling.

'I'll call her, hang on.' Sami reached into her pocket for her phone, and he grabbed it; he couldn't help himself.

'Just take yourselves on home now, OK, guys?' Ross winced again. 'Plenty of time to go over the paperwork. You can dump everything in here and take off. Go see your families. I know you've spoken to Penny, already, Sami, but—'

'I haven't, actually,' she interrupted, eyes flicking between Ross and her phone – Kris couldn't let it go. 'I assumed I'd see her here. I'm so sorry you've been left on your own to deal with this.'

'That's strange.' Now Ross was the one to frown. 'Andie said—'

'What the fuck else has Andie been saying?' Pink spots popped on Ross's cheeks as Kris exploded. 'That we're unfit for work? Like her, too busy running her mouth off in the most damaging ways possible? That we should be benched from sundown to sunset? Because if she is then we sure as hell should be too? Did Katja tell you what she said about Mohammed – in front of everyone!'

'Don't start, Gonzo. You've had the worst of it all, sure you have – but don't assume you're the only ones who've had a rough ride these past few weeks.'

Kris roared back, a bull in a pen. 'Oh, I know. I know all you have is our backs, I know you'd never have sent us out unless I'd insisted, I know Penelope Rhodes is about as clean a manager as the bedsheets in the Amman Intercontinental.'

The reinforced glass door crashed as it suddenly flew open.

'Ah, hey, guys,' Andie said pleasantly, as if she hadn't just put all her weight into trying to make their little glass cell shatter around them. 'How was the flight?'

'Hey,' Sami said brightly, smiling, even. 'I got your message. Sorry, I was going to call once I'd finished going through the gear—'

'What are you still doing here?' Kris cut her off, breathing hard. 'Didn't your flight land hours ago? Don't you have a connection to make?'

'Not for a few more hours yet,' Andie replied coolly, folding her arms across her chest as she surveyed them all. 'And once I saw the state Ross was in, I decided to wait it out here – the office is far quieter than the first-class lounge this time of year.'

'Like hell you did.' Kris couldn't contain himself, even as the questions wrote themselves all over Ross and Sami's faces.

'Why else would I be here?' Andie shot back, cold as ice. 'Why else might I want to speak with you, or Sami? In front of Ross?'

She had him then, but only for the briefest of moments as he suddenly remembered what was stashed back safely in his flak-jacket bag.

'Fine, I looted a carpet, OK? Are you happy now?'

Her brow furrowed. 'What are you talking about?'

He bent down, pulling the rolled-up Persian rug out of the lumpy bag at his feet. 'Saddam's finest, no less. Special delivery from the palace all the way to the back alleys of Soho.'

'What the hell is that?' It was Ross's turn to question now, grimacing further as he leant over his desk.

'A rug,' Kris replied, leaning it against his empty cargo pocket as if the carpet itself could physically protect him. 'I brought it back for Rory. I thought he might make better use of it than anyone in the office ever would.'

He held his breath as the four of them stood there, sweat trickling in slow motion down Ross's face, suspicion corrugated across Andie's, and total, blessed confusion wiped all over Sami's. Until Ross let out a roar of laughter.

'You were given that rug, right, Kris?'

'Not exactly, I—'

'Repeat after me, Gonzo,' Ross cut him off, trying to be serious but a smile still pushing at his face, no doubt a combination of genuine hilarity and the creeping effect of morphine.

'You were given it by a family who you had interviewed – they were merchants, I assume, with plenty still left to give?'

Kris stared at Ross's face, creased into a curious mix of agony and ecstasy.

'Because if you'd looted it,' Ross continued, 'and someone else confirmed you did, you'd most definitely get fired.'

Kris picked up the rug like it was a rolled-up towel.

'Exactly, skipper.' He fingered its rich, golden fringe. 'Exactly. It was a token of appreciation. That's all. A gift. You're right. It was a gift, which I don't need. Lucia won't tolerate anything she hasn't chosen herself.'

'Then I can think of no better recipient than Rory,' Ross replied, with another snort. 'There's a man who deserves so much more than just us buying him toast whenever we're back in town.'

'Happy now?' Kris turned to Andie, clutching the rug against his chest like armour.

'Royal Jordanian sure must have uncorked the good stuff,' she replied, eyeing him as she raked a hand through her hair. 'But I was actually waiting around to see what else we could do for Ross here. He's obviously in a great deal of pain.'

Kris's insides turned to ice as she continued.

'And we're specialists in that, aren't we? In pain? And suffering?'

'Is that why you wanted to talk to me, too?' Sami asked from somewhere to his side. He watched Andie's expression close over.

'That's right, except as usual, you were one step ahead of me,' Andie replied, nodding at the bulging, unopened trauma kit lying like an unexploded bomb on Ross's desk. 'Yah, I guess I'll have to get used to that now, won't I?'

Her gaze moved back to him, cold chips of blue, sharp as flint.

'Haven't you got anything left to give back to Ross too?' The chips moved to his sagging, empty cargo pocket. Kris suddenly felt as exposed as if he'd been naked. The carpet had been his only shield, and now it was clutched pointlessly across his chest.

'I gave what was left of mine to Adam,' he said, unrolling the carpet on to Ross's desk as if the more he gave her to look at, the less she'd see. 'He was nearly out.'

'Speaking of which,' Ross grunted, 'can you scan and sign for it while you're all here? I need the barcodes done pronto. We can do all the rest of the paperwork later, but that can never wait ... You too, Sami. Andie can show you where the scanner is.'

'It's OK, I can do it,' Sami replied, stepping gingerly around his chair to reach for the clipboard on top of the cabinet. 'I signed the trauma kits out the first time.'

Andie laughed suddenly, high and mad.

'Don't think you know this guy,' she hissed as Sami stared at her. 'Don't ever think you know him. Take it from me, you don't. None of you do.'

Kris let all his breath out into the crash of the door as Andie stalked out, the carpet's rich colours shining up from Ross's desk. The kaleidoscope was shifting again, that much he knew, but what kind of picture would he get this time? A shiver ran down his back as he rolled it back up, to leave only the gold threads shimmering between his fingers.

~~~

Drizzle had started to fall as they waited outside for their respective cars. Soho was as packed as the office wasn't, crawling with shoppers after their post-Christmas bargains. Kris knew how alien Sami would be feeling. She just wasn't used to it yet. And as soon as she felt like she was, it would all be lying in wait to ambush her in her dreams.

'So what happens now?' He realised it wasn't just rain beading her face as she beseeched him. 'We just go home and wait?'

'Exactly that. It won't take long though. I promise. Penny Rhodes isn't one to wait around.'

Sami didn't even have it left in her to sob, the tears just silently rolling out of her eyes. He tightened his grip on the carpet as his arm twitched to reach towards her. Not now, Kris. Not ever. No more complications.

'You'll get used to it. This part, the in-between, is the hardest.

All the trying to get back to normal when normal isn't what you thought it was.'

'There's just no way I can—'

'Sure there is. You're on to a winner. You've nailed your first two assignments, and they were in the only places that count at the moment.'

'But how do I get us back on the road? All I managed in Baghdad was to get us in trouble. No one will ever have a clue about Ahmed and his story unless I can convince Penny we've got enough. Everything feels so completely out of my control.'

'Occupational hazard.' Kris cleared a cough out of his throat as he replied. 'It only feels that way, mind. All you have to do is make it impossible for management to ever count you out. Speaking Arabic helps with that, but you're better off proving yourself somewhere other than the Middle East next.'

'I'll never be better off anywhere else.' She practically spat as she said it, finally able to wipe the drizzle out of her eyes.

'Well you won't go back in a hurry if anyone realises how personal it is.' Kris scratched at the stubbly patch on his head. 'It makes you look incapable of being objective. It'll happen again, of course it will, the war is too hot to bench anyone with the lingo for long. So just go make your own luck while you're waiting. Find something else to do. There's a world of stories we've all had to walk away from.'

A horn beeped just as his heart picked up speed, Mohammed's blood doing its job again. What would she come up with? Where would they go? He was suddenly revelling in losing control as much as she was panicking, memories of Andie and piercing little eyes buried tightly in the carpet under his arm.

'That's my ride. Be lucky, alright? I'll call you, I promise.'

A flicker of something else passed over her face then, but Kris slid into the car before he could do anything about it. He knew where he was going, even if she hadn't worked it out yet.

Chapter 21
Muscle Memory

I must have paced the roads in and around Holloway for most of that night, closing the front door on the bags I kicked over the threshold no sooner than I had opened it. Penny didn't call, nor Di, nor Kris, nor anyone – my brother and I hadn't spoken since Mum had been sectioned, and it was hardly the time to try and start again – all he would see was a collaborator. He only ever saw it Mum's way, and why wouldn't he? He only stayed with her in the Middle East because he knew how much she hated living there. He understood she couldn't bring herself to leave either. There was no escaping to boarding school for him, and it didn't take long for her to start holding that against me too. I dug fingers into my ears as his screams rattled in my head – Mum had nearly got her way by the time I dragged myself up the stairs to see why she was taking the world's longest bath. And my brother blamed himself for not being there as much as he blamed Dad for being the catalyst in the first place.

I did find myself looking up his old number, wondering if it was still the same. Wasn't there still a chance that being each other's only sane, living blood relatives trumped anything else? But with every white flash I blinked out of my eyes, I felt Kris's hand on my cheek. The heat of every imprint made the guilt flare just as hot. Never mind that I could tell myself it was in pursuit of a job worth more than anything else, for my brother, the business was as complicit as Dad.

I paced full circuits of the Arsenal stadium, majestic in the silence, reassuringly solid in the dark. Would I swap feeling wanted, purposeful and alive for existing like a phantom, only seen if I wore a more acceptable skin? I knew I never would. Muscles have permanent memories, and these were better than any mine had before.

I turned away from the corner of every street that would lead me back to the Holloway Road, where my studio flat awaited – vegetables rotting in the fridge, milk curdling on the countertop. I still had Kris's luck even if I had nothing else – a broken family, hardly any friends, not even a semblance of a functioning daily existence. I hadn't been able to bring myself to return Di's calls after our newsroom showdown, and then she'd just stopped. Round and round I went again, Gillespie Road, Highbury Hill, round to Avenell Road, and back, ears rustling with the ghost of a crowd as I passed the hulk of the football stadium for the eightieth time. Could it be that simple to be part of something else? A season ticket, the camaraderie of a crowd that cared as much as you did. But then I caught sight of the yoga studio, newly set up in neon, aspirational colours, waving from the far corner of Gillespie Road – and remembered how you can be in a room full of people, sweating over the same goal, and still feel as lonely as you ever have. Just because you're all working towards the same thing doesn't mean you are going to share it.

Exhaustion finally found its way into my legs as dawn shimmered on the horizon, bringing its optimistically pink edge to the outline of the Coronet in the distance. And as I dragged myself home, to my curious pocket of personal space floating high above the Holloway Road, I found him.

Wahid was slumped in a service alleyway behind the pub previously occupied only by dustbins – it wasn't big enough for anyone or anything to take up permanent residence there. His familiar bags of wares were nowhere to be seen, and his face looked like burned cauliflower, its usual colour drained away apart from in the gashes blooming from his eye socket and the corner of his mouth. He was wearing a puffy black coat, which made him look even rounder than usual – perhaps his bags were stashed underneath? But as I bent over him, frantically muttering his name as I patted his livid, blotchy face, I realised it wasn't all black. The sleeves were soaked through with blood.

My hands flashed forward before I needed to tell them to – wrapping around and squeezing down hard on the cuts to his wrists. Adrenaline jolted through me as I calculated: these were fresh cuts, and were horizontal rather than vertical, so we still had time, whereas there were crusts all over the gashes to his face, those were already healing, even though they looked anything but.

'Stay with me, Wahid,' I muttered, pressing my knee down into his wrist so I could free a hand to reach my phone. It would take minutes for the ambulance to arrive, only a few more to ensure his life didn't slip away into the steaming piles of rubbish he was slumped against, but the damage, the cause, that was irrevocable. I eyed his bruises as he murmured to me. What had happened? The scream of the incoming siren rattled round my head like so many I had heard before, my hands falling away as the paramedics swarmed.

'Do you know him? What happened?'

I blinked white flashes from my eyes as the man in uniform barked up at me. Where was I?

'I found him like this,' I gabbled, rubbing non-existent dust from my eyes. 'He's a regular on the block, I live across the street.'

'Drugs?'

'No, no...' Some glass crunched underfoot as I stepped backward. How would I know whether he took drugs? Just because we had some shred of background in common ... The stretcher clattered equally scornfully out of the back of the ambulance.

'Can I ride with you, please?' More glass crunched as I implored the paramedics lifting, strapping and loading, as if all the movements were happening at the same time. 'He's got no family here, and he won't be able to contact any relatives abroad without help—'

The rest of my sentence caught in my throat as a gloved hand pulled me roughly into the back of the ambulance.

'It doesn't matter to us what the story is here, lady,' the paramedic said as the ambulance squealed away, flinging me across Wahid's body. 'We're only here to try and change the ending.'

We both lurched again as the ambulance skidded.

'Just know this. He'll try again, they all do. So remove whatever it was that got him there in the first place, if you can.'

He faded as Mum's body, gravestone-white and limp, swam into focus on the stretcher. They literally brought her back to life, they told us afterwards. She was that close. Her cuts ran in the wrong direction. I blinked furiously as I stared down at Wahid – why was he giving up? Rubble and debris rolled beneath my feet even though the floor was slick with blood. What did I think I could possibly do to make any difference to Wahid here, when all he wanted was as far out of reach as the clouds of dust choking the skies over Baghdad and still inexplicably catching in my throat.

It didn't take long for him to regain consciousness. Almost as soon as we were inside the hospital, less than a mile away, his eyes fluttered open, as if the swish of the curtains closing around his cubicle was enough for him to sense he might be able to face whatever was inside. And just as he did, I felt my own means slip away – all the energy that had been blazing around my body just buzzing away into the floor as I clasped what I could of his bandaged hand.

'Wahid,' I murmured, crouching over his cot. 'Can you hear me, Wahid?'

He closed his eyes again, bruised brow furrowing as I squeezed his hand tighter.

'You're safe now, Wahid. You're in hospital, and you're going to be OK.'

A sob escaped then – mine or his? Guttural and harsh. I dropped his hand before I could stop myself, white flashes popping all again. Did I honestly think I was going to be able to explain to him why it was worth hanging on, why it was so lucky that I'd found him when I did?

'I'm so sorry, Wahid. I'm just so, so sorry.'

I knew then that he was the one sobbing, his dark eyes alight with fury as they reopened. What was I sorry for? Stopping him on his way out? He'd finally found the courage to end his own suffering even if he couldn't end that of the rest of his loved ones. And I'd brought him back for what? Did I need him to tell me again how what family he had left were being brutalised beyond recognition in the home they once loved? Or that he could no longer eke out an existence selling counterfeit cigarettes and worthless trinkets to drunks and addicts on some nondescript, forgettable corner of a city miles from anything he'd ever known? I realised I had no idea where he actually lived – sharing a house, no, a room in a house, with how many other people in a similarly desperate situation. Or was it even under cover? Was it a box in an alleyway? How was it my right to bring him back to that, if he'd chosen to leave it all behind?

'I just—' I jumped as he shouted, no words, just a piercing scream from his guts. 'I just couldn't leave you there.'

'You,' he hissed suddenly, rising and falling back on to his cot as we both realised he was tethered to it. 'You try to save me – why? Why did you do this to me? You think this is what I want?'

I wiped a kaleidoscope of memory from my eyes as he screamed in Arabic. He was right, I had made myself a witness to his private suffering. I had done it deliberately – for my own purposes, not his. And then I had made a choice on his behalf. What other choice could I have made, though? Who could have walked away without trying to stop him?

But you only ever see it your way, my mother whispered in my ear.

'They are all dead, Miss Samira,' he spat, straining at the leather straps holding him to the cot. 'Everyone is gone now, everyone – the occupation has taken everyone. And this country, these English people, they do not want me here.'

The bruises all over his face flashed livid purple as he raged.

'And now, because of you, there will be no peaceful end for me. Now, I must find a sharper knife, or I must wait to be beaten again. For me, there is only pain left.'

'I just couldn't leave you there,' I whispered again. And then I closed my eyes as I walked out, stumbling through the curtains out into the ward. Because how much more did I think it was fair to witness? What else could l learn about Wahid and his tortured life that would make my involvement any more reasonable? My eyes flew open as I crashed into a metal cart.

'I'm so sorry,' I mumbled to no one in particular, hands shaking as I tidied spilled boxes and dressings. *To bear witness is to compel action*, Dad murmured, deep inside my inner ear. *To stay silent, to stand by, that is to do nothing*.

But in that moment, Dad, the only action left was to walk away.

Once I got outside, that was it. My body just gave up, legs crumpling beneath me. I had to crawl to the nearest available bench, just feet away from the ambulance bay. I'm fine, I mouthed at quizzical staff, all with far more pressing things to do but still driven by the sight of a woman bent double until she lay prone, breath wreathing in cold clouds around my head. I stayed there for what felt like a lifetime, a chorus in my ears and flashback after flashback in my eyes, no matter how tight I screwed them shut. It was only when I realised the buzzing through my body was actually my phone rather than yet another echo from the past that I snapped back to consciousness. And by then the sun was fully up, blinding me all over again as I opened my eyes directly into it.

'Sami? Is that you? Hello? Hellooo?'

Penny still wasn't pausing for breath as I finally got my phone to my ear.

'Sami! Are you alright? I've been calling and calling.'

'Penny, hi, yes – sorry, it's me, I'm here...' I trailed off as a bus screeched past in a cloud of petrol.

'Where on earth are you? In the middle of a roundabout?'

'Sorry, no.' I wobbled as I stood. 'I was just grabbing a coffee and a paper.'

'I'm sorry I missed you yesterday,' she said. 'I so wanted to be there when you came back, especially after everything you went through.'

'It's really no problem,' I replied over the cracks in her voice. I'd heard them all before, even though she will have had no idea. You don't have to have your own kids to understand what it's like to have to let them down all the time. 'We just dumped the gear—'

'Yes, Ross said,' she interrupted with a cough. 'Then I trust you got yourself home OK? Did you manage a good night's rest? It's very early to be already up and about.'

I wrapped a hand over the mouthpiece as an ambulance siren blared closer. It wasn't so loud yet that I couldn't answer, but the words just wouldn't come.

'Sami? Are you still there?'

'Sorry, yes.' I rattled some change in my pocket. 'Just paying – hang on.'

I rubbed the mouthpiece again before continuing. 'My body clock is still a bit all over the place because of the overnight shift.'

'Ah yes – another thing I wanted to talk to you about.' She muttered to someone else in the background. 'First thing's first, though. I wanted to see you yesterday because I wanted you to hear directly from me how impressed we all are with your recent work.'

My face twitched into a smile then, I couldn't help it.

'I was concerned, I'll admit, when we sent you to Kabul with Jennifer but she was incredibly complimentary. And to have got yourself inside that women's hospital, even if we couldn't do the story itself justice, was very smart indeed. You clearly have a knack, Sami. You have a knack for spotting simple human stories. Truthfully, we could and should do better at showcasing that kind of journalism. It is often difficult, with political and military events moving at the pace they are. But it isn't an excuse. And I, for one, have been determined to do something about that for some time now.'

'Thank you,' I said, body catching up to brain. I suddenly felt able to stand, nodding at the paramedic hovering with a cigarette in the ambulance bay.

'It's been a personal bugbear of mine, not that I'd expect you to have known that. I have, truthfully, been trying to fix it for a long time. I want the network to stand up and be counted – to make a point of it, and not be scared of the consequences. Why else are we in the business, if not to shine the light at the people determined to turn it off? But unfortunately we have many pay-masters, and conscience is only one of them – which, by the way, is why I can't always use the reporters themselves to do it, I don't have enough of them to go around as it is.'

I swayed on my feet as she continued. To me, this was the lan-guage of love, the language of purpose and conscience, the language that had long stood for everything I had lost. I hadn't necessarily expected to hear it from Penny, but I'd come to the news industry expecting to find it somewhere. And to hear it so soon after questioning so much else was a literal rush of blood to the head. It turned the whole night around.

'Yes,' I breathed into the phone, even though she hadn't asked me any questions.

'I have to bench Kris for the foreseeable future anyway. Sending him back out after everything that happened in Iraq was always going to be a risk we would only ever just get away with. But it's more than my life is worth to restrict him to London-based stories, and he's too talented to keep off the road for good. I'd be on the rack from both sides.'

Penny continued ranting as if she was convincing herself. I wish I could have told her the one thing she definitely didn't need to do was convince me.

'So we might, just might, be able to get away with a side project, something left of the main agenda but just as impactful. I can style it as the "World's Untold Stories" or similar – and I should be able to skim the money together if the travel is lean enough. Kris'll do it, I don't even need to ask. And if you are game—'

'Yes,' I said yet again, but loud enough this time to cut her off. 'Yes, I am. I'll do anything.'

She laughed then, as high and loud as another siren making its way towards me.

'I've got you off the overnight shift for at least the next month. Make sure you take some time for yourself for the next couple of days – eat well, rest, catch up with your family, just be kind to yourself. And then let's start the new year with a bang, shall we?'

I laughed back at her. The sirens were coming closer and closer, but I didn't need to hear anything else she said. I knew exactly what I was going to do.

'Find a project with preferably as low operating costs as possible, somewhere off the beaten track but with just as much at stake. A story that everyone can relate to, no matter where it is. Think about charities that might let you travel on their aid flights, or other creative ways to move about that are not flying business class on a commercial airline. Engaging with the right organisations can often bypass official paperwork, as you can move around under the auspices of someone else—'

And with that, the ambulances, three of them, were upon me, squealing into the car park as stretchers clattered towards them.

'I won't let you down,' I cried over the commotion, even though no one, least of all Penny, could hear me. I knew exactly who I was screaming at. 'I won't let you down.'

Chapter 22
Pale Reflections

Kris cocked his head, gravel crunching as the van pulled away from the end of the path. Was that why he couldn't hear Trixie? Her barking would usually start long before any car had actually stopped outside – he gave the front gate an extra rattle, the van back on smooth tarmac by then, and still, only silence came back. Lucia had picked a cottage down a grassy lane so identical to all the other grassy lanes around that particular meadow that you could stick the same key into almost any door before you realised you were trying to open the wrong chocolate box. The perfect little village for him to escape home to, apparently. Kris had only agreed to it because it was that close to the airports he could get out of there fast. Lucia had it all figured out long before he'd ever had to explain anything to her – another reason why they worked, or at least, why he thought they still worked. But right then he found himself having to double-take, and not just because the last time he'd slept was dozing off somewhere in the sky over the Mediterranean sea, dreaming of old men mutilated by their wheelchairs and teenagers frying in oil. His key fitted, so why didn't everything else?

Crunch went the door as he pushed it open into the pile of wellies and other apparently essential child-related equipment. But where was the dog as he whistled, the low, singular pitch that, no matter how long he'd been gone, never failed to bring her out from whichever pile of mud or sticks she'd found momentarily more interesting?

He whistled again, stumbling as he got into the hall, looking through into the silent kitchen and the darkening garden beyond. Where was she? This was a dog that, as a puppy, used to wet herself, literally burst all over the floor with excitement, whenever he got back. Submissive urination; he'd seen plenty a human do it too, mind, but never when they were pleased to see him. Now, where was Lucia as well? Where were the boys? What part of the usual routine, the one they'd all rehearsed for so long that it felt as natural as it looked, had somehow tweaked out?

His legs buckled again; he told himself it was because there were even more, apparently critical, supplies thrown all over the place, but still the carpet may as well have been quicksand below his boots. Whether the place felt like 'home' or not, he was always expecting them to be in it.

'Trix!' A shout then, hollow and empty. The house didn't make a sound, another leaden few seconds of silence while he froze on the spot, an interloper caught in the act, until—

'Daddy!'

Kris could have melted then, plain slithered down onto the floor in a heap, save for the rolling ball of seven-year-old and dog that came barrelling through the kitchen as the back door flew open. Relief flooded over him – it took a second to process what it was, but yes, it was relief, a sensation he'd come to associate with something far removed from walking through what was apparently his own front door.

'You two ... where have you been hiding?'

He peered over two fluffy heads to the back door, only to find his reflection, thrown back at him by the lengthening shadows behind the glass.

'And where's your mother? Building a new doghouse out there for me?'

'Stop it, Tixie.' Tommy yanked his hand out of the dog's mouth.

'Tom? Where's Mum? And where's Nico? What were you doing out there in the dark?'

Trixie squirmed away from him as he looked around. Where

was the pudgy four-year old, due to be clambering all over him round about now? A cartoon strip flashed past as he blinked, small boys feeding mud pies to stray dogs, black on white.

'She had to pop out,' Tommy replied in the sing-song voice of a child repeating something he's been told multiple times. 'She's only going to be a few minutes.'

'What?' Trixie yelped as Kris grabbed for her.

'She just had to pop out,' Tommy mumbled, yanking at his trouser leg. 'She's going to be back soon.'

'She had to pop out?'

Kris asked himself the question as he repeated it.

'And she left you behind? To go where? Wait – is Nico here on his own too?'

'No, he's at Gramma's.'

'What?'

'Gramma's. Nico is. Come see my Christmas presents, come! Santa, he got me—'

'I know what you got, Tom.' The dog whined and scratched at the door as he dropped to his knees, reaching for his son. 'Listen to me for a second. Where's Mum? Did she leave you here all by yourself?'

Lucia's voicemail rattled round his head. Hadn't he told her he was on the way back? *Hola, you've reached Luceeeea, leave a message after the tone.* Tommy squirmed away as he held him, the sudden sour smell of fabric soaked through with urine nauseatingly familiar. His own son was scared of him, not the woman who'd left him here alone in the dark.

'She said she had to pop out...'

'Where? Why didn't you go with her? When did she leave? Was it still light outside?'

'She'll only be a few minutes,' the child said, eyes as dark and earnest as the now pitch black beyond the glass of the back door. 'She said she was going to play away from home.'

Kris blanched, grip tensing around the little shoulders in his hands. 'She said that? Mum did? To you?'

'I heard her.'

'Say that? When?'

'Gramma,' the child mumbled, trying and failing to wriggle free. The smell of urine was suddenly so pronounced Kris felt like he could almost taste it, a bitter mix of shame and regret. 'I heard her tell it to Gramma. She said you did.'

'Tommy, listen to me.' Kris had to wipe a clammy hand before cupping his son's face. 'Does Mum leave you by yourself a lot?'

'No! She said it's only when her friends can't come to play here.'

Trixie barked then, out of nowhere. Bang-bang-bang, one-two-three, like a pop gun.

'Her friends? Mum has friends that come to play?'

'Daddy, stop.' He twisted his head on his little neck.

'Who's her friend? Who's she playing with?'

'Gramma said to her, you get to play away so why, why can't she?'

Trixie erupted as Kris swore, barking like he was an actual fox in her living room. And then another door flew open, alongside the ones already swinging on their hinges inside his head, disgorging their filthy contents like vomit.

'Kris. You're back!'

And there she was as he turned, Lucia, framed in the doorway as frozen as the snowflakes starting to fall gently around her head, tiny little flakes lit in the dark sky behind her by the multiple bulbs he suddenly noticed dangling brainlessly above his head from a new light fitting.

'When? When did you get back?'

He froze too as he stared at her, poised as an ice sculpture in the doorway, even as Trixie flew past, leaping and slobbering as high as she could.

'Well, you should have called,' Lucia said, finally dropping to her knees to pet the dog, who slavered all over her. He felt the ice creep into his bones. Not his beloved Trixie, no. 'We've all been so excited to see you, haven't we, Tommy darling?'

'Did you already tell Daddy what Santa brought?' Tommy's voice quavered somewhere behind them. 'Mumma, you said it would be a surprise, you said—'

'That you'd only be a few minutes. Is that right, Mumma?'

He shivered as he heard himself, another voice chiming in from the past.

'Oh, Kris...'

The air crackled as she closed the door over the snow blowing in from outside.

'Let's talk about this later, you must have had a long flight. Baghdad, was it? Unless you're rushing off again somewhere.'

'Rushing off? Is that what you've been telling yourself? That it's OK to leave the kids on their own, because I keep rushing off?'

He batted away the dog, he couldn't stand to touch her. Whose house had he walked into? Even if it was a pale reflection of the unconditional love he'd had once upon a fairy-tale time, they'd had an understanding, he felt sure of it.

'You can go and watch TV if you want, darling.' Her voice was soft as she turned to Tommy, didn't even bat a fake eyelash at his painfully obvious accident. 'Daddy will be in in just a second.'

He stared as the child did exactly as he was told, piss-soaked trousers and all, the dog trotting after him. His dog, the one that was supposed to be overjoyed to see him no matter what.

'What is this, Luce? Did you honestly leave Tommy here on his own? And for how long?' He asked it as if it was still a question. 'I found him outside in the dark with nothing but a designer fucking dog for company.'

Lucia cocked her head to the side, unhooking the huge buttons on her coat, silver fur shimmering under her new light like something from outer space.

'Do you really think I have to explain myself to you? After all this time doing it by myself, just how you like it?'

'Where were you?' He could hardly hear himself as he asked. 'Tommy said—'

'He's seven, Kris.'

'But he was here all by himself,' he cried piteously. 'What could have been so important that you'd leave him alone?'

She rounded on him then. She still had her furry coat on – it was like being attacked by some wild alien animal.

'Did that bullet knock out whatever you had left in your head, Kris? Who are you to ask me a question like that? You've never stayed with us one minute longer than you needed to.'

She was suddenly raving, light bulbs flying as her arms whirled over her head. This couldn't be Lucia, couldn't be the woman he was so sure had wanted – no, had needed – the exact same foundations as him, no matter whether their reasons were galaxies apart. This was a changeling in her place, it had to be. He opened his mouth, miraculously found his voice, used it.

'Where were you, while our seven-year-old was hiding in the dark by himself? Where was she, Tommo? Playing away from home, was it?'

But all Kris could hear himself say was, *Should I shoot her, boy? Who'd miss her?* He looked down at his hands as if they were someone else's, tried and failed to unclench them from fists.

'That's it, isn't it? That's what she said. She's just popping out, she'll only be a few minutes, because her friend couldn't come to play at our house today, could he?'

Of course it was only when Lucia screamed that the child came rushing back. Trixie growled as his hands flashed out, not his dog anymore, never again. A hunk of ceiling crashed down, chunks of splintering plaster turning his hair grey, Lucia's hair white, and Tommy's little head as powdery as a snowman. And just like that, here he was again, blinking dust, dust and more fucking dust out of his eyes as he stared down at the fistful of wires and bulbs sprouting from his hand. He'd yanked out her entire light fitting and stilled them all, a plaster-cast of a family suspended in a scene he'd witnessed so many times he could have cast it himself.

The tears streamed as it hit him. Not the dust-in-your-eyes variety either. Because that's exactly what he had done. He'd made himself the star in his own private war, building a family just so he might try not to lose it, and hadn't known it would matter until now.

Clouds flew as Lucia fell forward, Tommy coughing his lungs up as she swept him into her dusty arms. Kris swooned for just a second. Who was that? And where was he? Another seven-year-old picked himself up off the floor inside his head. But the only whimpers he could hear came from his wife and son.

'Daddy!' Tommy dissolved into another cough as Kris stumbled and fell backward, threshold between the door and porch slicing worse than a flak jacket into his back.

'It's OK, fella.' Kris spluttered as he staggered to his feet. 'Mummy will have this mess cleared up in no time—'

'Yes, I will,' Lucia interrupted, shards of cut glass in the dust. 'Daddy's got to get back to work now, darling, OK? Come here, sweetheart, don't worry.'

And the dog didn't even try to stop him as he lumbered out, back up the path that could have been anyone else's, along the grassy lane that led to nowhere. All he could remember about what happened next is when Sami called.

Chapter 23
Untold Stories

She finally answered the phone on the third try – of that particular round, I mean. I'd been calling Diana on and off since hanging up on Penny, every morning and evening for the best part of a week, all times I knew she'd be awake. I'd been in and out of the newsroom to make arrangements but had only caught sight of her the once, an unmistakable flutter of immaculate hair and coat as she whipped around the corner on her way out early on New Year's Day. Even when we were closest – creeping into each other's rooms while at her family home during the school holidays, probably, before everything got so complicated – there was still a part of me that would always find a part of her resolutely out of reach. But the only way I could move on without her was by knowing I'd at least tried. She was the only constant I had left.

'I'm so sorry – did I wake you?'

'Something like that,' she replied softly, even though it was already perfectly obvious I hadn't.

We sat in silence for a moment. I watched a bus deflate on the road below, passengers streaming out into Holloway Road Tube station.

'How are you doing?'

'Me? Oh, I'm fine.' I could hear the squeak of a tap turning on in the background. 'And you?'

'Good, yeah. Good...' I trailed off, fiddling with the zip of the bag at my feet. 'Look, Di—'

'Hang on.' The tap roared for a moment.

I tried again. 'I'm sorry about everything. I'm sorry for going off at you in the newsroom, for not returning your calls, for just generally giving up after you stopped returning mine.'

She sighed into the phone, white noise blowing into my ear.

'It's just all I've ever wanted to do, and I still think there's a chance, no matter how tiny it is, that Mum might finally understand it all—'

'I know,' she cut me off. 'We've known each other for long enough that you don't have to explain yourself to me. I'm just not entirely sure that you realise what you're getting yourself in to. It's all moving so fast – you've gone from zero to hero in less than a month. Ask yourself whether any of these people – Penny, Ross, Kris, whoever – whether any of them really understand, much less care about what you've been through? Or whether you can cope? And if they did, whether they would think it was a good idea to keep repeatedly exposing you to similar situations?'

'It's the job, Di. They don't even know. Can you imagine if I wept all over Penelope Rhodes and said, by the way, you should know that my dad was a journalist, he was killed covering a story. Oh, and my mum's been sectioned for her own protection after trying to do the same to herself. And get this: my brother hasn't spoken to me since—'

'That's exactly what I mean. I'm not saying they need to be taking an entire mental and physical history, but these people are supposed to be managers, and these are life-or-death decisions. Don't you find it alarming that you've travelled to both Kabul and Baghdad in the space of a month on the back of being able to speak a bit of Arabic without as much as a by your leave to anyone else?'

'You know it wasn't as simple as that.'

'These are the facts, Sami. People are being hung out to dry on this, and you can't or won't see it for what it is. Everyone's heard about what happened to Andie, and don't get me started on Kris. I can't be part of it, I'm sorry, but I just can't. I love you more than you'll ever know—'

'Di, don't—'

'Let me finish. We've never talked about this, and I never want to again, but if it will convince you to protect yourself then I'll do it.'

By then I was slumped on the heavy black cases at my feet – the only support I had left. It was as if she'd been holding her breath for years and finally decided to let it all out in one go.

'What do you think really got me to stop sticking my fingers down my throat? Do you think it was when Bunny found out? Or Matron? You were there for that too, remember? Or do you think it might have been when I realised there were other ways I could control how I was feeling? And who taught me that? We were both sent away to be raised by people who didn't love us, but you may as well have been sent to the moon. And yet you were the only person I remember whose family still loved them as much as you loved them, and when I worked out why—'

'We don't have to talk about this, Di...'

'You were the first role model I ever had, Sami. And you'll be the last, if you just take a step back and treat yourself with the love and care you deserve.'

I ran a finger over the tears glistening on the cases, face burning as it remembered Kris's fingers on mine.

'This is the only thing that makes me feel like I am,' I said shakily. 'And that's why—'

'Oh, God. God, Sami.'

'It's going to be different, this time, Di. Penny asked me to plan it myself, every last detail. We're going on our own, just me and Kris. We'll be making our own decisions in our own time. There's no one to trust but ourselves, and don't you trust me? We're not even going to the Middle East. There's practically no journalists where we're heading, even though, by rights, there should be hundreds.'

'You're about to get swallowed whole, Sami. The business is about to chew you up and spit you out, just like it did to your dad.'

'There is nothing that would make him prouder of me than

what we're about to do. And Penny, she's ... I hadn't realised. It's all she wants too, she wants to use the business how it should be used, and not just pander to the West's war the whole time. She wants to stand up and be counted with us. That's why she's doing it, that's why she's said—'

'What exactly has she said? You have a blank cheque to fly on a wing and a prayer round the world with?'

'She's calling them "The World's Untold Stories". I stood up, turning on the spot as I said it, eyes travelling the four blank-white walls of the flat no longer threatening to close in on me. 'She can't spare any correspondents to do them, that's why she's asked me. And she wants to find something for Kris that will keep him on the road—'

'Sami, Kris was shot in the fucking head!' I jumped as she swore, pulling the phone away from my ear. Di almost never did. 'The translator who was sitting next to him is still catatonic. And she wants to keep him on the road?'

'Kris isn't a manager,' I interrupted, the flicker of anger that had sparked when she brought up my father breaking into flame. 'He just wants to keep working, and why shouldn't he? He's earned that right after so long keeping on doing it. Half this country wouldn't have a clue what goes on beyond the North Sea if it wasn't for his rolls of tape.'

'That's it, isn't it?' Di suddenly sounded as far away as she really was. 'I can't believe I've been so stupid. That's what this is all about. It's all about Kris. It's about him just as much as the job...'

I pulled the phone away from my ear again. I knew if I said anything it would be unrecoverable. It took a couple of minutes for her to finally run out of road.

'Where is it that you're going?' she finally asked, sounding further away than ever. 'Pray tell me which untold story is going to find airtime on our network when you couldn't even get more than a headline for the girl who tried to burn herself away from the Taliban? Dammit, Sami, don't you see? This is madness. It's negligent at best, and at worst ... I don't even want to think about it. There is no worthy end to this, none at all—'

'Darfur,' I interrupted, eyes finally settling on the shape-shifting slice of winter sky just visible through my window above the balcony. 'We're going to Darfur. There's a genocide under way, Di, and we're damn well going to tell people about it.'

'The Sudan? Are you kidding me?'

'Darfur.' I drifted with the clouds as I said it again. 'It's the semi-autonomous region to the west. The Sudanese government is arming Arab militias to—'

'I know where it is, Sami, for goodness' sake, and I know full well what is alleged to be happening there. But no one else does, nor cares that they don't—'

'There's a genocide underway, Di. A genocide – and there's blood money behind it too. Where do you think the weapons are coming from? Not to mention the starvation, the disease. We're flying in with the World Food Programme. Perfect, Penny said, as we'll be under their security protection too.'

'This is a suicide mission, Sami. If it's a perfect anything, then it's that. I can't believe what I'm about to say to you. God, I don't even think I can.'

'Some stories are, Di.' I made it easy for her then. It felt like it was all I had left to give her. 'Some stories are worth dying for. But I'm not going to, I promise. And if we can just get enough eyes on what's really happening there, then we might be able to stop thousands of other people dying too.'

A bus squealed somewhere far below, just as I realised she had hung up.

Chapter 24
Wolf Moon Rising

In the end it was Rory who finally answered the call. Kris was somewhere else, huddled next to him, his body under a blanket, but his mind so far gone it may as well have been past Pluto. Uppers, downers, sidewinders – his medical miracle constitution usually made mincemeat out of serious benders but couldn't even produce a sausage out of this. Nothing was responding as it should, and he'd spent years practising. The year had even changed in the time he had spent digging around in his mind – faceless crowds everywhere, celebrating or commiserating? Who can ever tell on New Year's Eve?

Why had Lucia finally cracked? More to the point, why had her cracking made him do the same? There was no dust to blame as Lass licked the tears from his eyes. He had nowhere else to go but back out, and now he didn't even know if he could. Gonzo's own specialised brand of gonzo journalism was suddenly worth less than blank tape, and he could never have predicted why. Finally his eyes focused only to find a Wolf Moon, impossibly wide and high in the sky, howling silently at nothing as Rory held the phone up to his ear.

Sami didn't know where they were going yet, just that they were. There were probably a thousand other things she said in the moment, but that one was enough to propel him up and out of Rory's pit, across the few steps through the back office door and into the crew room.

And that's where Ross found him, sometime after the first sun of a new year.

Kris fused his eyes shut into the volley of swearing, but his eyeballs were rolling so hard behind his lids there was no fooling the guy.

'C'mon, Gonzo. I know you're in there. Just get the hell up, would you?'

Ross swore again as Kris coughed, eyes still closed.

'What are you, half human, half dog? Get up, Kris, now, come on.'

He coughed again, rolling onto his side.

'You want me to change the locks? Make it impossible to hide in here? I'll do it.'

Kris cracked an eye only for both to fly open. Ross was practically eyeball to eyeball with him, right down on the floor. No wonder he looked like he was going to throw up. Kris must have coughed right into his face.

'Get up, come on.'

Kris rolled himself to sitting, letting a box of cables take his weight as Ross backed away.

'You stink worse than a slag heap, you know that?'

'Can't say I'd noticed,' Kris croaked through a mouth drier than the Sahara.

'You want to talk about it?'

A thousand possible replies clattered through his head as a cage door clanged open on the opposite wall. Did Ross think it was in any way ironic that the network's photographers were literally kept in cages? Even if these were man-sized cubicles of chicken wire only made so equipment could be neatly stored and separated. What did he think about his own life's work? How did he feel about being paid to record other people's suffering, only for the paymasters to look away when they brought home the evidence? How about all the pontificating they did to themselves and each other – how it was all in the name of accountability? And how about that cliché to end all clichés – the one about making a difference?

But he said none of this. Instead he said: 'Do you have any soap?'

'Soap?'

'Yes. Soap. Lather. You know the stuff. Imperial Leather, that's what I fancy. Goes up like shaving foam.'

He stood up then, stretched as far as the cages opposite would let him.

'I could use a couple of rounds of toast too, buttered to the corners, mind.'

'Kris, come on—'

'You've never gone to work a day in your life on an empty stomach, DeVito.'

'Who said anything about work?'

'Why else would I be in here? You think I don't have better places to spend the night than with the carpet?'

Ross stared him down then, to his credit. He wasn't going to make Kris say any of it.

'Don't you even think about moving till I get back,' Ross finally growled. 'Breakfast, shower, a change of fucking underwear. I'll even throw in a fresh T-shirt. But then – then we talk.'

He didn't need to wait for the nod. Ross had been somewhere close enough to where Kris was to know he'd won that round at least.

'You'll get Rory a round too while you're at it?' Kris called after him, flexing his fingers against the bars of the cage. He didn't need to ask, but wasn't going to let Ross know that.

~ ~ ~

'So what'd she tell you?' Ross mumbled at him through a mouth-ful of toast.

'Who?' Kris unwrapped a new T-shirt – black, standard, may as well have been uniform. They were still alone in the crew room.

'Penny – who else?'

'Did I speak to her?'

'She said...' Ross's brow furrowed as he looked up from his steaming paper bag. 'Never mind. We can talk about all that upstairs. She'll be in soon enough.'

Kris pulled the shirt over his head. It was still creased and scratchy, but like everything else, he could barely feel it.

'I talked to Sami. At least I think I did. Not Penny.'

He turned away as he said it, reaching for and downing the coffee Ross had brought him in one fluid movement. It was still boiling but down it went, one gulp, bang.

'And how do you feel about it?'

'What?' Kris swallowed again, even though it was all gone.

'The project, Gonzo, come on. I buttered the toast myself, corners and all.'

'OK, OK, OK.'

Ross balled his paper bag into his fist as he swallowed. Kris fiddled with his dirty T-shirt, winding it around a wrist, pulling as tight as it would go. In the moment or so of silence that passed, his hand turned from brown to white and then to a weird shade of blue. He finally let the T-shirt go loose when Ross started up again.

'So you spoke to Sami?'

'Yeah.' Kris jumped in spite of himself as he turned to find Ross perched on the case cross-legged and wide-eyed. 'Jesus, DeVito. Who are you trying to be now? The Buddha himself?'

Ross scowled as he swung his legs off the case onto the floor.

'Sorry.' Kris pulled the towel tight again. 'I don't remember what Sami said, though. I just know it was enough to get me in here.'

'Right,' Ross replied as Kris slumped back down against another case. 'So do you want me to tell you about it?'

'Hit me with it, go on.' Kris lolled his head back and forth against the chicken wire until he finally focused. Ross had the tiniest of eyes but they saw everything.

'Honestly, Kris.' Ross practically deflated as he sighed. 'If it was any other story, I would have quit over it. I feel that strongly about you staying out of warzones for a while. But Penny is on to something, for sure. And she, for all her faults, is the one person who can make the rest of this company listen to her when it counts.'

'You really think that? About Penelope Rhodes?'

Kris forced himself to hold Ross's gaze. Even the older man didn't need to look away, and he'd had to learn how to walk again because of her.

'I do,' Ross replied softly, those tiny eyes firing like darts. 'You learn from your mistakes, Kris. That's why I trust her. I did then, and I still do. Of course I wish things had turned out differently, but only an idiot would blame her for that. She made the best decision she could with the information she had at the time. Should she have had to make a decision like that? I have been over that more times than I've taken breath, and it didn't get me out of the wheelchair any faster. Sometimes you just have to let stuff go, else it will always hold you down.'

Little pricks broke out on the back of Kris's neck as the darts got to him.

'But this is about you, Kris. It's not about me. You're one of the most talented – no, *the* most talented photographer of your generation. I'd put my neck out and say that to anyone who asks. They'll be able to fake photographs soon enough. I'll say even then they won't be able to fake shots like yours. And this is the generation that counts, where video has really come into its own. It won't always be this way – they'll invent something else. But for now, it doesn't matter if it's Tiananmen Square or Live Aid, it's the pictures that always do it. And so many of them are yours.'

Kris knew Ross was still talking, but all he could see were the pictures he'd taken. How many kids had there been? Starving, dying, no legs, no arms – they all became the one infant in his head, and if he stopped blinking for more than a second, it had either Tommy or Nico's face on it. The women, there had been

just as many – raped, enslaved, tortured, some of them, and wait
– there she is, terror all over her face, iron-red hair in his filthy fist:
Should I shoot her, boy, what d'ya reckon? And that was the only
man he could see, the man he had done everything to never remember, only to end up becoming in so many ways—

'You've hardly been home, though, Kris. It may be the most
worthy story to come your way for months, but most of those
months have been somewhere else. How do you feel about Lucia
and the boys? Especially after missing Christmas?'

'How do I feel about them?' Kris asked himself, like a robot.
'How do I feel?'

'How do you feel about going back out again so soon?' Lord
Buddha prompted, from high on his cable perch.

For all Ross's hundreds of meaningful examples of this outsized
talent Kris apparently had, Kris could have thrown him back thousands. In that moment he could not think of a single picture of
someone dying that had meant others didn't. What about the ones
where someone had died in the process? No one ever seemed to
talk about the translator who had gone too, or the other lackeys
that got caught when they weren't even meant to be part of it.
He'd met plenty of them too, and never forgotten a single one.
Off came a shred of skin from around his fingernail as he watched
Mohammed's blood pinprick out, onto his thumb. And as he
blinked again, there was Ali, a corpse on a stretcher save for the
beeping machines keeping him alive.

'Kris? If you can't tell me yourself then—'

'Me? Oh, I'll be right,' he interrupted, wiping a bleeding finger on
his wet hair. 'Never better, honestly, skip. You know me. What else
would I do? And where are we going, anyway? Now you mention it,
the one thing I do remember telling her was no more sandpit.'

Finally Ross laughed, belly quivering as he uncrossed his legs.

'It's a sandpit, for sure, but it's not one you've played in before.'

'Huh?' Kris flinched as the hand raking through his hair hit the
scar somewhere underneath.

'We're finally going to do it,' Ross said, smile lighting up the whole of his face. '*You're* finally going to do it, I mean. You're going to get to do the job we all want to be doing.'

'Enough of your poetry, DeVito. What's she come up with this time?'

'Africa, Kris. Darfur, to be precise. Sudan's dirty, filthy little secret. If you come back with the right shots, it will be...'

Ross faded again as Mohammed's blood took over, firing around his body like it was suddenly overjoyed to be there.

And if it wasn't for the tiniest seed of guilt needling like the prick in his finger every time he thought about Sami, Kris might have said it was too.

Chapter 25
Black Dogs and Slaves

The baby had a tummy bigger than its head, so swollen it seemed absurd that we should still be able to see its ribs, except there they were, harp-string sharp against the skin. It seemed equally absurd that the rest of its body would resemble nothing other than a bundle of sticks awkwardly caught together in a torn muslin knotted between its legs. There was an adult hand wrapped around its miniature fingers – so wizened I had to look again: surely it wasn't wearing a leather glove? Through the tent flap, a line of hessian huts shimmered so bright in the Saharan sun as they streamed away into the distance that, just for a moment, I wondered if they'd been cast in gold. But this was Darfur, a land invisible to all but its government, bent on ridding its sands of anything other than the purest grains. The only common language was absurdity. There was nothing taking place in those tortured desert dunes that was anything less.

'Come check this,' Kris muttered to me as he fiddled with his camera. 'The light's not perfect, but I think I can get away with it.'

Sour deodorant stung my nose as I leant into the viewfinder. Lynx Sahara. He will have worn it just for that. I was fast becoming fluent in our other common language: gallows humour.

'You're all good,' I murmured with the lightest brush to his arm. Another absurd word to use under the circumstances. But we had our instructions: we were to bring back untold stories. These were tales that no one had been able to listen to before.

'Tap me when you're done,' he mumbled, giving a thumbs-up

to the only other man crowded into the squalid tent. Damon, our UNHCR escort, gave me the last nod I needed with his bright-blue head. By then it just seemed appropriate rather than absurd that he was wearing a box-fresh blue cap.

I summoned up some Arabic with a gulp of air so thick it felt like water in my lungs.

'Yousra,' I murmured, reaching out to brush the scars of the arm wrapped around the baby. 'We're ready to start now, if you are?'

Her headscarf fluttered a yes.

'Ahmed, your son – he's nearly two now, is that right?' Another flutter. 'How long has it been since he had something to eat?'

She replied with the tiniest inclination of her head. 'Some supplies came in last week, but it was just powdered milk, peanuts. Nothing more. They say there was another truck, but it never came. We are still waiting.'

Ahmed stirred like a moth in her arms as she sighed. *Hush, little man*, I wanted to whisper. *Don't wake up.*

'Who would do that? Who would stop food trucks from coming into these camps?'

'Janjaweed. They kill the drivers, then they take the trucks.'

I brushed the scars on her arm again, I couldn't help it. The hairs on my own arms reached out to Kris next to me.

'Could you tell me what happened the last time the Janjaweed came into this camp?'

'They come on their horses,' she said, words floating with the dust on the air. 'During the day, they bring food, sometimes clothes. They ride around, they laugh, they try and joke with us – we are refugees, we should be pleased to see them. But there is no one who laughs back. We are not refugees. We have been driven from our homes, homes that are not far from here at all. But we cannot go back. They will never let us go back. Then at night, they return. They come for the girls. Sometimes they burn down the tents, they don't care if we are still inside. They shout Sudan is for Arabs, not black dogs and slaves. Only then do they go. When they are finished.'

'Do you think…?' I had to pause, swallowing the heartbeat accelerating up my throat like vomit. 'Do you think you could tell me what happened to your daughter?'

'We tried to hide under the blankets,' Yousra whispered, more fragments on the air. 'But there was nothing they couldn't see. I begged them to take me instead, but they beat me until I dropped her. When I woke up, she was gone, the tent was burning, Ahmed was still under the blankets. We had to run. And now he will die soon too.'

She stroked the arc of his swollen belly as gently as breath.

'Now, I wish only for death. Nothing can bring peace here, except death. This is all that we pray for. We pray for death.'

There were no words left, not even fragments, as we packed up and edged out of the tent. The sand felt like lead in my boots, even though I knew we'd nailed it.

Kris mumbled as we trudged away, sand and grit in his voice too. 'That better have been good enough. I may as well have been focusing on their last breaths. That baby, his little chest – every time I zoomed in I thought it might stop puffing and we'd just be standing there watching—'

'You did great.' I cut him off with a damp bottle of Fanta from my bag. 'And Yousra did even better. While I was too busy choking on my questions.' I traced out the top of my bottle with a fingertip, rubbing sand and sugar together. 'At least we've put a face on these attacks. Even better, a mother and her baby. This is why we came, it's exactly what we need. Soon enough, no one will be able to call it anything other than ethnic cleansing.'

I flicked orange scum on to the ground just as Damon caught up with us, panting.

'We need to hustle, guys – come on. There's a couple of horsemen coming over the horizon. There's no way we can let them see the camera.'

'Wow – how do you know?' I turned on the spot, playing for time. The blue hats of the UN gaggle teemed like butterflies.

'There.' Damon pointed into the distance at a cloud of sand, only distinguishable from the rest of the desert glare because it was most definitely moving. 'Come on, guys, seriously. The van's pulling round now.'

'What am I looking at?' I stood perfectly still while he hurried away, shading my eyes as I peered at the horizon. 'How can you be sure that's the Janjaweed?'

Kris grabbed roughly at my arm. 'You heard the man. We need to move, and pronto.'

I shook him off as I planted my feet.

'We need to put a face on them just as much as on her,' I whispered urgently. 'A victim like Yousra, like Ahmed, in the context of an aggressor like that? The Janjaweed are stuff of legend.'

Damon was shouting now, almost at the main gate a few yards ahead. The thunder of hooves coming closer was unmistakable, as were the brown legs galloping and moving the cloud of sand inexorably forward.

'We just need one shot. It will be worth all the gold in Darfur. One clean shot of the horsemen will make our story a thousand times more impactful and you know it.'

'Get in the van,' he hissed, shouldering his camera. 'And then I'll do it. But only when you're inside the van.'

'Sami!' Damon screamed from the open back doors of the white UN van careening as it reversed towards us.

'But Kris—'

'If you want any of this on tape, Sami, then you'll get into the fucking van.'

And then they were upon us, all at once, the horses shuddering to a halt just feet away inside the main camp gate. Flowing white robes billowed with the clouds of dust settling round the horses – huge, oiled-brown stallions, as impassive in standing as they were electric in charging. I dared not even blink as the riders came into full view, pristine white robes only marked by the sleek, polished rifles slung round their backs. Were they an extension of the horses themselves? One man was wearing gold aviator sun-glasses, flashing teeth the clean white of new piano keys as he leered down at me. Finally I was able to blink, as there I was, looking back at myself from the mirror of his glasses. And there too was Kris, camera pointed at them like a weapon.

'*Salaam aleikum.*' I stared at myself as I said it. 'My name is Samira. We are here with the UNHCR.'

My face split in half as the man cocked his head, looking inside the van.

'So where is your badge?'

I jumped as my reflection came back into view. The man was speaking in perfect, practically accent-less English.

'*Salaam aleikum,*' another voice said: Damon, crouching inside the back of the van with a fistful of notes. 'They are with us, please, have a look at this paperwork. We are preparing a video of our work in the camp for our headquarters in Geneva.'

My reflection disappeared along with the piano keys as the man turned to Kris, still stock-still and filming beside me, camera humming with the nerves in the air.

'Turn that off,' the man said, aviators glinting for good measure as he tapped the lens with the tip of a long, brown finger. 'Turn that off right now.'

For a moment, we were all statues, frozen in a cartoon strip. Then I don't know which came first: Damon's cry, the backfire of the engine, a whinny like a high-pitched scream. We bounded into the back of the van just as a rifle butt smashed into the windows, shards of glass twinkling around our feet as we accelerated away.

'I'm sorry, Damo,' I gabbled as the van bumped over the sand, willing Kris to stay quiet. 'I know we pushed it, but Yousra's story is worth so, so much more set against pictures like that. No one has been able to see the villain of the piece before, and the Janja-weed ... the Janjaweed are stuff of fable.'

'The villain of the piece?' I flinched as Damon exclaimed, crunching an empty plastic bottle into his fist. 'Jesus, Sami, you've either not been hearing me, or you've not been listening. These aren't actors we're dealing with. It's not some slapstick black comedy. Imagine something so depraved it tortures you to the bone. Then imagine how these fabled warriors are licensed to do it by their very own government. You do not play chicken with people like that. We've made them angry, and they were jacked up enough to start with.'

The bottle suddenly snapped, broken pieces of plastic joining the glass quivering on the floor. I turned to Kris, only to find him slumped and staring against the other side of the car. Silence hung in the putrid air as the van sped up, desert tracks finally joining the only road back into town.

~~~

'You did well to speak English,' Kris finally grunted, glass crunching underfoot as we climbed out of the van back at the UNHCR compound. 'As soon as I heard the guy speak I knew we were in the clear. Those guys are pros. Whacking a bunch of aid workers isn't their game. How else would they get their kicks if the doctors didn't show up around here with their bags of tricks from time to time?'

Kris frowned in the direction of the blue hat disappearing into the compound. Damon hadn't been able to say anything else, much less look at us since we'd made it to the road.

'I didn't deliberately set out to defy him,' I sighed as the gates clanged shut behind him. 'There was just ... oh, I don't know. We had one shot and were we honestly not going to try and take it? I wish it had happened differently, but...'

'So do I.' Kris winced as he heaved his tripod onto his shoulder. 'You can make it up to me with another Fanta, mind. Cold...'

'What?' I hurried to keep up, reaching out to stop the entrance door bashing my face as Kris bowled through it.

'Next time I tell you to get in the van, you get, do you hear?'

'I don't, actually. How would you have kept filming if anything kicked off and I wasn't at your back?'

'That's my problem, not yours. I wasn't planning to take that picture with you on my elbow.'

'Why not?'

He swore as we stopped outside the door to his room.

'Kris…' I persisted. 'Those shots are going to be massive, better than anything we've got here so far. The Janjaweed … even the name fits. You couldn't even draw a more perfect cartoon villain and now—'

'Spare me, would you?' I followed him into his room even as he kicked the door closed towards me.

'I don't understand—'

'Of course you don't fucking understand.' He kicked the small fridge in the corner, finding it empty. 'You think it's as simple as printing a magazine cover and then, bam, in rolls the cavalry.'

'Isn't it sometimes?' I reached for the camera he'd thrown onto the desk, a plastic trestle table opposite the only power point in the room, practically sparking it was so overloaded with extension cables. 'Let's have a look, shall we? No one has been able to put a name to a face on this story and now—'

'Knock yourself out,' he sighed. 'But give us your key first, would you?'

I threw it at him as I flipped open his laptop, connecting up the camera. He had far more need for the Fanta in my fridge than I did.

Close up, the menace of the Janjaweed leapt off the screen. The man in aviators looked almost handsome, gold frames glinting atop a sculpted profile, neon-white robes setting off his smile. I jumped as Kris snorted from behind me, door banging as he came back in with a lurid-orange bottle in his hand.

'See?'

'Whatever you reckon,' he said with a slurp. 'Could be the start of a bad Western, if that's the look you were after.'

'Wait till Penny sees it,' I said furiously, hands flashing across the keyboard as I clipped up a still and emailed it to her before he could stop me. 'You just wait until she sees—'

The door banged again as he disappeared into the shower.

Chapter 26
Outriders

Sami was dead right about that, even if she had the rest of it six ways to sundown. The Janjaweed were like no other villain Kris had ever seen. Thoroughbred horses, glossy enough to race at a derby, better-than-American teeth and sunglasses to match. Yep, Sami had known full well something was going to change the game on Darfur. She was just wrong about what.

Kris squeaked the washroom tap shut just as Damon tapped on their door. He'd come to apologise. He knew they were only doing their jobs, he just didn't think they understood how much danger they'd put themselves in. Come join us on the roof, have a few laughs, there's plenty of moonshine to go around. It didn't take much for Kris to grip and grin. The blue hats were actually putting in the yards on the ground far more than the likes of journalists, no matter what any of them told themselves. Had Sami flown in with food, medicine or portable shelters? Had Kris brought along anything of practical use other than a camera or microphone? No, they had not. Worse, all she planned to do was tell everyone about it, then walk away.

But not him. Not this time. Not ever again.

So up they shuffled, onto the compound roof and out into the velvet dark, black enough to blot out everything, even though the florid horror of the camp sat barely a mile out. Out came the moonshine and rancid tobacco, along came the same old jokes – here they go again about the cook roasting a chicken only to find an egg still inside. Haha, yeah, hilarious, like they'd all forgotten where eggs really came from.

And then, there it was. The only thing able to light up a dark as intense as that.

Fire.

This one came with the crack of gunshots, the squeal of horses, the distant soundtrack of agony. A huge blaze, bursting luminous orange through the dark, with the crackle and hiss of bonfire. No air to gasp, only smoke, rolling thick and invisible through the black sky. This one came so soon that the camp dust still clung to his boots, coated his throat, gritted up his eyes, even though all there was for him to focus on were flames, sprouting faster than he could blink.

And this one came with a firetail like none other. They all knew what was burning. They could all smell barbecue, they could all taste blood. This was as close to the fires of hell on earth that any living being could ever get to.

But none of it was a surprise to Kris. None of it. Because what he'd known, from the moment he laid eyes on them, was that those horsemen were outriders for the apocalypse, not the cavalry.

'You're looking at the camp we visited earlier,' Sami choked out as he reached for his camera and focused behind the viewfinder in one fluid movement. They were spread as flat as possible on the roof to avoid the worst of the smoke.

'We're barely a mile away at the UNHCR compound in El-Geneina, the regional capital of Western Darfur. We know it's the camp that's on fire, because there is nothing else but sand for hundreds of miles around. What we can't tell you for sure is how it started, but we've heard from multiple eyewitnesses about similar attacks all over this land at the hands of the Janjaweed militia. What we also can't tell you for sure is what's gone up in flames. But all that's inside the camp are rows and rows of hessian tents and straw-woven huts, all full to bursting with displaced women and children. It's hard to imagine what could be burning other than those dwellings, if you can even call them that.'

There came the tremble in her voice just as he clicked the

camera off. The air was still crackling as they hauled themselves
backward down the roof shaft. Kris had seen enough long before
the attack started. But it turned out Sami still hadn't, not even
close.

'We need to call Penny,' she gabbled, trying and failing to grab
the camera from him as he barged them into their room. 'It's news,
we can prove it – we visited that camp earlier, we saw Janjaweed
casing the place, we can—'

'So?' He hawked up a glob of tar. 'What do you think she's
going to do – dial 999? We can't prove a fucking thing – not until
we go back.'

'It's news, Kris. It's news! No one has been able to prove these
raids are happening the way the victims say they are.'

'And suddenly we can? Because we watched a bonfire in the
dark in the direction of a camp we visited today? Where we got a
couple of cowboys to laugh in our faces?'

'We go back in tomorrow.' Sami practically spat then, black
streaked all over her face as she wiped sweat into soot. 'We search
every tent till we find Yousra, if she's still alive. We film what they
did, every last bit. We take her testimony, along with anyone else's
we can find. And then we take it back to Khartoum. We show
those clowns the evidence. I bet you all the money in the world
we get them to say, on camera, how it's just some dirty black Africans. How Sudan is meant for the Arabs. How the Janjaweed are
just doing their job. Then I promise you, when that goes public,
you'll get to watch the cavalry arrive instead.'

'You can hear yourself, right?' Kris opened the window even
though bonfire was still stalking them. 'We're part of this. You
think they picked that camp at random? There's every chance they
decided to hit the place because we waved a camera at it.'

'No!' She shouted then, as much to herself as at him. 'No. Kris,
how could you—'

'And you're the one who thinks what we're doing is actually
going to change one single rancid thing about it all.'

'I won't stop until it does. I can't. How can you?'

'You're not hearing me, Sami. I'm not the one stopping. I'm just done watching, recording, signing on to be the witness that's never allowed to speak. We just watched humanity burn to its end out there. There's nothing left but dust, and all you want to do is tell everyone about it? You think that's going to do the trick? The clouds will clear, it will all just melt away? Let me promise *you* something, for once. If she's made it, then I'm getting her out of there.'

And just like that, it was out. As careless as she was clueless. What the hell had he done, forgotten this was the only formula he had left? How would it ever make sense to anyone other than him? He'd lost Lucia, he'd lost the boys, he'd basically burned his own house, his unconditionally loving unit, down to the ground too and now ... Kris gulped and gulped, only to find bonfire. If there was ever a moment, if there was ever a chance, that someone would see his side of it all, then surely this was it? Smoke writhed between them from the open window, the quietest assassin of all.

'She? Do you mean Yousra? Are you out of your mind? You think you're Moses, sent to bear her aloft above seething hordes? You want to start a stampede? Get all press banned indefinitely?'

'Do you think anyone would ever know that it was us? And don't you think it's worth it, even if they did? Just to get one person the peace they deserve after all this? It'd be one and a half, if you count Ahmed. Plenty of room in the back of those massive medical trucks. Nice and dark. We could sneak them inside. It would be so easy – wrap her in a sack, light as a feather, into the back, bam. They've even got fridges inside, for fuck's sake, food, water, the works.'

'She won't stand a chance, Kris. She'd be dead on arrival in Khartoum, or wherever the truck made it before it was carjacked and they killed her anyway. This is nuts. I can't even believe we're having this conversation.'

'Neither can I. You know they made her watch as they raped

her daughter, right? They had a go at her first, and then they made her watch, held her eyes open, made her suffer a thousand times more pain than if they'd done it to her again themselves. And then they torched her tent with that baby inside. When they had the misfortune to survive they left them all to starve. And you just watched whatever's left burn to the fucking ground.'

'I know it hurts, Kris. I know it's worse than anything we could ever imagine...'

'Then tell me why I shouldn't just jack up her morphine drip? If she's had the misfortune to make it, yet again? Why the hell shouldn't I just end it, for once? If Ahmed hasn't croaked already, they'll stick her as soon as he does. And then why shouldn't she go too? Why shouldn't she be given the dignity of a painless, peaceful end? After all that? You give me one reason why I'm not the one making sense of all this dust out here.'

Sami recoiled like he'd hit her, upending the flimsy cot behind her.

'Because it's murder, Kris! You think knowing you're a killer will feel any better than this? That suddenly you'll become the Archangel Gabriel? You couldn't do it even if you wanted to—'

'What, you think I don't already have a stash? How much horror do you think I can take?'

He brandished the bulging black case he never went anywhere without, stuffed full of every medication that could ever be needed, anywhere.

'Whatever works, right? How else do you think I could keep doing it, again and again? Don't pretend your little blind eyes see through it. Everyone watching, they think it's just another Ahmed, but let me tell you, I remember every single one. Every single fucking one.'

He reached for her as she stumbled. Had he actually hit her?

'You just can't, Kris. You can't. We can't...'

He held on to her fists as she clubbed at him like a baby. His own personal chemistry set, he'd finally shared it, and for what?

Here he was yet again, parked in the moment before it could all blow up in his face, except this time there was no gunfire to run from, no bomb about to go off, no hostile takeover waiting just outside the door. It was just him and his conscience, suddenly desperate not to be alone in the fight.

So he did the only thing left he could possibly have done next.

He kissed her.

Chapter 27
Don't Wake Up

Every single caress felt like a betrayal. My mind raged every time my body responded to his touch – idiotic, brainless nerve endings, how could I be losing myself when everything around me demanded so frantically that I hold it together? He pulled me to him as I pushed him away, until I found myself pressed up against him so hard I might as well have been trying to climb inside. There was so much left to say, but every kiss made the words evaporate, and they felt so poisonous in my mouth that all I could feel was relief they'd never come out, that they'd just hovered at the edge of my tongue – all the things we both knew but never said, and wouldn't have to confront if we just kept kissing, kept letting the physical sensations rinse the mental ones inside out, back to front and upside down. His hands, they marauded everywhere, uncoiling my body every time I tried to wind it tighter, the silken breeze from the ceiling fan clicking randomly into gear just in time to chase away the guilt, ever-present at the edges. We tumbled together in a pile of clothes until it was over, fan clicking off right as the tell-tale wetness pooled between our legs, so we could both write it off as sweat if we wanted to.

Since it certainly wasn't sex. I finally understood that part, at least. All we'd done was communicate in the only way we had left.

Eyes still closed, the memories cascaded: the muffled crying as my mother discovered yet another indiscretion, the final, tight hug-and-kiss from my father before he left us for another story, only to never come back. Then came the blood pooling under the bathroom door when we realised Mum had gone inside with the express intention of never coming back either. After that, there was nothing left but fevered dreams about what might come next.

I woke first, dawn blazing in the sky like the fire was still raging. Kris lay next to me as he'd fallen, arms still tight around my chest, breath hot in my ear. I'd never lain naked for so long with a man before, much less a man whose thin band of gold on his wedding finger weighed heavy on my stomach with every breath. If it wasn't for the smell of bonfire, still acrid on the air, I could have told myself that all the rest of it had just been a nightmare. Except there was Kris, still solid, warm and alive, a protective shell curled round my back. I wanted the moment to mean something else so badly I felt faint. And I was still lying down.

I rolled myself out from his arms to the floor, where I found most of my clothes, dressing as I crouched. It couldn't have been more than 5:00am, I guessed, but I knew I'd find Damon and the others up. There could be no hiding from what had happened. We had to make sure we went with them when they went back into the camp. We had to finish what we'd started.

Kris stirred as I cracked open the door, a shaft of light falling across his face so he couldn't help but open his eyes.

'Mine's a Fanta, if you're going,' he grunted, pushing himself up onto his arms to blink. I shook my head at him. Everything I'd had to say a few hours earlier came clattering back into my head, but my body was still warm from his. I couldn't get those particular words out even if I tried.

'We'll be leaving as soon as they do, OK?' I coughed as I said it, guilt so sour in my mouth I could have thrown it up. 'So look lively, will you?'

I turned away before he could say anything else, closing the door to find Damon lolling outside in the fetid corridor.

'Hey.' I brushed down my shirt self-consciously. 'I was just about to come find you.'

'Great minds.' He slurred as he replied, eyes and head rolling on his neck under a clean blue hat. 'I thought you jokers might be spoiling to see your fable come to life.'

'I'm so sorry, Damo,' I found myself whispering. 'I know this is harder for you than we'll ever understand.'

'You got that part right, if nothing else.' I flinched as he banged the wall behind him. 'By rights, we shouldn't take you anywhere except the fucking airstrip. How am I supposed to trust that you won't go where you're not wanted?'

'Damo—' I reached out to him as he stumbled. Alcohol steamed off his shirt, still streaked with soot and ash.

'I just want you to know...' he mumbled as he steadied himself against the wall. 'I just want you to know that I'm only taking you back in there because there is an outside chance you might be able to change the record back home.'

'There's more than just an outside chance, there's—'

'And that's the only reason why you're getting anywhere near a UNHCR van. 'If you so much as cough while we're in there without asking me first then—'

Damon's jaw dropped as the door flew open behind me.

'You make the rules, boss. We'll do whatever you say, I can promise you that. Show us what you can, and we'll do the rest.'

My skin prickled as Kris boomed behind me. He smelled so ostentatiously of mint I instantly felt like I couldn't possibly open my mouth again.

'You point, and I'll shoot. OK, my man? We'll be out front in ten minutes?'

'Just...' Damon kicked the wall with a heel as he trailed off, looking between us for a moment. Under his new-day-blue cap, his face looked nothing but grey. 'Just get us noticed, OK? Instead of yourselves.'

I nodded vigorously as he wobbled off.

'Poor bastard.' Kris sighed. 'Still thinks he'll find the answers in a bottle of moonshine.'

I flinched as he laid a hand on my shoulder.

'See you out front, then,' he said lightly.

I couldn't even murmur back, hating myself all over again as I pushed open my own door. As if clean clothes and a toothbrush could possibly sanitise anything that we were about to see.

~~~

Time took on a visceral quality as the van bumped along the road to the camp. Every jerk over a pothole made the journey feel familiar, as if we knew where we were going, knew what to expect at the other end. The dawn's fire had already burned out to desert glare – another cheat, another joke at our expense – the sun rolling her ever-present eye at the idea we might be able to shift the sands below. There came the clump of Sudanese desert flowers, beguiling in their incongruous beauty – how could such blossom keep root in sands like these? But as we rounded the corner to the main camp gate, the absence of bustle hung in the air like a threat. Kris looked into his camera from the moment we climbed out of the van rather than look directly at anything else.

The mouth to the camp yawned open into a blackened crater where row upon row of tents had been. Ridges of scorched sand fringed the edges like the muffled cries lapping at the edges of my consciousness – surely this was the work of a meteor, a random piece of space junk. The sudden slap of rough desert wind whipped torched fragments of still-bright cloth into a dance in the shelter of the furrows on the ground – yet another joke, the breeze laughing along with the sun, for we were to find no hope here.

I stood in motionless silence, even as the sand flew into my eyes, because just to blink would be to acknowledge what had happened. Not so for Kris, flitting with the wind as his camera clicked and whirred. Nor for Damon, murmuring and plucking at my arm like a terrified child.

'Yousra made it,' he whispered, hat blurring to a blue smudge as my eyes gave up their fighting. 'But we don't have much time. She's with Ahmed in the medical tent. His organs are failing. The MSF doctors just arrived.' He waved a hand at the black hulk of a truck reversing through the gate.

'Say what?' Kris still had the camera to one eye. 'Who's that?'

'MSF. Doctors.' Damon beckoned us away from the crater into what was left of the camp. 'They'll talk to you for sure once they've done what they can, but...'

What they can? The question stuck in my throat, so parched I could barely open my mouth.

'This way, come on.'

I jumped as the camera banged into my leg, Kris finally looping it around his shoulder rather than staring into it. We hurried behind Damon as he disappeared down a row of tents.

'MSF,' Kris muttered, camera ricocheting between our legs. 'M ... S ... F.'

'Don't go there,' I hissed at him, every bash from the camera an echo of the night before, poisonous words about to find oxygen again. 'I know what you are thinking. Stop it, and stop it right now.'

'You do?' His maniacal laugh rattled in my ears. 'Everyone thinks they know what I'm thinking – you, Ross, Andie, the dog probably does too. But you know what? You don't know jack.'

'Stop it, Kris. Stop.' My words stumbled with my feet. 'It won't help anyone. It's a fool's errand – what do you think will come of her when she's found at the other end? If she's even still alive by then?'

Another mad laugh, another corner, Damon's blue hat popping like torchlight ahead.

'Please, Kris—'

He suddenly howled into the wind, sand whipping around us as we began to jog. Who was trying to keep up with whom? I still don't know.

'I film as people burn to death, Sami. People watch it happen because of me. Then they turn it off, eat their dinner, sleep the dreamless sleep of the dead. But I can't turn it off. I can never fucking turn it off ... I can't even turn it down. You think I don't deserve some peace? You think Yousra doesn't deserve peace once Ahmed's gone? You'd rather leave her to burn alive in the next raid than give her the end she's begging for? That's your real, journalistic objectivity?'

I couldn't answer him for panting, as by then we were running, borne forward by the beginnings of a haboob, as if the desert could sense the sandstorm my mind had turned into, as we wandered as far away from the reasons we'd been sent here as the breadth of the Sahara itself. The wind slapped me round the face, again and again and again. For this was the only reason Kris had left.

'This time, it's about both of us,' he shouted into the howling dust, sky darkening in reply. 'This time, I'm taking a double hit. You, and me. We're actually going to save someone, instead of mincing around and watching.'

We hurtled around the final corner into the shadow of an open MSF truck, its cavernous insides as inviting as the cool hulk of its shade.

'When we're done interviewing Yousra, you take the doctors away. Talk to them on background, away from the camera – that's all they'll do for us, anyway. Just make sure to leave me alone. Leave me the fuck alone.'

'Kris ... Kris, please – you can't save yourself by saving them.'

I croaked helplessly as the haboob raged, the only thing that I thought could stalk these desert plains with the same blind ferocity as the Janjaweed. Except here was Kris, blinder even than that, licking dust from his lips as he shouldered his camera, a desert dog on the hunt. From then on, I felt like a phantom, one that only he could really see.

It's true that I was inside the medical tent, the scene of the crime, even though I can't remember how I got in there. It's true that everywhere we looked were either cots lumpen with corpses, or bloodied young girls with bandages leaking between their legs. It's true that I deliberately summoned the doctors, that I got everyone else away from the camera while Kris took our final shots. All I remember seeing of him was a posture of infinite tenderness, one that knows the love of a mother with nothing left to protect her son. And it's true that even in a crucible of a war so helpless, I still saw purpose in bringing this unspeakable horror show home.

Until I saw her.

Afterwards.

How in death, all her body radiated was soul.

The only real truth I witnessed in that tent was Yousra, finally at peace.

Because he killed her.

Chapter 28
Just Another Ahmed

It turns out you never know what you're going to feel until you've felt it. Kris had no doubts, not even a whisper, until afterwards. The needle slid in, so fine and sharp it could have been invisible, yet so overloaded with morphine it could have taken out half the tent, and the thinnest of dividing lines snapped, just like that. He watched as the light returned to Yousra's eyes, willing that some might flicker in his own, but not so much as a glimmer came. Her suffering just melted away, but his? Kris was suddenly throbbing with it, from the centre of his knackered soul to the ends of his shot-off hair. He stared at her still and peaceful expression – that complete absence of pain, a total blank – and felt his own distilling into an equally inescapable sensation.

Envy.

Because, as it turns out, all he actually wanted in that moment was for someone else to understand too. Kris had wanted Sami to understand so badly that all there was left to feel afterwards was despair. There lay Yousra, a victim of so much, finally at peace in the most rancid place on earth. Surely this was as close to mercy as anything could ever be? If there was a definition in a textbook, wouldn't this be it?

But it also turns out that they don't write textbooks about humanity. Only about the rules of engagement.

And Sami didn't understand, not one single bit. Instead she fought him like a wild animal.

The blue hats were horrified – who was this madwoman making a scene? Discovering another corpse in that tent was no surprise to anyone, but some obscene meltdown from the allegedly objective observers? The doctors were not there to take care of overfed Westerners daring to lose their composure when all around them were shadows of people who had lost everything in circumstances beyond even imagination. Surely they could see this was more than just a distraction – that it was delinquent behaviour, it was a crime? Only when one of them made to give her a tranquiliser did Sami finally calm down. By then there was nothing else left to do but leave.

But there was no walking away with a clear conscience for Kris. Not this time. There was way too much sand in the air for that.

None of the blue hats rode with them back to the compound, not a one. Damon closed the back doors of the van like they were animals he'd caught at last, rats in a trap. Finally Kris was able to clear some of the dust from his throat.

'It was painless, Sami. It was all she wanted. Don't you see? All she wanted was to make the pain go away.'

She laughed then, high and mad, like he had been joking. Some feeling came back, but only anger. He was so disappointed it flamed into rage. Practically every shot he'd ever taken suddenly hit him between the eyes – flash frames like strobe lights, bam, bam, bam.

'Let me tell you something, Miss Objective Observer. I've seen hundreds, thousands even, of people get the opposite of what they deserved. I've recorded it happening, put it to tape to prove it, and for what? Kids left without parents, parents left without children, dogs left without legs. I took a photo of a baby without a head once. I walked into that compound – a UN shelter, no less, in the arse end of Lebanon – and I slipped on a human hand. A whole hand, intact apart from the fact it was no longer attached to a wrist. Then I got to skate straight down onto my back plumb into a pool of blood, litres of the stuff. We told everyone about that, the world even screamed bloody murder, but nobody did a damn thing about it, not a one. And the business made more money off my pictures than went to the relief effort, but that's a whole separate conversation that I'm pretty sure you'll never have with me—'

She crashed into him then, both flying from side to side as the van bounced across the desert.

'Do you think I don't know that already? That you hold the monopoly on understanding why some things never change no matter how hard you try? That you have to have seen it for yourself to believe it? Have it burned into your eyeballs, have it tattooed into your brain, so you can never see anything else?'

'Well, if you do, it's only because I took the fucking pictures. Gonzo Gonzales, that's me. If there's a headless corpse, I'll film it, even if it means I may as well take my own head off in the process. There was a soldier, he was holding the baby, staring through the space its head should have been – I got that shot too, by the way.'

'The Israelis shelled that compound knowing full well there were civilians inside.'

'And did anyone give a shit? Did anyone even care where it was? Do you remember that part too? I suppose you think because you can draw the map from memory that everyone else can too? Those facts, that information, those pictures – not even in black and white; in full glorious technicolour – they didn't move the needle, not even a bit. The Israelis will do it again, you just see if they don't. They all will, doesn't matter who they are, or why. The UN report into that whole bloodbath wasn't even an excuse for a whitewash. That town – Qana, since you ask, although it may as well have been an outpost on the moon – the only reason people even remember its name is because some idiots still think Jesus turned water into wine there. And I can tell you the only red stuff running in that town was blood, rivers and rivers of the stuff. So tell me this: what do you think was left for the families? For the relatives of those victims? Huh? Let's say you were that baby's mother, you got the body of your kid back in that condition, the whole world screamed on your behalf, but nothing happened? Let's just say—'

'Ask me then!' she suddenly screamed, mile-high; by rights the windows should have broken. 'Ask me, go on, ask the question, instead of answering it for yourself. Did I want to die? Did I want the rest of my life to be taken out of my hands, after my dad was gone?'

She crumpled then, like a paper cut-out. He found himself shaking her.

'We took her choice away,' she wailed. 'I never wanted that. You could have asked me the day after Qana and my answer would still have been the same.'

'What the hell are you talking about?' He shook her again even though she was limp, flying back and forth with the car like a rag doll.

'He saw it all too,' she whispered. 'I like to believe he never saw anything, but we got his body back. He died of his injuries. It wasn't a clean break – he was still alive for half of it. And I thought ... I thought that being with you, after all this time, would—'

'Who? Who died?' By now the van was buzzing, so hot with tension it could have exploded and no one would have been surprised.

'He only went inside that compound so he could bring the story out, he didn't even have his camera on him. I know that's the only reason he would have done it, that he would have even been in Qana to start with. There were families with children, tiny babies even, they all thought they were under the protection of the UN. The survivors said he went in to translate for them.'

'Wait a second. There was a man in that compound who—'

'Who was the only one who spoke English. The only one who could make sure the testimony inside would make it out.'

And then Kris saw it, heady as a clear dawn, even though the air was still thick with the settling sandstorm, the windows were still coated in dust. A broken body in a pool of blood sheltered in the crook of wall that kept him alive for long enough to tell them everything. One of hundreds of bodies he'd seen before, except...

'That was your old man? That translator ... that was him? But I thought—'

'What, that he was just another Ahmed?'

Kris rubbed an eye as he mumbled, old cries in his ears, blood-rust tang on his fingertips.

'I remember them all, Sami. Every single one. I never forget them, not a hair on their heads, not a scar on their faces. I focus on them – I see it again, and again and again, with every frame. That man – that Ahmed, your Ahmed, as it turns out – he cried out to me. He was the only reason I saw what I saw. I had to walk away from him, and look what happened when I did.'

'What, and you're going to kill me, now, too? Gonzo Gonzales, bringer of peace, destroyer of pain, decision-maker-in-chief?'

Kris dropped her then, suddenly red hot, his fingertips burning.

'You've known all this time that I was there too? You planned this all along?'

'I don't know what I planned anymore. I just—' She screeched as she hit the window, by rights it should have cracked in two. 'I just thought there was a chance you'd be everything he was, and that if I could just change Mum's mind about it all, she might get her own soul back, even if it was just a tiny piece. She might even love me back, for once, in spite of everything I've done to remind her of him.'

Crash went the van as they finally hit the road and sped up. Her Thuraya suddenly started to buzz between them, a live grenade on the back seat.

'But now there's only one interpretation. No one will ever understand, least of all her. There's only one word for what you just did to Yousra, Kris.'

'What, that it's a better story now she's dead?'

And then time seemed to stop, right as the car accelerated, long enough for even Kris to see the end of the road.

There would be no new mission, there would be no renewed purpose.

There was no sudden sensation of floating, lighter than air, high on the rush of seeing he'd truly made a difference to someone who deserved it the most.

No. Kris may as well have pitched head down into some canyon where he would never stop falling, the only accompaniment a hard physical longing, all bone-jar and smack, for the only person that had ever loved him. He rubbed his head again only to find nothing except a seven-year-old, blisters bursting in his palms as he cut his father down from the rope before he got to die. He'd seen enough by then to know for damn sure a man like that did not get to just escape and leave the consequences behind. A man like that did not get to just waltz through the valley of the shadow of death with anything less than unimaginable pain and suffering at his heels. No. He was coming down off that rope to face every last second of his fucking waste of a life in agony.

Sami picked up the phone, pulled out its overweight aerial, opened and closed her mouth, nodded a few times. The buzzing was still keening in his ears even as she turned it off.

'Penny got our pictures,' she said dully. 'Management have gone nuts. They want everything – a long cut, a short cut, a magazine-length interview, as soon as we can do it. Every last detail, no matter how graphic. They don't even care about giving the state the right to reply, or about having any politicians on camera. It's enough to just say we've asked. And she's going to sell on the lot – the pictures of the Janjaweed, of Yousra, every single roll of film.'

Somewhere outside the van the gates of the UNHCR compound clanked open as he stared at her gazing into the dust.

'I'm going to do it,' she continued evenly, 'and you're going to help me. But know this. When it's done, I'm going to tell them everything.'

The gates crashed again as she got out of the van. Were they open or closed? Kris couldn't tell. He was still falling; down, down, down.

Chapter 29
Devils on Horseback

Sometimes I allow myself to question if I said it out loud. It only happens involuntarily, a muscle reflex against all that I do to ensure my mind never turns that way. Can I write another script, work on a different story, investigate some new allegations, however harrowing? Can I occupy myself right down to the synapse of my nerves?

But when you are in the business of who knew what and when, who said what and why, by default you end up with a measure of doubt. And even the most agile of mental acrobats can slip up in the darkest recesses of a sleepless night.

Is it a dream, or is it real? I can never be sure. My father is always there, so it must be a dream, and yet I can never see his eyes, as I never could when I was young, his glasses constantly misty as we lurched from life in one overheated Middle Eastern city to the next. I flinch, an engine backfiring somewhere, burned rubber in my nose – now Mum's there too, and she's how she used to be: loving, confident and supportive, even if she always wore a slight frown, a question mark permanently drawn in the line between her eyebrows.

Where have you been? And what did you do? Please, don't leave us so soon, not again...

So it's a dream, it must be. Except here she is again, staring into space, blank and vacant – anyone who didn't know her would say she's been wiped clean, but the question mark, it's still written on her face.

Where have you been? she asks of me, this time. She doesn't

need to say anything, just incline her head a fraction away from the open window of her all-white mental institution, devoid of colour, of memory, of any evidence of humanity. Perhaps she's luxuriating in the breeze on her face, so cool and refreshing, a world away from the physical quality of the air in Beirut, in Amman, in Cairo. Is she considering how the fragrance of meadow after the rain is over-rated compared to the heady mixture of petrol and pavement barbecue, the scent of life undeniably on the move? Except I know that she's not. She's asking. And she's asking us both.

Where have you been? And what did you do?

She's Penny now, crumpling instantly against the glass wall of her office, folding herself into her tiny, betrayed centre. Much as the news business as a whole surely will, if this matter isn't set to rights the only way it can be. It's then that the thought creeps out, an ear worm of a thing, nagging and insistent. And suddenly the texture of those moments is as limpid as the present itself – the air as sandstorm-thick as Darfur, as laced with just-fired explosives as Baghdad and as steaming with humid sorrow as Kabul. Suddenly that's the air I am gulping all over again, alone in my bedroom in the dead hours before dawn.

Where have you been? And what did you do?

I turn for my father but he's gone – he's dead, he's not even a sprite, there's nowhere to hover unnoticed inside this box made of glass, a domain of mirrors and reflections, no humidity to turn anything to fog. There's nothing but clarity, even as Ross unlocks his polished cupboard like a man possessed, rifling through paperwork, fumbling with barcodes, howling as vials, blister packs and syringes shower to the floor. He's creating chaos – amplified by sirens, shouts, uniformed policemen – as if it might somehow exonerate us all, as if counting and recounting the contents of the not-quite-bulging-enough black leather medical packs might somehow cause the huge number of missing drugs to reconstitute themselves from nothing but shadows.

But there's no chaos that can muddle the answers to these particular questions as Kris willingly lifts his hands to be cuffed and led away.

Multiple crimes have been committed here, of the most ghastly kind, and you've surely heard enough by now to understand how it all came to pass.

There are no questions left except one.

Did I know what he was doing? Did I ever see the gleam of a needle, a lethal shot in his hand? Or did I just see a moment ground down to its atoms of anguish, disbelief and despair?

Did I ask him: what are you doing with that? Or did I just ask myself as I watched in my mind's eye, hovering above the needle, the finest of lines dividing us, willing that I choose to come down on the right side.

This is the thought that hovers at the edge of my tongue, the thing we both know that I never said.

What did you know? What did you know, Sami?

What did you know?

~~~

'It's important we're all crystal clear on this point, Miss Nassar, so let me ask you again.'

The barrister, my barrister, pauses to look around the packed courtroom. She's the lawyer for the prosecution, so technically, we're on the same side, even though sitting in this witness box feels anything but. Kris is the one in the dock, but who is really to blame? This court doesn't care. She just wants to win.

I clamp my mouth shut. The question lingers, even as I swallow. What am I going to say if she asks me outright? I still don't know. And we've rehearsed it a thousand times.

'When did you become aware that all these people had been killed deliberately?'

'I only knew about Yousra,' I reply softly, gazing at the magazine cover lying in the laps of almost everyone I can see – her eyes, dark, never-ending, unmistakably still alive. 'I had no idea he had killed anyone else until—'

'Let me stop you there, Miss Nassar. To be clear, you are saying you knew nothing of the other two murders until the defendant himself confessed to them, here in this courtroom? During this trial? The deliberate killing of Habiba Soltani and Ahmed...?'

She trails off instead of saying last name unknown.

'Ahmed Aziz,' I reply. 'His name was Ahmed Aziz.'

'Ahmed Aziz,' she repeats, with the smallest of frowns. Her wig is so low on her forehead that only I can see it. It's meant for me, as I'm supposed to be following her script. Her opening statement laid it all out – paint-by-numbers, one to two to three. But even she couldn't have foreseen where those numbers would lead.

This is a murder trial that's gone from one body to three.

And Kris has confessed to killing them all.

'Miss Nassar?'

'That's right,' I say, blinking blinding white flash from my eyes. 'I only found out about Bibi and Ahmed when you did. I mean, I only found out Kris had killed them too once we confronted him about Yousra.'

'Let's back up a moment again, Miss Nassar. To be clear, for the purposes of this court, Habiba Soltani – Bibi, as you referenced – is the eighteen-year-old girl you interviewed in a hospital in Kabul, Afghanistan. Ahmed – Ahmed Aziz – was an elderly gentleman you spoke to in what was left of his home in Baghdad, Iraq, in the aftermath of a suicide bomb attack?'

'Yes,' I snap. These were my stories, but now they sound like hers, told in the space of ten seconds with no perspective or under-standing.

'So you became aware that these two victims had died after you had interviewed them. You had no idea how, only that they had. Why didn't you question it?'

She's still frowning as I stare at her, motionless black-on-white, like a chess piece.

'If you could just answer the question, Miss Nassar?'

'Answer the question,' I mumble as I reflexively rub my stomach. Suddenly all I can see are Bibi's horrific scars.

'I'm sorry?'

'Bibi was catastrophically injured,' I say, digging a finger into my waist. 'She had deliberately covered herself with boiling oil, to escape life under a forced marriage. Even without the doctors backing it up, it was obvious that she might not have survived.'

'If you could just stick to the pertinent details, Miss Nassar—'

'Surely there are no details that aren't pertinent in this case?'

'Your Honour, I'd like to play a tape for the court, if I may.'

Black robes swish, a curtain going up, as she steps out from behind her polished desk. The desk covered in folders, but she won't open them, just tap them with a finger, more acting.

'You may, counsel.'

The judge, also a woman, has a sore throat. Either that or she's been coughing to hide how she really feels this whole time. She lets out another splutter as the barrister twirls on the spot, brandishing a remote control.

'Ladies and gentlemen of the jury, you have heard Miss Nassar describe, in moving detail, her encounter with Habiba Soltani. Indeed, some of you may have read the original news report, which was published last year. But the video of her interview was never broadcast, and serves to elucidate an important point.'

The crowds on the benches rustle in anticipation as she presses play, except all I can hear is Ajmal. His gentle voice compelling Bibi to tell us her story, and whispering it back to the camera. I blot away the sweat starting to film across my forehead, suddenly back in the fetid hospital even though the courtroom is freezing.

'Here,' she says with a click, the tape pausing mid-wail. 'Ladies and gentlemen of the jury, it is here that you will see the evidence, crystal-clear, that Miss Nassar walked away from the defendant and was outside the room while the victim was still alive.'

The tape rolls again, and I watch myself following Ajmal through the choked ward, the shot pulling close on the door as it swings to. Then the sweat starts to run, stinging my eyes as the realisation rolls over me.

Kris did it deliberately. He made sure there was proof that I wasn't there at the time.

I bang a fist into my chest, furious at my heart for fluttering. For what this video also shows, in blazing technicolour, is that I am the one who walked away. I am the one who got up, turned away, and left her behind. It's playing out on the television in front of me, but no one else will register it as I do. In that moment, I deserted Bibi, and Kris didn't. He took away her pain long after I had left.

'Miss Nassar? Could you please confirm for the court that it is you walking out of the room on the screen there? Closing the door behind you?'

I blink furiously as she points the remote control at me and then at the gigantic monitor set up in front of the jury.

'I closed it so the edge wouldn't be in the shot...'

'Just the pertinent details, again, please, Miss Nassar.'

I whisper a yes, nodding as I drop my head. I can't bear to look anymore. The barrister places her remote back on her polished desk with a triumphant click.

She is so sure we're winning. But right now all I feel is lost.

'And just to be clear, again, for the purposes of the court, Miss Nassar: the first you learned of Habiba Soltani's death was on your return to the UK, during your preparation of the news report, whilst in contact with the various military officials that had facilitated your trip inside the hospital. And you didn't question it, because she had suffered unimaginable injuries.'

'Yes.' I clear my throat. 'That's right.'

She taps a folder as she gives me an almost imperceptible nod.

'Let us turn to the case of Ahmed Aziz, then, Miss Nassar. This was a gentleman you also interviewed, but we have little evidence left of that. In fact, there was no specific news report of his particular story, even though there was coverage of the bomb attack that killed the last surviving members of his family—'

'We were ambushed,' I snap, the courtroom rustling in surprise as I interrupt her. 'Our vehicle rolled over an IED. We had just seconds to flee for our lives – by rights we should never have made it. That took over, even though I wish it hadn't.'

'The events of that particular ambush have been perfectly established already, thank you, Miss Nassar.'

Her eyebrows disappear under the rim of her wig as she raises them at me. A reminder we're following her script, not mine. That in this room, her script is the only version that matters.

'What I am asking you is this: by all accounts, including that of the local Iraqi news agency that originally interviewed Mr Aziz, he was not as catastrophically injured as Bibi had been. Not at all, in fact. Indeed, he had survived this particular bomb blast because of the protection of his wheelchair – a metal frame that encased the entire lower half of his body, where the original blast radius was concentrated. So when you later learned of his death, why didn't you question it too?'

'He was an old man,' I whisper, rubbing a kaleidoscope of memory from my eyes. 'His entire family had been taken from him, he had no surviving relatives left. He'd suffered the agony of the accident that had left him paralysed to start with; he'd watched the city he loved go down in flames. And he was left in the ruins of his home with no means to get himself food, medicine, even water when he needed it. Even if that wasn't enough to convince me he might have died of natural causes, it wasn't inconceivable that he could have died of a broken heart.'

'How did you find out he had died, Miss Nassar?'

Another frown, another interruption for straying into the realms of impossibility. Except I know you can die from a broken heart. That's what really did it for my mother. There are dead bodies, and then there are abandoned live ones.

'Hamdi told us. He was the local journalist who met Ahmed first, on the day the market was hit. Hamdi was how I managed to get access to Ahmed in the first place. Hamdi called into our office after the ambush to check we were OK – he had no way of knowing whether we'd been affected at the time; he only narrowly missed being hit himself. After the dust settled he'd gone back to check on Ahmed and found him dead. What was left of his house had basically crumpled around him. It could have been shock, it could have been impact from falling rubble, in that situation it could have been anything.'

'Except it wasn't, was it?'

'No,' I say, so softly she asks me again. 'No, it wasn't. But no one who had witnessed anything of what happened there, what was going on in Baghdad at the time – what's still going on even now – would have questioned it. All that was important in those phone calls was that Hamdi was safe, and so were we. It wasn't even me who spoke to him, it was Andie—'

'Andrea Quinn, the senior field producer stationed in Baghdad at the time.'

I nod instead of saying anything else.

'So let us return to this question of who knew what, and when, Miss Nassar. I don't think we need to establish any more details about the horrors you witnessed in Darfur. Your extraordinary news reporting and the coverage on your news network have taken care of that.'

Another prop waves through the air, this time a rolled-up magazine. One dark, unblinking eye, Yousra's, stares round the court.

'But let me ask you this. You didn't immediately report Yousra's death to the authorities. Instead you put together the news story first, allowed your superiors to license all the material, let the reaction roll in – quite considerable, and rightly so, I might add. Now why was that?'

I look into Yousra's liquid eyes instead of hers. They're closest on Katja's lap in the front row, as black as her customary voluminous skirt and cardigan. The answer to this question is so obvious I cannot believe I have to say it out loud.

'There was, in fact there still is, a genocidal regime operating in Sudan, and we were the first to have direct evidence of that. The government is purposefully arming Arab militias, men on horseback known as the Janjaweed, to rid the western region of Darfur of ethnic Black Africans, three particular tribes, to be precise: the Fur, the Masalit and—'

'Miss Nassar.'

'I'm sorry,' I say, but I'm not talking to her. All I can see is Mum, propped vacant in her all-white room in her all-white mental hospital, covered in scars inside and out.

'My point is, we had the proof. Once I realised what Kris had done, I had to make doubly sure this one death hadn't been in vain. We had taken the first known pictures of the Janjaweed, and now they are known the world over. Whether you like it or not, the fact these people are so telegenic actually matters – if you asked someone to put paint to canvas and come up with a devil on horseback, it's not inconceivable they'd paint the same thing. It captures the imagination, for better or for worse, and it spurs action far, far more effectively. It shouldn't, but it does. And you only need to look at what has happened since. There's still so, so much more to do in Darfur, but the pictures of Yousra, and her unimaginable story, alongside the images of those men...'

The words stall in my throat as I catch the glint of gold aviators in another lap. But then I find Diana, shivering next to them, holding Yousra's beautiful face in her slim hands.

'Those pictures brought home the horror of what is happening in Darfur. And now we at least have the beginnings of a massive humanitarian intervention, if not yet a co-ordinated peacekeeping effort. The world is watching far, far more closely than it was, and it will come, it is only a matter of time. There is no definition of genocide that these horrors do not match. And in the second that I knew I had the microphone, I knew I had to use it – how could I not?'

I linger on Penny, face shining with tears that she isn't even trying to hide as she gazes up at me from next to Katja.

'If I didn't tell the story first, I'd have abandoned everything just at the moment I could have salvaged something. I owed it to Yousra. I owed it to everyone.'

'And once you'd put your report together, you'd sent through all your pictures, that's when you reported the other side of what you knew.'

'Yes,' I say. 'Yes. I just made sure the real news got out first.'

But the question still lingers, even as I look up for Di and the green light of her eyes.

What did I know?

Chapter 30
No More Questions

'Mr Rusholme? Might I remind you that you are under oath here? Could you answer the question, please?'

There's a snort as the man surveys her, colossal wig the colour of bile under the artificial lights. The defence didn't bother asking him any questions – what could they possibly have been? But this woman, this lawyer for the so-called Crown, isn't going to stop until it's his blood running over the floor. And Mohammed didn't give it up for that.

'I told you, it's Gonzales – why do you keep calling me Mr Rusholme?'

'It's on your birth certificate.' The lawyer waves a piece of paper at him. 'Yet another fantasy of yours? A different name, a different life?'

The man turns inward: *Should I shoot her, boy? Yeah, Dad, you go right ahead.* A door slams someplace, Lucia finally walking out. Her unconditional love suddenly covered in so many conditions that it's choked on its own sick.

'So now we've established that, Mr Rusholme, let me ask you one more time. You are admitting, in the presence of this court, to the premeditated, deliberate murder of three individuals.'

There's Ross, so puffed up with fury he's practically blistering in the front row.

'Individuals you identified, yourself, in the course of your front-line work as a journalist. Individuals you targeted deliberately...'

Katja now, third from left, wrapping herself so tight in her usual black cardigan he's surprised she doesn't snap.

'Vulnerable, defenceless individuals, already so brutalised in the inevitable course of war – and yet, you made a deliberate choice to take whatever rights they had left out of their hands.'

Should I shoot her, boy? What's she worth, to you?

'And you claim that Samira Nassar – catapulted into the limelight after your shots of the Janjaweed militia were published all over the world – you claim that she knew absolutely nothing of your murderous intentions?'

'Yes,' Kris replies softly. *Go right on ahead.*

Everyone in a wig pauses for good measure. Someplace else, a clock ticks down on a wall.

'Mr Rusholme, is it correct that you also claim that these were acts of mercy, rather than cold-blooded murder? Because – let me recall this correctly – you claim these were people that had nothing left to live for? That in their own words, all they wished for was death?'

Did I raise a pussy, boy? That's all you got?

'These, of course, were words you claim were issued, voluntarily, to you and Miss Nassar, in spite of the fact this court has heard the tapes, watched the video, and seen the evidence of what can only be described as leading questions.'

You want to play chicken with me, boy? You think I won't blow her brains out?

'And yet, still you claim you were doing them a favour? So disillusioned with the craft, with the industry on which you've predicated your life's work, you claim you were the one making the real difference here? By giving them the peaceful end they deserved?'

I'll fucking do it, boy!

A scream then, hers – the only scream Kris has ever heard since. All the child in him knows is failure. He should have let the old man shoot her. His mother had nothing left to get herself off a bridge, over a cliff, into the path of a steamroller. There was no one else on earth who more deserved the numb comfort of the blinding white flash. What she got instead was years of pain and terror, followed by nightmares until the pills finally ended it.

'Mr Rusholme?'

'Yes.' Kris coils an imaginary rope through his fingers as he says it. 'And I'd do it again.'

Another gasp, yet still all he can hear are screams. They never stopped, even after the old man was put away. Even after Kris cut him down so he didn't get to escape the rest of his life in a cage. The sun would blaze and she would shiver. The harbour wind would whip salt off the water, and all she would smell was gunpowder. Someone would reach out to her and she would flinch. It was all she could see. Even when she closed her eyes. After all that, his mother still had to do it for herself. He gropes his way back to reality as the lawyer's questions start up again.

'Let's return to this issue of who knew what, and when, Mr Rusholme. You've told this court you tried to protect Miss Nassar. That she knew nothing of your plans, that you took deliberate steps to ensure she was kept in the dark. But isn't it true that you targeted her in the same way? That Miss Nassar was a means to an end, for you?'

'I wouldn't say that, no.' Kris regards her, steely and frozen as the brainless curls on her wig. But he can't look at Sami. Or Andie, or Lucia's empty chair. There's nothing left to see there. Nothing that can change his story.

'So how would you describe your relationship?'

'It was work. It was professional.'

'So you have sexual intercourse with everyone you work with?'

'It doesn't happen like that.'

'Then how does it happen?'

He considers this, as he considers each strand of artificial hair hiding her head. Telling the courtroom how what goes on the road stays on the road will make as much sense as them.

'Isn't it true, Mr Rusholme, that this was just another way that you used Miss Nassar? After you had been shot, you identified a way to manipulate yourself into situations that would serve your murderous purpose? And Miss Nassar was the conduit crucial to this?'

'Not exactly...'

'So what would you say? That you preyed on her vulnerabilities, just as you preyed on the vulnerabilities of all your victims, for your own purposes?'

'It's not the same thing.'

'What's not the same? You didn't identify a vulnerable young woman, in a tremendously charged situation, sometimes terrified for her life, and manipulate her emotions to suit you?'

'Sami, your Miss Nassar, she went into it with her eyes open. She wanted everything she got, she just never understood what she was looking at.'

'So you're admitting to manipulating her?'

'If it puts her in the clear, then yeah, sure, I manipulated her. I used her. In every way possible, even physically.'

'Ladies and gentlemen of the jury, I put to you that we have a fourth victim here.'

The lawyer sweeps round so she's standing directly between them. Kris couldn't see Sami even if he wanted to.

'Miss Nassar herself was, too, a victim of Mr Rusholme's deliberate, premeditated, predatory behaviour. She was as innocent as all the other victims in this, and we have her to thank for bringing Mr Rusholme's perverted agenda into this courtroom to face justice – indeed, something she did only after she ensured she had done right by the only other victim she could...'

On cue, all heads in the courtroom swivel down at the magazine in their laps, at the face gazing up at them in more pain than any of them think they could imagine.

'Indeed, Miss Nassar has been shown to have behaved as responsibly as Mr Rusholme has behaved irresponsibly.'

Kris laughs then, high and mad.

'Irresponsible? That's the best you can do?'

'Oh no, Mr Rusholme, I can do far, far better.'

'And so can I.' He sees the lawyer's wig slip, her disguise imperceptible to anyone but him. 'You can all call it whatever you like because I'm not arguing the toss on this. I killed those people. I planned it out, every last detail. I killed them all. But I made damn sure that no one else got snarled up in it too. You're right that I made deliberate choices – hey, let's call them responsible ones, so I'm in a language even you can understand.'

'Mr Rusholme!'

A shout somewhere to his left, but still, there are only screams in his ears.

'I got everyone out of the way.' He looks to Andie then, white as wax, four from right in the back row. 'Everyone who could have been directly accused of a crime – all of them. I did what I had to do to make sure they were nowhere close.'

'All of them? So you had quite the entourage, did you?'

'Propaganda is big business, lady. State media has got to be able to cover state interests. There's a whole lot of cash in the wings for operations that hold the microphone – we had cooks, bodyguards, translators, you name it.'

'So there were others? That's what you're saying?'

'No. I'm saying I got everyone out of the way. Everyone who could have been directly accused of a crime. The shame is, there are so many more that should be in this seat.'

'If you could just stick to the facts, Mr Rusholme.'

'These *are* the facts!' His eyes find Penny, head bowed, dressed for a funeral. 'Everyone with me on the ground, everyone actually doing the company dirty work – the warm bodies, if we're sticking to the factual terms – none of them had a clue what I was doing. I made damn sure of that. They all called me Gonzo with no shade of irony, like the agenda-setting they reckon is gonzo journalism actually does anything other than puff the right egos. Loads of them thought we were in the business of giving voice to the voiceless, holding power to account, shining a light into the darkness – note, each one of these clichés is factually fucking correct – and I went along with it, hook, line and sinker. Ask them, why don't you; they're due up here too, when you're finally finished with me. But ask yourself this: who put me there? I've told you how it all happened, every last detail. So you should know. Who sent me back, again and again, even after it was obvious—'

'Are you arguing you were not sound of mind, Mr Rusholme?'

'Well, I had been shot in the head.'

Silence then, no one dares gasp. Not even her.

'Yes, I suppose you had. And yet, from everything you've willingly told this court, these are murders that you planned from the outset. You found someone to get you to where you needed to be, you deliberately carried enough morphine on you – obtained covertly, we've also established – so that when the moment came, it was a simple matter of needle in, needle out.'

'Do me a favour, lady, would you? Just for a second, instead of asking me all the damn questions, ask yourself what you would prefer. Let's say your baby was ripped out of your arms and raped – yeah, they do that first – and then thrown onto a fire?'

'Mr Rusholme—'

'Let's say you heard that story again and again, like it was your favourite tale at bedtime, chased all the nightmares away, milk and cookies, same old verses, same old songs. Then let's say Ma and Pa told you if you sung that song enough, you'd get more cookies, more milk, the nightmares would stop happening, because you'd told enough people about it—'

'Mr Rusholme!'

A bang then, a hammer this time, like he's not wearing a skin that has fielded far worse blows before.

'They just do it again, it doesn't matter what you do. I could give you more examples than you've had hot dinners, except you don't care about any of that, you just get to turn it off, like all the other robots.'

Bang, bang, bang, goes the hammer, go the bombs as they blow overhead.

'This is not a moral court, Mr Rusholme, this is a court of law, and in a court of law, justice will prevail. The facts are that you have admitted to the premeditated murder of three individuals.'

'Ask yourself what you would want, under those circumstances. Ask yourself what you would deserve, if you'd gone through all that.'

And then a scream, mile-high and tuned perfectly to the acoustics of this particular courtroom, amplifying rather than fading as it echoes back and forth. Sami. On her feet, behind an overturned table. She stares at him, unblinking, even as the uniforms descend.

'I am the one who made the difference!' Kris screams back at her through pandemonium. 'It was the only difference left to make. You know better than anyone else that all they deserved was the peace they were begging for.'

The courtroom door slams behind him as they drag him away, but not before he hears the one with bile all over her head laughing about how she really has no need to ask any more questions.

Chapter 31
The Last Stand

The court breaks for lunch, as if any of us are going to eat it. My barrister, the lawyer for the prosecution, turns on me the minute the hammer stops banging.

'Pull yourself together,' she hisses as she adjusts her wig. 'What on earth was that about? I warned you that the sex could over-complicate matters, and then you only go and behave like some heartbroken teenager. I couldn't have established any more perfectly that you had nothing to do with it only to have you risk being held in contempt.'

Diana's hand finds its way into mine from the row behind. I grip it so tight I hear her gasp.

'All I need to worry about now is the rest of his defence,' she mutters, bending to scoop up the papers scattered all over the floor from the fallen table. 'This is nothing less than a murder conviction – anything else will be an abject failure for the Crown. We'll be skewered by the press – hah! No doubt with no hint of irony. But he's made himself look so unhinged they'll go for diminished responsibility. I just know they'll have a character witness limbering up in the wings. Hell, they might even chance insanity.'

'Wouldn't that be the fairest outcome of all?'

I jump as Diana addresses her directly.

'Excuse me? Who is this?'

Miss Field, the barrister, stares at me instead of asking Diana herself.

'By his own admission, he witnessed more horror and suffering than any human being ever should. He recorded it just so others would learn about it, putting his own life on the line countless times in the process. He almost died as recently as six months ago, and was sent back out into the heat of it again and again and again.'

'Di...' I try to squeeze her hand but realise she's the one gripping mine, not the other way around.

'He knew what he was doing, of course he did. But isn't the context just as important? Isn't what he did the very definition of diminished responsibility?'

'Who are you? And exactly what is your relationship to my client? Or this case?'

Miss Field, on her feet now, squares up to Di.

'It doesn't matter who I am,' Diana says. 'What matters are all the facts, not just the ones that suit you, and—'

'If you'll excuse me.' Miss Field holds a hand up in her face as she glares at me. 'Go get yourself some fresh air, would you, Sami? And do see to it that you can keep your emotions under control for this afternoon. I'll be back in half an hour if you've any questions before the defence gets going. You won't be called. There's only one possible variable here.' She pauses to run a finger under the rim of her wig. 'Oh, and take your friend along too, would you?'

Diana stares after her with a rueful smile as she sweeps away in a rustle of robes and paper.

'By rights, the news business should be on trial too,' Di says, dropping my hand so she can walk round to meet me on the other side of the front bench. 'Kris should never have been sent out after he was shot, at least not for months and months.'

'He's a grown man, Di.' I wipe a hand on my skirt. 'He's more experienced than half the managers making decisions on his behalf, and he went along with them all.'

'And what does that tell you?'

'Just...' I look at my feet. 'Oh, I don't know. We're the ones who are supposed to be the adults in the room.'

She shrugs. 'I don't disagree with any of that. I just find it difficult to accept that a matter of such nuance is going to be settled in the least nuanced way possible.'

'He killed them, Di.'

'Yes, he did.' She gazes at me as the courtroom empties round us. 'But even you don't believe it's as simple as that.'

'In some ways, I really do.'

Yousra's eyes weigh on me from every seat in the room.

'Sometimes I think, as journalists, we spend so much time considering stuff from every possible angle, weighing every last piece of information, that we lose sight of the foundations. And some things really are as binary as they sound. You don't have to be neutral about it to be objective.'

'None of that sounds simple to me.'

'I just...'

I trail off as a door slams. We're the only ones left in the courtroom.

'He killed them, Di.' I say it again, even if it's mainly to myself. 'I've gone over this so many times in my head that I feel like I'll never be able to compute anything else. Worse, he made their stories about him.'

'Yes, he did. And he'll pay for it for the rest of his life. But don't you think we should too?'

'Us? What do you mean?' My breath stills in my throat.

'Pain sells, Sami.' She plucks a magazine from the seat behind her, crumpling Yousra's face in her fingers. 'But only one type of pain – the kind that the people reading about will almost certainly never have to experience. Otherwise they wouldn't watch it, they wouldn't read about it. It would hit far too close to home. It's voyeurism as much as it is journalism. You know it's not quite as binary as you're making out. This magazine cover has made millions out of her...'

'But that's not the point, at all.'

'...that she'll never see. Even if she were alive.'

Now it's only her eyes I can see, piercing green, staring into my brain.

'Of course it's wrong that he killed her. Of course it's wrong that he killed them all. But isn't it just as wrong that the business used him, just like he used you? Wouldn't it also be completely wrong for no lessons to be learned from any of this? Aren't we, ultimately, all in the business of perspective? There are costs to all of this, every last column inch of it.'

I try to look away but I can't. I never can when it's Di who's staring.

'Kris can't be blamed for it all. You know that, even though it hurts more than I can imagine, than anyone can imagine. It's true you are another of his victims. But it's also true that he is too.'

'Well they're about to roll out a character witness anyway, aren't they? It must be Andie ... or Katja...' I trace a finger over my lips as I consider it. 'And there's nothing I can do about it now.'

'No, you can't. But I can.' She places a finger over mine, stilling the gasp in my throat. 'And I'm going to. I'm his character witness. I'm the last on the stand. I just wanted to make sure I told you about it first.'

~~~

Miss Field blusters and grumbles, all swinging robes and sleeves, as we take our seats behind the now-restored prosecution table. Instead of asking any more questions of Kris, the defence is staking the rest on Di, and the courtroom has suddenly gone from sub-Arctic to uncomfortably hot.

'Could you state your full name for the court, please?'

The clerk brandishes a bible as he approaches the witness box.

'Diana Octavia Emerald Yardley.'

These are names Di has previously gone to extreme lengths to hide. But no one, not even the unrelated members of the press in the public gallery, dares utter even a hint of a snigger as she rests her smooth, white hand on top of the bible, perfectly manicured nails flashing proud red.

'Thank you, Miss Yardley.'

Di stays standing as the clerk scuttles away, surveying the courtroom with her customary poise and grace. Miss Field taps a finger on the folder in front of her, to demonstrate if only to herself she's still in control of proceedings.

Fear kicks at my chest. I feel like my conscience has separated itself from my body to take the stand against me.

'For the purposes of the court, Miss Yardley, could you please also state your occupation?'

Di pauses for another moment, as does the barrister for the defence, a birdlike woman whose tiny hands move with the precision of a conductor.

'I'm a supervising news producer,' Di answers as she sits. 'Sami and I were made permanent members of staff after a successful internship together nearly two years ago.'

'To be clear, you are referring to Miss Nassar?'

'Yes. Miss Nassar and I have known each other since school.'

Another pause, as the defence brief steps to the centre of her stage. I blink away flash frames of memory, of Diana, practically the only family I have left.

'Isn't it true, Miss Yardley, that you also know the defendant?'

'Yes. I first met Mr Gonz—, I mean, Mr Rusholme, on his return from Baghdad last year.'

'To be clear, you met him just after he'd been seriously injured in an ambush that also critically injured another colleague?'

'Yes.'

There's complete silence in the courtroom, except all I can hear are machines, beeping and wheezing as they keep Ali's body alive.

'And could you take us through the basic details of your relationship?'

Di's head inclines on her neck like a ballerina, away from me.

'Mr Rusholme and I were lovers, for a very brief period of time.'

'Lovers? Do you mean he engaged in an extra-marital relationship with you?'

'I suppose so, yes.'

Whatever was pummelling my chest moves up to choke me, so hard I can't even gasp. Diana and Kris? For how long? When? And why didn't she ever tell me?

'Could you tell us what happened the night of November the twenty-first, 2003?'

I flick backwards through my mind and come up with nothing except night shifts, all of which Di was there for except…

'I had met Mr Rusholme the previous week. He'd come straight off the plane into the newsroom to a hero's welcome. Everyone had moved to the pub across the street to toast his return. He'd escaped with his life, and risked it in the purview of the business a thousand times before. We got talking, and eventually he came home with me, although I took steps to make sure no one saw us leave together.'

'Why was that?'

'He was married. And it's not the sort of thing that I wanted anyone to know about.'

'What do you mean by that?'

'The news business is competitive on all fronts. It was commonplace to find people doing whatever it took to get themselves where they wanted to be. I was determined not to be one of them.'

'Whatever it takes?'

'Yes. Drugs, sex, favours, you name it. It was seen as par for the course, it still is.'

'So what made you break your own rule and become involved with Mr Rusholme?'

'I was drawn to him.' She tucks away an escaping strand of hair. 'He was magnetic, especially so after the incident. He seemed almost superhuman in survival. I'm not proud of it. I knew he was married, but there were rumours, there always are, and I had plenty of my own insecurities humming in the background. He had a way of paying attention that made me feel like he could see into my head, and none of it mattered. Only one other person in my life had ever done that, and she had her sights set on far further horizons.'

She looks straight at me, but only for a second.

'Back to the night of the twenty-first, Miss Yardley. Could you tell us what happened?'

Di takes a deep breath, the first time I've seen her take any. Tap-tap-tap go Miss Field's fingers, a tattoo of despair.

'I had arranged to meet Mr Rusholme at my flat after work. I was on the overnight shift, so we were meeting early the following morning. Once he'd arrived though, it was obvious that he'd also been awake all night.'

'Obvious? How do you mean?'

'He was under the influence of both drugs and alcohol.'

'And how do you know that?'

'He ... he smelled of it. It was unmistakable. It emanated from every pore. And there were more illegal substances in his pockets than you might find in a police raid.'

'I see. And were you also under the influence?'

'No, I'd been at work all night, countless others can testify to that. And I don't drink.'

I close my eyes, just for a second. I thought I knew Diana better than if she were a sister, and yet I don't recognise the woman in front of me.

'So you met, as scheduled, at your flat. And what happened next?'

'He was high, but he was lucid,' she says. 'I wouldn't have let him in otherwise. It happened very quickly once he was inside.'

'What did?'

Finally she drops her gaze, shifting uncomfortably in her seat.

'Miss Yardley?'

'We had sex almost immediately,' she says. 'There wasn't much talking, or preamble. We just ... fell on each other. It didn't matter to me the condition he was in, and it was almost as if he sensed that, making him even more passionate. All I cared about was how much he wanted me, and in that moment he wanted me more than anything. But then his behaviour completely changed.'

'His behaviour? Do you mean his demeanour, or—'

'We were both just lying there, afterwards,' Di interrupts, a renewed flash of steel in her green eyes as she lifts her head. 'By then, we were in bed, under the covers, I was exhausted, and I assumed he was too. His eyes were closed, he was motionless, breathing regularly. I was almost asleep, but then heard him murmuring. Then it started. He began to thrash about. I can only describe it as fitting, really. His head was rolling from side to side, his arms kept flying out, catching me all over my body. He began screaming, unintelligibly – no words, just howling, and then his eyes opened only to roll straight back into his head. I tried to extricate myself, but I was trapped – every time I moved away his arm would catch me, and hard, and that's when...'

I watch in a trance as a hand flies to her throat.

'He suddenly stopped jerking and turned on me. It was as if he had woken up somewhere completely unexpected and immediately assumed everything around him was a threat that he needed to overpower at once.'

A cry then, mine? I twist round to see Andie clap a hand over her mouth, unmistakable recognition in her eyes. Di continues as if she'll never start again were she to stop.

'I couldn't fight him. I was completely pinned to the bed by his hands wrapped around my neck, and I was in total shock. In the moments before I had felt curiously elated yet disgusted – this man had chosen me, and repeatedly, when he could have had absolutely anyone else he'd wanted, and yet I felt sick at what I'd done, and how I'd been lying about it. I remember kicking like mad, trying to punch him, but his elbows were holding my arms away from me. Very quickly I just started to fade, I couldn't breathe...'

'Do you think he was trying to kill you?'

'No,' she says softly, resting a hand against her delicate collarbone, so defined it looks like it's been shaded on. 'I think he had no idea what he was doing. Because it stopped almost as suddenly as it started. Just as I thought I was going to pass out, there was no air left in my lungs, he dropped me like a rag doll. When I'd finished coughing and spluttering, I found him completely comatose next to me again. He was out cold. It was as if it had never happened.'

'That must have been terrifying for you.'

The barrister mimics Di's gesture, placing a hand on her robes.

'It was.' Di rubs her neck before she can continue. 'But all it really did was confirm the disgusted part of the equation to me. I was so angry with myself for falling for it in the first place, some clandestine relationship with a married man, with a work colleague. I was already suppressing how seedy it felt, even if it made me feel wanted. In that moment, all I could do was punish myself, rather than him.'

'What do you mean by that?'

I close my eyes again. For the first time in this wholly bewildering episode, I know exactly what she is going to say.

'I spent a long time in hospital when I was a teenager, recovering from – or fighting, I should say – anorexia and bulimia. These are conditions that never really leave you, but I'm pleased to say I've got them under control now, rather than the opposite way round. But that morning, I just ran to the bathroom and locked myself in. He'd have had to batter down the door to get to me, and I didn't care if he did, I was so disgusted with myself. I made myself sick until there wasn't even bile left. By the time I had finished, he was long gone.'

'Ladies and gentlemen of the jury, if you'll allow me, I'd like to recap the timeline of these events with Miss Yardley. To be clear, you first became involved with Mr Rusholme almost immediately after he returned from being shot in the head on assignment in

Iraq. He had been in similar situations but not been injured count-less, if not hundreds of times before. This episode – and we will hear from a medical professional in due course – took place within a week's return from that assignment. Is that correct?'

'Yes. It is.'

'And isn't it also correct, Miss Yardley, that when you finally came out of the bathroom to find him gone, you also found this?'

The barrister swoops a piece of paper in front of the jury, a bird's wing in the sky, stilling Miss Field's fingers mid-tattoo on her folder.

'Yes.'

'Your Honour, allow me to enter into evidence this medical as-sessment of Mr Rusholme, dated November eleventh of last year.'

She hands the piece of paper to a member of the jury, reaching for a duplicate on the table behind her.

'From which I will now summarise the salient portion aloud, for the benefit of the court.'

She meticulously unfolds a pair of glasses then places them on her nose, prolonging every last drip of tension in the air. I want to look away, to find anything else but Di, but I know if I find Penny, or Andie, or anyone else connected to the network, I might lose the shred of composure I have left.

'This is the second page of a two-part evaluation of Mr Rush-olme, conducted on his return from Baghdad in November. The first page denotes his physical condition, which, despite the sig-nificant lacerations left from the shot to the head, is apprised as fit to return to work. The second page is, however, a recommen-dation as per his mental health, and labels him as at exceptionally high risk of developing severe and complex post-traumatic stress disorder. It goes on to list the symptoms, which range from night-mares, substance abuse and hyperarousal, to the risk of full-blown psychosis.'

She removes the glasses from her nose to look up at Di.

'Miss Yardley, what did you do with this piece of paper once you'd found it?'

Diana positively shrivels, curling in on herself.

'I kept it,' she whispers. 'I couldn't bring myself to give it back, because that would have meant admitting I'd seen it, and then facing up to how it had come to be in my possession. I told myself that it couldn't be the only copy, it was a matter of medical record – this was an assessment conducted by the network itself. There was a doctor on roll that fulfilled the network's contractual obligations in terms of medical insurance.'

'And that's it? You just held on to it?'

'Yes,' she says softly. 'Until I gave it to you.'

'And why did you do that?'

Silence, as Diana uncurls again, quivering like a sapling.

'Because I know first-hand how damaging a culture of silence can be. As journalists, we tell ourselves we have to speak up on account of those who can't, we have to shine a light into the darkness, give voice to the voiceless, hold power to account. That should apply to everything, and everyone. You don't have to be in a warzone to bear witness. Some of the worst battles can be inside your own head. And we're not allowed to feel it, we haven't suffered enough by comparison. This business, our business, it has to be as good at recognising it when it happens to us as it is at when it happens to other people. The truth is that silence is the ugliest sin of all. And we're all guilty of it, especially me.'

She pauses for a moment, but no one interrupts her, not even Miss Field, whose fingers have hovered, frozen above her folder, since the piece of paper came out.

'There will be others you can ask about how much the network knew, whether they'd deliberately disregarded the psychological evaluation. I never asked, I was too ashamed, too concerned about my own position to worry about the very real dangers to others. I will always feel appalled that I didn't speak up earlier, whether they knew or they didn't. And it's true that no one was dragging him kicking and screaming anywhere other than to the doctor. In a crucible as competitive as ours, there is only so far you can worry about the state of minds other than your own. But to stay silent about it? That is the only binary matter here. And I can't. I won't.'

With the merest flick of her sparrow's hands, the barrister thinks she lands her killer blow. No more questions of Kris. No more questions of anyone else. She's confident enough has been said for this story to end her way.

Except there's someone else still standing.

Someone else is going to have the last word.

And it isn't who I'm expecting at all.

Chapter 32
Paperwork

'A rebuttal witness?'

'With your permission, Your Honour, yes.'

'What's going on?' I ask, but Miss Field is already swooping towards the bench, a carrion crow coming into land. My mind lags, my powers of reason are delayed. A rebuttal witness? I know what it means, so why am I asking the question? Who could possibly refute Di's statement, much less the accompanying medical report?

The courtroom rustles and murmurs as I strain to hear the conversation at the bench. I know Di is in the row behind me, but if I couldn't look her in the eye before, I definitely can't now.

Miss Field turns, a triumphant pirouette of black, as she raises a hand to the witness box.

'Your Honour, the Crown calls Miss Andrea Quinn.'

Only as my vision starts to darken round the edges do I realise I've been holding my breath.

Andie? How could she fall on my side of this particular line?

My fingernails scrape at the table in front of me as Andie takes her place in the witness box, sharp and angular in a crisp white shirt and black trousers, her face a mask of control. I swallow as a finger of acid steals up my throat.

'You'll be familiar with the protocol for the examination of a rebuttal witness.' The judge addresses Miss Field. 'But for the benefit of the jury and the purposes of the court, let me state that any line of questioning must be solely confined to the subject matter of the evidence in dispute.'

'Of course, Your Honour.' Miss Field bows her head. I watch the small smile playing around her mouth. This is just a game to her. We're the chess pieces, not them. And she's just unleashed her queen, capable of moving in any direction.

'Could you state your full name for the court, please?'

'Andrea Lea Quinn.' A hand flutters to tuck away a stray strand of hair, but it's a bluff. Andie isn't nervous. We're all about to find out why.

'Thank you, Miss Quinn, and for the purposes of the court, could you please also explain your relationship to the defendant?'

'We're colleagues,' Andie replies. 'I'm one of the network's senior field producers, which means all my work is done on the ground, where the story is. And I was more often than not paired up with Mr Rusholme.'

No mistake on the name; she must have already known what it really was. More cold creeps through my insides. What else does Andie know?

'Miss Quinn, could you tell us what happened last year, on the morning of November fourth?'

'How is this relevant to the evidence in question?' The judge interrupts with another cough, but there's no hiding how she's feeling now.

'Your Honour—'

'Let me remind you again, counsel, your witness is only here to refute the evidence that the defendant was unsound of mind for the duration of the period in which he allegedly committed these crimes. Does that include the morning of November fourth?'

'It does not, Your Honour, but—'

'Then let's get to the point. And unless it is directly relevant, please do not try to make it.'

'Of course, Your Honour.' Miss Field turns on the spot to collect herself, but Andie does not flinch, her mask fixed on some faraway point in the distance that only she can see.

'Miss Quinn, could you tell us what happened after the defendant returned from Afghanistan, where the first of these crimes is alleged to have been committed.'

'I was still in Baghdad,' Andie answers; flat, calm. 'Kris had left after the ambush only to head back out to Afghanistan two weeks later. I was surprised to learn of the deployment. Kris was never one to shirk an assignment, even with an external injury.'

External? Wasn't this all internal, as far as injuries were concerned, anyway? Still I can't look away, locked in Andie's thrall.

'But I'd expected him to come back to Baghdad. He had a lot of unfinished business to attend to.'

'What do you mean by that?'

'Kris never walks off a story.' I flinched as her eyes bored into me. 'And by then, we had been involved for some time. I expected him to come back rather than choose to go anywhere else.'

'Involved? Could you be more specific?'

'When we were deployed together, we stayed together,' Andie replied. 'It was never anything more than that.'

A rustle swishes round the court. Another one of Kris's former lovers? Whose character witness was Andie supposed to be?

'Isn't it perfectly reasonable, though, that he was sent somewhere else? You are employed by one of the biggest news networks in the world.'

'Yah, certainly.' Andie gave a little nod. 'Which is why I looked into the story he came back with. I assumed there must have been a subtext for it to have trumped the war in Iraq.'

'And what did you find?'

'The unexpected visit from the president made sense,' she continued, 'but the story from the female burns unit most definitely did not. I would never question the merit in a story like that – you can never do enough of them – but it didn't add up that the girl had died. There was no reference to why or how, and I was curious. The point of our story seemed to have been that she had survived her attempt to kill herself. So why had she been found dead shortly after we spoke to her? That to me was the real story.'

'Put like that, I can't see why everyone wasn't asking the same question—'

The judge sustains almost as soon as the defence objects. My ears tingle so hard I'm sure everyone can see them turning purple. I never thought to ask. I thought it was just a better story.

'I'll rephrase, Your Honour. Did you question either Mr Rusholme or Miss Nassar about what had happened?'

Andie replies with another nod. 'I spoke to Mr Rusholme as soon as he answered my calls. We didn't usually speak outside of field assignments – he had his own life, I had mine. I must admit I was furious he hadn't come back to Baghdad, but that wasn't why I kept calling him. Something just didn't sit right about the whole thing, and like any decent journalist, I was determined to find out what it was—'

Any decent journalist. I rip at the skin around a fingernail.

'Where is this going, counsel?' The judge interrupts again. 'This is your last warning. You must direct the witness only to the evidence in question, which, need I remind you, is what we heard from Miss Yardley a few moments ago.'

'Yes, Your Honour.' Miss Field has to clear her own throat to reply. 'I am just establishing, for the purposes of this court, why Miss Quinn felt she had to do what she did next—'

'And what was that?' The judge is on her feet now, both hands on the bench.

'Miss Quinn, could you tell us what happened when you left Baghdad along with Miss Nassar and Mr Rusholme at the end of last year?'

Miss Field is gabbling now, flustered, even though she still seems to hold the upper hand. But to what? I still don't know...

'I was already due to leave when Miss Nassar and Mr Rusholme were sent home too. They had got themselves into a spot of bother on the way back from interviewing Mr Aziz.'

'Ahmed Aziz, the defendant's second victim?'

'Yes,' Andie answers. 'I found Mr Rusholme going over the only tape back in the newsroom. Most photographers go back to their pictures again and again, but not him. It was really out of character. He would always say once was enough, he didn't need to look again. And the truth is it always was – he was the best photographer at the network. He never needed a second shot. But this time, he was just sitting, spooling tape back and forth. I couldn't understand what he was doing. I kept seeing the same shots, again and again, and just as we started talking, Hamdi called in to check on their welfare.'

'Hamdi?'

'The local journalist at the Iraqi news agency who Miss Nassar had used to set up the interview.'

Used. Everything about Andie's answers is loaded, but I can't tell where Andie is pointing her gun.

'And what did he say?'

'That it was strange,' Andie continues. 'That it didn't add up. The blast that took out our vehicle was pretty small. There was a short firefight afterwards, but again, it was all too far away to have made any difference to the building Ahmed was in. He had no visible new injuries, he just had no pulse. Hamdi was mainly re-lieved that our crew was OK, but when I kept asking if he'd seen anything unusual, he remembered he'd noticed a syringe in the debris on his way out. He only noticed because it was still intact, unlike all the rest of the glass in the building.'

I take a breath along with the courtroom, but Andie doesn't relent.

'I was standing next to the edit deck when he said it. There was no such syringe anywhere I could see while the interview was still under way.'

'Surely that single piece of video couldn't have shown you every angle of the building?'

'Surely,' Andie repeated agreeably. 'But there was an easy enough way for me to check what I suspected. An easy enough way to establish there was no doubt at all Mr Rusholme knew exactly what he was doing.'

'And what was that?'

The courtroom stills as Andie finally pauses, inclining her head in an unmistakable direction.

'Paperwork,' she says simply. 'And Miss Samira Anne Nassar is the one that gave it to me.'

And with that all the oxygen in the room instantly diverts to Andie, every word that follows just as damning, every subsequent explanation making it harder and harder to breathe.

The locked cupboard, its clipboard, the bulging leather pouches. The scanner and its log sheets, recording each individual barcode on every vial, every blister pack, every syringe.

The toxicity of ambition.

I gave Andie all the evidence she was looking for, just because it was her who asked.

'And what about Miss Nassar?'

I start at my name, but Miss Field is still addressing Andie.

'Judging by the paperwork, she had no idea what he was doing. Kris had been stockpiling long before she came on the scene. There's no doubt, as you'll see...'

A trolley rattles as it is wheeled in, groaning with paper. There must be hundreds and thousands more sheets than the one Diana fluttered. All that's missing is a bow tied with red tape.

'...that Mr Rusholme couldn't have been more deliberate, nor premeditated. He knew exactly what he was doing.'

And with that, Miss Field ends it. Quickly, just as the judge specified. Andie never knew where I really stood, but it doesn't matter.

Because I did. I saw the same paperwork.

I just didn't understand.

Chapter 33
Look Again

The man, he's standing tall in the dock, but with a near-transparent posture, so limp without the mascot of a camera on his shoulder that he has to rest a hand on the low wall in front of him.

It's almost over, but this is an end that even he couldn't see coming. Something is lifting, as evanescent as the light changes with the clouds, stirring shadows so fast even his shutter would struggle to capture their shapes. A tinge of beginning just as the fly closes, changing the perspective, toying with the final frame.

The man sees himself, so he knows he is there, in the dock, accused of murder, surely guilty as charged. But he also sees something else – the cool eye of judgment, morphing and shifting, hovering with the light as it decides which side to fall.

The girl, she's there too, her stance equally curious. She's not in the dock, but looks just as defeated – her figure shrunken without its customary aura of determination, her gaze downcast and haunted. He sees her reflected in the face staring up from the hundreds of news magazines blanketing every lap in the courtroom.

Are they still looking at the shot that ended a war and launched a career? Or do they finally see it for what it is – a deserving soul about to be set free?

When the verdict comes, even it can't land, surely the word 'manslaughter' belongs on the opposite side to 'diminished responsibility'? There's insanity too, somewhere high up there, floating as it is absorbed into the clouds suspended over the lot.

The man, he listens intently, but can't hear anything that means understanding. There's mitigating, there's dereliction of duty, there's murder, and there's mercy. These people, they read the report, they argued the toss, they weighed the risks. They went back to the scenes of the crimes. They tried to establish whether the picture was different. They tried to find the families, to talk to officials, to unearth new evidence.

But it was all gone. They were all dead too.

So the man stops listening and starts looking again. It doesn't take much to turn him deaf, he's a man who's only ever heard screams, who's only ever lived with a soundtrack of pain. But the looking, it's suddenly agonising, so unfamiliar – here, high in the dock, there's no viewfinder, no shield other than the tears welling behind their long-held seal, falling invisibly and silently as mist. And the seven-year-old in him finally remembers.

It was a dusty afternoon, a stifling hot apartment, his mother, his paint-box, her camera. He was too young to watch what happened most nights his father came home, so he painted her a thousand different pictures. Brown dirt, red blood, blue eyes.

The darkest part of the human body is the pupil, she'd said, as they'd hunched over his drawings on the table. If you want to make your painting realistic, you've got to use black in the eye. And if you're framing a shot, she'd added as she passed over her camera, that's where the shadows have to be perfect.

You know I could never paint you anything real, the boy had answered. So use this instead, she'd replied, tapping the worn front of her beloved black case. Then you can show yourself the version you want, show everyone a different picture, even me.

And never stop looking for beauty, she'd added, as she wiped a tear out of the bruised eye he'd pretended not to see. You'll always find some, even in the darkest of places.

But it was only when he saw death up close that he knew she was right.

Because it's only in death that light finds its way into the eyes. They become spectral, with depths suddenly as transient as a last breath. A permanent mark of the moment when possibility becomes impossibility, when hope fades to peace.

The giveaway is always in the pupil.

As the courtroom rustles and murmurs, he sees it at last.

It's the girl. She's finally looking at him.

There's no light in her dark eyes, but there is the merest flicker of something else. The ephemeral reflections of light off water, as rare and transient as flowers that bloom from dust.

He looks back at her, affirming the emotion in her tears, and feels the unmistakable sensation of weight leaving his shoulders.

It no longer matters that everyone else sees a different picture. Because at last someone understands his own.

The cuffs take his hands, wrapping their cool calm circle around his wrists, as he is gently taken down. Beneath them, at least one scar has finally stopped hurting.

But who is really to blame? Where does the true fault lie?

You decide. You've got all the facts now.

Acknowledgements

It's hard to write thanks for *The Shot*, as it is, in so many ways, the product of other people's pain. The sum of not just my own experiences, but others I have no right to inhabit.

Bearing witness is, rightly, an uncomfortable place to be. As journalists, we can tell ourselves it is in pursuit of a higher goal – that shining a light into the darkest of corners might chase some of the pain and suffering away. As novelists, it is a harder sell. The truth is I could not have written this book without the sacrifices of so many people, thousands of whom I will never meet. And those I have may feel I have appropriated experiences that weren't mine to share.

My best answer – as both a journalist and novelist – is that it comes from a place of empathy. To imagine how it feels is only to try and understand it better. To vocalise what happened is only to try and make some peace with it, when it's impossible to forget.

To that end I owe thanks to so many people.

To Scott McWhinnie. No amount of window seats, chocolate bags, nor promotions to senior international cameraman could ever cover it. Thank you for taking me with you for some of it. Please make this the second ever book you read. Even if you're not in the library, it will feel a lot more familiar than *Siddhartha*.

To Diana, Terence, and the rest of the early noughties overnight crew. We have nothing to lose but our health! Cheers to the alcoholic breakfasts, the microwave lasagnes, the sleepless days and nights in the inappropriately named Coffee House.

To Ingrid, Tommy, Arwa, Jomana, Nic, Mohammed, Hamdi and Sarmad, RIP. At the time things were moving so fast I thought

I'd never remember it all, but it turns out I can recall every single deranged moment. Thank you for all being there too.

To Sebastiaan, Adam, Todd, Matt, Clarissa, Tim, Salma and Dominique. This isn't really thanks, but just, you know.

To Dr Wahid and Ajmal, for making Afghanistan feel like home while it had to.

To Damian, Debbie and Chris, some of the finest humanitarians in the world, for making Darfur hospitable. Which came first, the chicken or the egg?

To Tony Maddox and Chris Cramer, RIP. Thank you for making it OK to feel it. And to everyone whose privacy we invaded, who spoke up through the pain and the fear. I was part of your lives in an unforgivably fleeting way. Your influence will forever be a part of mine.

Lastly to agent extraordinaire Jon Wood, the Grande Dame of publishing Karen Sullivan, and the immense Team Orenda – bloggers, readers, writers alike. When I left journalism, I thought I'd never find a worthier tribe. How wrong I was. Thank you for being the most supportive, generous and downright unhinged team around. There's no more white-knuckle ride than your imaginations.

And to my family – Mum, Dad, Ben, Liora, Oli, Guy and Trixie. Thanks for it all. It's worth nothing without you.

Reading Group Questions

How does Sarah highlight the issues around reporting on the victims of war?

What is the role of a war correspondent and are they ever justified in intervening in the lives of the victims of war?

The Shot throws up some big ethical questions about the role of journalism in conflict situations. What answers, if any, does Sarah offer the reader?

Samira believes she is wholly invested in giving voice to the voiceless. Do you agree?

Samira 'saves' Wahid from his suicide attempt, but do you think Samira's actions were actually selfish?

Mercy is one of the book's core themes. Do you see Kris's actions as merciful?

What role does the homeless man, Rory, have in the story?

How does Sarah use Samira's relationship with Diana to explore the themes of trust and betrayal in the book?

At the end of the book, the reader is left to decide Kris's punishment; what do you think the result should be and why?